# A Second Chance for Happiness

THE IOWA CONNECTION

# A Second Chance for Happiness

Lisa Smelter

gatekeeper press™
Tampa, Florida

A Second Chance for Happiness

Published by Gatekeeper Press
7853 Gunn Hwy., Suite 209
Tampa, FL 33626
www.GatekeeperPress.com



Library of Congress Control Number: 2023946017

ISBN (hardcover): 9781662940019
ISBN (paperback): 9781662940026
eISBN: 9781662940033

CHAPTER

# One

Trish told her mom and sister that she needed some candy. Since they didn't have any in the house, she volunteered to walk to the only grocery store in town to buy some. As she started the three-block hike, she remembered the hundreds of times she had done that when she still lived in Iowa.

Trish was a small wiry woman who never gained an ounce, despite her sweet tooth. She loved chocolate. If there was no chocolate to be had, she made do with suckers and hard candy. For years, her family and friends teased her about her penchant for sweets, but she just grinned engagingly and shrugged.

When she arrived at Rush's Grocery Store, she was stopped by Mrs. Rush, the owner. Mrs. Rush was the town's mouthpiece, who knew everything that was going on in the community. She passed the news on to others, but she was kind and only shared the truth, not like other gossipers in town.

"Trish, I didn't know you were back in town. I hope you're here to stay. You came back because of your mother's health, didn't you?" Mrs. Rush asked compassionately.

The whole community knew that Mrs. Newberg had been seriously ill. Her stroke two months ago left her temporarily paralyzed on her left side and in a wheelchair. She was finally home from the hospital under Jenny's care. Jenny was Trish's older sister. She and her twelve-year-old son, Joshua, lived with Mrs. Newberg for the last seven years. They moved back home after Jenny's husband, Jack, was killed in a local farm accident.

Jenny called Trish and asked her to come home for a while. She needed Trish's help to take care of their mother. Trish was grateful to Jenny for letting her know about their mother's health. She hadn't been home in three years, ever since taking a job in Brazil.

"Yes, I'm back for a while. I want to help Jenny take care of Mom. I'm not sure how long I will stay in Dalton. My boss is holding my job open for me in case I want to go back to it." Trish's response was guarded because she didn't want to tell anyone about her job in Brazil. That was a closely kept secret.

Trish saw several older customers come in the door, so she felt okay in saying, "Well, I'm here to buy some candy. I'll see you in a little while."

Mrs. Rush chuckled and said, "I guess you haven't lost that sweet tooth of yours, Trish." She turned to greet her new customers.

Trish walked directly to the candy section. It had swollen and now took up two whole aisles. There was almost twice as much candy as there had been three years ago. She grabbed a grocery basket from the stack that sat conveniently on the endcap because she planned to stock up. If she was going to be in town for a while, she wanted to have a stash of candy at the house. Of course, she planned to buy some for the rest of the family, as well.

She found all her favorites on the shelf. After she put four packages of chocolate candy in her basket, she added Jenny's favorite hard candy, Josh's sour gummies, and red licorice for her mom. Trish wasn't sure if Mom could eat that anymore, but she didn't want her to feel left out.

Trish was carefully looking over the shelves one more time when she became aware that people were about to come around the corner into the candy aisle. She looked up expectantly, with a ready "hello" on her lips. She knew most of the people who lived in this small community.

Trish looked at the beloved face of the man she had run away from three years ago. It was Shaun, her dear Shaun. He looked so handsome. His thick strawberry blond hair was neatly combed, and he was wearing his "date night" clothes. He smelled great, too. She had always loved his after-shave cologne.

Her glance also took in her good friend, Mary Walsh. She was in Trish's class, and they had been good friends since kindergarten. Mary was a sweet-looking pretty woman with a sunny smile that made most people forget about her clubfoot. Mary had come to terms with her foot, which dragged a little behind its fellow. She wryly called it her "gimpy leg".

Mary's joy was obvious as she looked at Trish and exclaimed loudly, "Trish, it's so good to see you. I hadn't heard that you were back in town."

She moved forward to give Trish a fierce hug. Trish hugged her back. She had felt terrible about leaving Dalton without saying goodbye to Mary, having fled in the middle of the night.

Trish thought back to that terrible night. It was a fine summer evening. Josh and she had just finished a game of cribbage. Jenny came in the door looking very pale and quietly asked Trish to come into her bedroom to talk. Trish concernedly followed her into the bedroom because Jenny looked like she wanted to cry. Jenny directed Trish to sit down on the bed.

Jenny came over and took her hands. She squeezed them hard.

"Trish, I just heard from three different people that Shaun had an affair with Sheila Warrant. Before she left town, Sheila told a bunch of people that she was sorry to be leaving, especially now that she and Shaun were physically involved in a love affair. I didn't want to believe it, but one of the people who told me was Mrs. Rush. You know that she doesn't make things up."

Jenny's voice was shaking. This was not news that she wanted to pass on to her little sister.

Trish sat stunned, trying to process that information. It couldn't be true—her Shaun wasn't like that! They had already been engaged for six months. The wedding was only four months away. They had agreed to have a pure relationship until they were married. Shaun was fine with that. He had even suggested it, since he guessed correctly that Trish was an innocent woman.

Trish gave him the benefit of the doubt. She knew that Sheila very likely initiated the affair. That was what she did. Sheila Warrant was an attractive thirty-year-old woman from Chicago who came to stay with her cousin, Jonah, every summer for the last ten years. Sheila laughingly said that she needed to decompress somewhere quiet after living and working in such a big city.

Jenny couldn't stand her because Sheila had flirted with Jack about nine years ago. He rejected her because he was the happy husband and father to Jenny and Joshua. Shella just shrugged and moved on to another hapless man in the community. Now, it appeared that Sheila was back to her old mischief, only this time it was with Shaun.

Jenny could never have believed it of Shaun. He was one of the good guys, and he seemed to really love Trish, too. She had been so happy for them when Trish and Shaun became engaged six months ago.

Trish was so hurt and angry that she wanted to leave town that minute. After ranting and raving at Jenny for an hour, Trish was worn out. She had no feelings left. It was like she was an automaton. Trish was determined to leave Dalton right away and never see or speak to Shaun again.

Jenny and her mom tried to reason with her, but they couldn't overcome Trish's indignance and unsubstantiated anger. Jenny had affectionately and sometimes frustratedly called Trish "an independent little cuss" many times over the years.

Jenny worried that Trish had nowhere to go and no job. Just then, Trish remembered the ad they saw in the *Mason City Times* that afternoon. Mason City was the nearest large town. Trish and Jenny knew Mason City well. They both had gone to college there.

The ad was promoting jobs at a mine in Brazil. They were looking for a general helper, miners, and a doctor or registered nurse to go and live there for three months or more. The wages were fantastic, and there was free housing for the workers. Trish and Jenny had laughed about it that afternoon. Now, Trish looked for the ad, found the number, and called. She was desperate to get away, and she was willing to do almost any job for three months.

A sleepy voice answered the phone. It was almost midnight there. Trish talked with a man named Ted for ten minutes. He told her that she would be interviewed over the phone in the morning. Ted instructed Trish to fax her credentials to their office by 9:00 a.m. Central Standard Time.

Trish packed two large suitcases full of clothes that she thought would be suitable, her favorite books, some pictures, and her sketchbook and colored pencils. Being an artist, she never went anywhere without the tools of her trade. She regretfully took one last look at her simple, but beautiful, wedding dress, bought just a week ago. It remained in her closet, never to be worn.

She told Jenny that she didn't know how long she would be gone, but she would be in Brazil for three months for sure. Trish promised to call Jenny every other week, just to check in. She made Jenny promise not to tell anyone where she was, not even Josh or her mom. She didn't want anyone—especially Shaun—to know that she was in Brazil. If Josh and her mom didn't know where she was, no one could try to wheedle the information out of them. Jenny would be the only one who knew where Trish was, and she wouldn't tell anyone.

Since Trish was adamant about leaving Dalton that night, Jenny drove her to Mason City. The two sisters found an open motel and settled in for the rest of the night. Trish used the motel phone to call the Brazilian office the next morning. She faxed her credentials to that office, interviewed, and was offered the job. She would take over as the general helper as soon as she arrived. It took a day and a half before she could get an airline ticket there, so she stayed at the motel until it was time for her to fly to Brazil.

She sent Jenny back to Dalton right after she accepted the job. Jenny hugged her tightly and told her to take care of herself. She had always been around to make sure that her impetuous little sister stayed out of trouble. Trish was dry-eyed and determined when Jenny said goodbye.

Jenny drove home, thinking about Trish. Her little sister had always done things on a whim. She was an independent and outspoken young woman who championed the meek and those who could not stand up for themself. Her heart was as big as the outdoors. She had taken in every stray animal she found, became friends with all kinds of lonely hearts and forgotten people, and would give the shirt off her back to anyone in need.

Jenny loved her even more for the sweet and feisty person she was. Trish's impetuous nature had gotten her in enough trouble in the past, but Jenny stood up for her through every single problem.

She understood Trish's need to leave town but wished that her sister would have confronted Shaun before she left. Jenny had Trish's engagement ring in her pocket because she was going to return it to Shaun on Trish's behalf. She strongly wanted to yell at him for his stupidity, but Trish had quietly pleaded with her to just give it back and not get into an argument. It went against Jenny's nature, but she agreed, since it meant that much to Trish.

* * *

Trish came back to the present. It seemed as if she had been gone for a long time, but it was only a few moments. She looked again at Shaun and said very quietly, "Hello, Shaun."

Shaun looked at Trish. She looked wonderful—a bit too thin, but she had a nice tan. Her eyes and face were somber, but otherwise she looked like his sweet Trish. He had to restrain himself from rushing forward, taking her in his arms, and kissing her. They were not engaged anymore.

Still, he had thought of her and dreamed of her for three years. It was torture to act like they barely knew one another. He had been in love with her for five years. It was difficult to turn off that love just because Trish believed a bunch of nonsense. She should have talked with him about the situation before fleeing from Dalton, although it was typical of Trish and her impulsive nature.

"Hello, Trish," he said, just as quietly as she did. There was so much more he wanted to say, but now was not the right time.

Trish looked back at Mary and said, "I see that you're buying candy, too. Are you guys going to the movies? I saw on the marquee that *The Terminator* is playing tonight."

Mary laughed and said, "Yes, both Shaun and I wanted to get out of the house tonight. I've already seen *The Terminator* five times, but it's a classic. I could probably see it five more times."

She peered into Trish's basket and chuckled when she saw all the candy. As one of Trish's oldest friends, she knew about her love for candy. "Looks like you're stocking up on candy. I hope that means that you'll be here for a long visit. By the way, would you like to come to the movies with us? It would be like old times."

She stopped talking and looked guiltily at Shaun. He might not want Trish to come with them.

Before Shaun could say anything, Trish hurriedly said, "No, thanks, anyway. Mom and Jenny are expecting me back home in a few minutes. I told them that I was just going to buy the candy and come right back. You two have a fun time, okay?"

Shaun didn't say anything, but his blue eyes looked sad. He abruptly nodded and turned to Mary. He told her to pick out the candy that she wanted for the show. Mary told Trish that she would stop by in a few days if that was okay with her. Trish nodded, clasped her grocery basket tightly, and left the candy aisle.

Ten years ago, the local movie theater had closed because the owner couldn't make a living. After it sat closed for a year, it was bought by two young brothers. They totally revamped it, keeping the old red velvet curtain and plush comfortable chairs. Everything else was streamlined. Because they knew that people snuck in their own candy, they didn't stock any. They told people to bring in their own candy, provided they properly disposed of the wrappers.

They only offered popcorn, Coke, Diet Coke, and Sprite. All seats were $5.00. Sundays were set aside as Disney-themed nights, Saturdays were for classic love stories, and the rest of the week was for action and science fiction. They were all older movies, but the townspeople gladly dropped their $5.00 to keep the movie theater open.

There was little to do in this small town. The movie theater, the bowling alley, and Dalton's Cafe were all next to each other on Main Street. They were the only activities in the small community, other than the bars in town.

Mrs. Rush, who had been quietly observing the conversation, asked Trish if she found everything she wanted. Trish's silent nod conveyed her reticence to talk. Mrs. Rush rang up the candy, told Trish to say hello to her mom for her, and smiled encouragingly.

"Come in, again, Trish. Maybe we can have a little talk when you have more time." Trish's expression saddened Mrs. Rush. The Trish she knew was funny, confident, and outspoken. *To see Trish silent and sad is just not right,* Mrs. Rush thought.

As Trish slowly walked home, she thought about Shaun. She knew that he was very likely still angry with her, and she deserved it. Three years ago, she thought that it was best to leave without talking with Shaun, but those long years convinced her that she had been unfair. She should have talked to Shaun instead of breaking up via Jenny.

If he had the affair, Trish was sure that he would have confessed it to her. He had always been truthful with her in the past. Up to that moment, she had never been a coward. She should have looked him in the face and given him back his ring. There could have been closure.

If there was a mistake, he could have explained that, too. Maybe the rumors were wrong. She could have prevented those long difficult years of separation. It was possibly too late to ask for forgiveness. She saw how stubborn and aloof he looked in the grocery store. He probably had no intention of letting her ask him for an explanation. In his mind, she had already pronounced him guilty without giving him a chance to defend himself.

When they got engaged, they had laughed about his stubbornness and her impulsivity. They hoped that their poor children wouldn't inherit both of those traits. Then they just kissed and hugged each other at the thought of having children together. They were both very much in love with each other. Children would be the perfect addition to their loving circle.

# CHAPTER
# Two

Trish and Shaun grew up in the same small town. Shaun's family lived on a farm about four miles from the Dalton city limits. The Newberg family lived in a big old white house on the edge of the main street in Dalton.

The population of Dalton was just under a thousand people. It was a farming community. Most of the farms around town were dairy farms, cattle farms, or forty-to-eighty-acre soybean or seed corn farms.

Shaun was two years older than Trish. He had grown up admiring the spunky skinny little Trish. She never backed down from a challenge. An indomitable grin could be seen on her face after every altercation. She often took on other people's challenges, as well. Her sense of right and wrong was very strong, and she just could not stand idly by and watch injustice happen.

Shaun was the only son of elderly parents. When his father lost a leg in the same farm accident that killed Jenny's husband, the Healy family sold off most of their farm. Shaun could not handle a large farm by himself. They now only had three dairy cows, with the milk going mostly for their own consumption and weekly gifts to their next-door neighbor. The neighbor had a house with little acreage, four children, and not much money.

The Healy family grew seed corn on forty acres. After the harvest, Shaun sold most of it to his neighbors for their cattle. With the proceeds from the sale of the other two hundred acres sitting in the bank gathering interest, they were doing fine financially.

Trish was famous in Dalton for her long rambling walks with their Old English Sheepdog, Nolan. She usually walked for about five miles or so, and she visited with neighbors while she walked. The townspeople and surrounding community were used to seeing the duo walking briskly along the road. In the five years that she was away at college, a young teenage neighbor walked the dog.

When Trish's father died the year after she graduated from college, she moved home from her comfortable apartment in Mason City to help her mom. Not even a year after Trish moved home, Jenny's husband was killed. Trish helped Jenny with Josh, who was lost without his dad. With Jenny, Josh, and her mother all still grieving, Trish felt that she had to stay at home with them. She was anxious to get back to Mason City and her old life, but she was stuck in Dalton. Because her family needed her, Trish reluctantly settled back into Dalton for the long haul.

Trish started to work part-time at the library in town. There was no work for her in her chosen field. She had an art degree and drew lovely pictures, and she worked with pottery, metal, and other mediums, as well. Happily, Trish occasionally got work in her field when someone in town wanted a portrait done or a mural made.

To relieve her boredom at home, she resumed her long walks with Nolan. The poor dog was quite old by now, so Trish had to walk much slower with him. One summer day, the twenty-six-year-old and Nolan were walking along the gravel road that led to the Healy farm. The sky turned black, and the wind started blowing hard.

Trish hated storms, especially the ones that generated tornados. It was unfortunate that Dalton was smack-dab in the middle of "Tornado Alley". Tornadoes were something to contend with in the community in and around Dalton.

Trish had heard the tall tales about various tornados her whole life. She also remembered the tornado that tore the roof off her house when she was five years old. These things combined to make the independent and confident Trish deathly afraid of tornadoes that came down in her community.

As she saw the black clouds forming, she tried to hurry Nolan into running for shelter. She knew that the Healy family had an old shed at the end of their property. Part of the shed/shelter was underground. They stored tools and other things there for use on the farm.

Trish had previously investigated it one time when she was walking down this road. It was a hot sunny day. She saw Shaun Healy on the old red tractor in the field. He waved at her to come and chat with him. He brought them to the shed, where he had some cool bottled water stored in the underground section.

Now, as Trish hurried Nolan along, the rain poured down. She was drenched, but that didn't bother her. What bothered her was the lightning that continued to streak across the sky and the ominous thunder. They seemed like the predecessor to tornadoes. She didn't see Shaun, who was hurrying from another direction. The two people and the dog arrived at the shed at almost the same time. Shaun opened the door and held it open for Trish and Nolan.

He grinned at her and said, "Wow, what a gully washer! I saw you walking down the road with your dog and hoped that you would reach the shed before the storm. Come over to the underground section. I have some water and granola bars there. I think there is also a blanket or two. You should dry off a little. I don't want you or your dog to catch a cold."

Now that she was inside, out of the bad weather, Trish's happy smile came back to her face.

"Thank you, Shaun. It's nice to be inside a shelter. I hate storms," she said.

He nodded and smiled at her. After she dried off Nolan and gave him some water, she wrapped a blanket around herself and accepted a bottle of water from Shaun. There was a rough wooden bench in the underground section. She sat down on it and laid out part of her blanket for Shaun. He had no blanket and would have to sit on prickly dry wood in wet clothes. She was comfy, and she wanted him to be more comfortable, too. He gratefully sat on the blanket.

They talked generally about Dalton and the town library. All at once, they heard the tell-tale sound of a tornado in the distance. Trish clutched her blanket and fear drained her face of any color. She couldn't speak at all. Seeing her fear, Shaun moved right next to her. He spoke softly, as one would to a child. "Shh. It's okay. I won't let anything happen to you. We're safe in this underground section."

He wrapped the blanket around them both and hugged her tightly. She was stiff with fright for a few minutes. Finally, his body heat, comforting arms, and calm demeanor started to relax her. The storm lasted another twenty minutes. Both felt safe and warm in contrast to the crashing crescendo outside. It seemed so natural for Shaun to bend his head and softly kiss Trish's pink lips. She didn't protest, so he pressed a harder kiss on her lips. He found that he liked kissing Trish Newberg.

The storm overhead seemed part of the urgent kiss that they shared. They pulled apart and stared at each other. Neither had expected the feelings that came over them when they kissed. Shaun took off the blanket. He rewrapped it around only Trish but kept his arms around her. He was quite warm right now. He still wanted to hold her, though.

As the storm passed, Trish regained her independent spirit. Even though she was still quaking inside because of the storm, she made a joke about the weather. Shaun, who knew that she was still terrified, once again admired Trish for her courage in the face of her fear.

Looking tenderly at her, he reflected on the excitement of kissing her. She was so responsive. It could have been her fear, but he thought that she was very likely a passionate person.

They tried to talk normally until the storm passed. Shaun reluctantly withdrew his arms from around Trish. He gave her face a quick look. It seemed as if she was hesitant to leave his arms, too.

She returned the blanket and looked like she was going to leave. Shaun peered out of the shed and saw the large amount of standing water on the road. He thought that they may have gotten up to an inch of rain.

"Trish, it's only half a mile to my house. Let me get my truck. I'll pick you up here and drive you home. It'll take you a long time to walk home on that wet road. Your dog would probably appreciate the ride. What do you think?" His voice was warm and friendly.

Trish saw that he was right, so she said, "Thank you, Shaun. That's nice of you. I could walk to your house with you, though."

"No, stay here. Your dog won't want to trudge through the mud all the way to my house. I can be back here in half an hour. Sit down and relax."

She agreed and watched him leave; she wanted a few minutes to think about their kiss. It was the best kiss that she had ever experienced. Trish admired Shaun. She never thought of the two of them dating, but now the thought came into her head. *Why not?* His warm and caring arms made her feel safe, even when she was terrified. No one else had ever made her feel that way.

By the time Shaun came back with his truck, Trish decided that she would definitely go out with him if he asked her. Now, he just had to ask her . . .

Shaun dwelt on their kiss as he made his way home. He wanted to kiss Trish again. Rushing into the house, he told his mom that he was going to give Trish Newberg a ride home because she and her dog had been caught in the storm. He grabbed his keys and headed back to the shed, wondering if Trish would go out with him if he asked her.

They settled old Nolan in the bed of the truck before getting into the cab. It only took about five minutes to get from the shed to her house. Shaun grinned at Trish and jokingly said, "Aww, another exciting adventure in the big city of Dalton."

Trish's grin was there, too. "Yup, that's one for the books. Thank you, Shaun, for everything. You must have known that I was terrified. I have this huge fear of bad storms. You helped me more than you could possibly know." Her voice and face were now somber.

Shaun smiled at her nicely. "You are welcome, Trish. I would do it again. You're a great companion." A little imp inside him made him add, "I wouldn't mind trying that kiss again, either. You're a great kisser." He looked intently at her. Any sign that she wanted to kiss him again, and he would ask her out.

Trish laughed and lightly replied, "Yes, it was a nice kiss, wasn't it?" Her reply was brief because she hoped that he would ask her out. Since he didn't, she would just be as friendly as she could toward him.

He let her go without saying anything more. Maybe there would be another occasion when he could ask her out. In the meantime, he planned to think a lot more about their time together.

Trish went into the house and told her family what happened. She omitted the part where Shaun held and kissed her. That would be her own private memory. She hoped that Shaun would ask her out sometime in the future. As it was, she went over their kiss a hundred times in her mind.

Sunday evening, Trish and Mary were getting ready to leave the movie theater after watching *Toy Story*. They saw Shaun, who was laughing and talking with his parents. Trish, clutching her boxes of chocolate, nervously greeted them. The Healys made a comment about the storm, and she blushed when she caught Shaun's eyes. He grinned slightly, remembering their kiss, too. They said goodbye and left to go home.

Shaun thought about Trish every spare moment since the storm. He couldn't erase from his mind the feel of her small body in his arms, nor the thought of her courage even though she was so scared. But mostly, he remembered their kiss. It was the best kiss he ever experienced. He looked forward to kissing her again, to see if they had the same magic without the drama of a thunderstorm.

Her blush tonight made him think that she remembered it, too. Maybe she enjoyed it just as much as he had. That was enough of an incentive for him to ask her for a date. However, he didn't want to have an audience, so he decided to wait until she was working at the library. She told him in the shed that she worked by herself from one until three o'clock on Mondays and Wednesdays.

On Monday, Shaun found that he couldn't get away from the farm. He told his mom that he had an appointment at 1:00 p.m. on Wednesday. She nodded and said that they could eat at noon that day. Shaun often had farm business, and she wasn't even curious about his meeting.

At 1:05 p.m. on Wednesday, Shaun walked into the Dalton Library. It was a small building, and the only person he saw there was Trish. She noticed him and gave him a big smile.

"Hi, Shaun. What can I help you find today?" she asked him, engagingly.

He grinned at her and came over to lean on the counter. "I came in to ask you something. Will you go out for a meal with me at the Dalton Cafe on Friday night? After that, I thought we could go bowling. They have laser light bowling from 8:00 until 10:00 p.m."

Trish's smile was huge, now. Her heart was beating fast. "Yes, that sounds fun. What time do you want to go to the cafe?"

Shaun smiled warmly at her and said, "If I pick you up at 6:00 p.m., would that work for you?"

Trish's smile was still evident. "Yes, that will work."

Now that he asked Trish out, he didn't know what else to say. He was usually not tongue-tied around women; he prided himself on his glib comments and easy conversation with others. There was something about Trish today that had him tied up in knots.

It must have been the fact that she was looking particularly fetching in a pale blue sundress. Her hair looked very soft and curly as it lay on her bare shoulders. He hadn't really noticed what she looked like before, but now he noticed every little thing about her.

She wasn't wearing any makeup except for super shiny pink lip gloss. Her eyes were bright and happy, as was her face. Long silver earrings danced back and forth as she moved her head, and her fingernails were painted a soft pink.

Shaun cleared his throat, smiled at her again, and said, "Well, I only had a minute. I need to get going. I'll see you at 6:00 p.m. on Friday night, okay?"

Trish nodded and smiled back. "Okay, see you at 6:00 p.m., Shaun. Bye."

After Shaun left, Trish thought about him. He seemed kind of shy today. She had never known him to be hesitant before. Of course, she wasn't usually shy around people, either. Maybe they both were nervous about their upcoming date on Friday.

Friday night came quickly. Since it was a beautiful summer evening, she wore some tight white cotton shorts and a pretty, ruffled top. She left her thick curly hair alone. Some pink lip gloss and flashy earrings were all the adornments she added. Trish looked cute and fresh, and she hoped that Shaun would think so, too. She didn't usually wear much makeup. *My face looks better au naturel,* she thought.

Shaun thought that Trish looked wonderful. He didn't think that women needed to wear makeup. In his opinion, most women had nice faces without all that makeup. If they wanted to wear it for themselves, that was okay with him. But if they chose not to wear makeup, he liked that even better.

Shaun could see beauty in almost every face. Trish had pretty eyes and a wonderful smile. He liked her freckles, too. Her body was petite and wiry, and she looked cute in her shorts and ruffled top. He especially liked her thick curly hair. It gave her a defiant and sassy look.

Shaun was a man who liked to have lively discussions with people. In fact, he liked a bit of sass in a woman. He learned in high school that girls who agreed with everything he said bored him. He had gone out with a pretty and meek blonde but got quickly bored with her non-conversation. She and her family were apparently quite hurt when he broke up with her after a few months. To this day, they barely spoke to him, even though the girl had long since married.

Trish and Shaun had burgers, fries, and chocolate shakes at the Dalton Cafe. They amicably argued whether *Toy Story 1* was better than *Toy Story 2* and about other general things.

Shaun enjoyed lightly sparring with her. She had good arguments for why she thought certain things. They were both in a good mood after their meal. The bowling alley was right next door, so they slowly made their way there, stopping and talking with everyone they met.

It was not unusual to see any variety of young people together. Dalton was such a small community that most of the young adults in town went out with each other at one time or another. It was only after seeing the same people together for five or more times that people started to wonder if they were seriously dating.

Laser bowling was a lot of fun. They both were quite competitive, and their scores were nearly identical. Shaun won the first two games by a very small margin. Then Trish really worked at it and won the last game by eleven points. They had a great time.

At 10:00 p.m., the bowling alley staff ushered everyone out. It had barely gotten dark, and Shaun didn't want their fun evening to end, so he suggested that they drive around for a while. Trish was enjoying herself, too, so she agreed.

Shaun took the highway toward Mason City. They drove with the windows open in the truck. Soon Trish's hair was all over the place. She laughed and pulled a hair scrunchy out of her purse and put her hair in a thick ponytail. There was a scenic site off the highway, so Shaun pulled into it. They sat down on the park bench to continue their conversation.

At one point, Trish pulled off her scrunchy and tried to comb through her wild hair with her fingers. Shaun gently stopped her fingers. "Leave your hair. It looks awesome like that," he said softly to her.

Trish looked up into his face. She was surprised at his words, but she nodded and smiled a little at him. Shaun bent his head and kissed her. It was a very thorough kiss. His hands went into her hair, and he gently caressed her head while they kissed. It was just as magical as their kiss had been in the shed during the thunderstorm.

Trish kissed him back, just as thoroughly. She felt his hands leave her hair and pull her closer to him. When he had both arms around her, she sighed blissfully and stretched her arms around his neck. Their kiss lasted a long time. When they pulled away from each other, their eyes were dark, and they were both breathing heavily.

Shaun breathlessly exclaimed, "I hoped that our next kiss would be as wonderful as our first one. I'm very glad to say that it was. Trish, your kisses are amazing! I could kiss you all night."

Trish grinned knowingly and said, "Now, Shaun, you know that people will talk if they find us kissing the night away. Although, I do agree that it was a great kiss. You are a wonderful kisser, too."

With that, they kissed again, many more times. Each kiss was just as enthralling as the last. Eventually, they came up for air. Trish pulled away first. She was not accustomed to this extended amount of kissing. Feeling a little out of her depth, she decided they should cool down.

Shaun felt her pull away, physically and emotionally. He was glad that she had the strength to pull away. They were going way too fast. This was their first date, and he was shaken by the intensity of his feelings for Trish. He had never felt that passionate about any girl before.

It was getting late, so they decided to head back home. Shaun pulled into her driveway, grabbed her hand, and squeezed it tightly. "Will you go out with me again, Trish? I really enjoyed the evening—and not only the kissing. We seem to have a bunch of things in common."

Trish nodded happily. "Yes, Shaun, I will go out with you again. Just name the time and the place."

Shaun said, "I'm not sure which evenings I'll be free next week. Is it okay if I call you or come into the library to see you in a few days?"

"Sure, that will be fine. Shaun, thank you for a wonderful evening. I liked everything about it. I'll look forward to our next date. Good night."

Shaun didn't try to kiss her again. He wasn't sure he could stop kissing her once he started. Besides, they were in her driveway, and anyone could see them. No, he preferred to do his kissing in private, like the shed or that lonely bench in the scenic area.

Trish told Jenny and her mom about her date. While not revealing anything about their kissing, she enthusiastically talked about the meal and bowling. She said that he was going to ask her out again next week. Jenny watched her intently. Trish looked like she had been thoroughly kissed. She had never been so bright-eyed after a date before, either.

Shaun came into the library the following week and asked her out for that Friday. He snuck in a quick exciting kiss as he leaned over the library counter. They had another great date that Friday. It was the beginning of a sweet romance. Shaun could tell that Trish was an innocent woman, and he never asked her to do more than kiss him.

They became an established couple. They often took Mary with them when they went out. She didn't go out very much, otherwise. While she was great fun, many men could not see beyond her clubfoot. That she hankered after one man was known only to Shaun and Trish.

Mary had never gotten over her high school crush on James Regan, a tall dark-haired young man who was Shaun's age. He ran his folk's farm, just like Shaun did. His dad was in poor health, and James lived with his parents. James was a kind and decent man, who cared for his parents and the cattle on his farm. He quietly came to church on Sunday with his parents, but people never saw him out with a girl. James mostly stayed at home and took care of the farm.

Mary always thought that he was deep. He got good grades at high school, and he could talk about a wide variety of topics when he wanted to. Mostly, he was quiet. He watched people and listened, but he did not pass on any comments unless he felt like it. Mary always laughed and said that she would make him smile and talk if she could just get the chance. James seemed accepting of his circumstances. She wanted the chance to "shake him up" a little.

Mary's parents were lovely people. They gave her as many opportunities as possible. She attended the same college as Trish. The two friends met often while they were undergraduates. When Mary earned her agriculture business degree, she went back home to help her parents with their farm.

Trish asked Shaun if he minded if they sometimes took Mary with them on their dates. He understood Trish's penchant for helping others. That was one of the things that he loved about her. She cared about so many people. By now he knew that he loved and adored her. He was patiently waiting for the right moment to propose to her.

They hadn't yet pronounced their love for each other. Shaun wondered if Trish was just waiting for him to say it first. He was often a little unsure of her. She seemed as if she loved him, but occasionally her independent nature led to his uncertainty. They went out for more than a year and a half before he felt sure enough about her to propose.

Shaun proposed to her on Christmas Eve that following year. He had come over to celebrate it with Trish and her family. They were going to spend Christmas Day with his family. Her family had gone to bed, and Shaun and Trish were all cuddled up on the couch, just watching the twinkling lights on the Christmas tree and listening to the quiet music.

Trish's face, full of love, gazed at Shaun. He finally realized that she loved him, too. Kissing her deeply, Shaun then slowly rose from the couch. He knelt before her, gently held her hands, and looked her straight in the eyes. Trish sat up straight in anticipation of the long-awaited moment.

"Trish, I have loved you for a long time now. Will you marry me?" he asked in a quiet hopeful voice. He watched her face intently as he spoke.

Trish could not stop the delighted smile that came onto her face. She had waited an awfully long time for Shaun to get himself ready to marry her. She would have married him six months ago.

"Yes, Shaun. I will marry you. I have loved you for a long time, too."

Shaun kissed her hands and joined Trish on the couch. They snuggled up on it while they talked. It was the most magical Christmas that either one had ever experienced.

Everyone was so happy for them the next morning when they heard the good news. The excited couple planned to marry in ten months' time, after the seed corn harvest.

Things had gone wonderfully well for them until Sheila came to town and made a mockery of their love. Trish despised Sheila's cavalier destruction of their happiness.

## CHAPTER

# Three

Trish walked into her mother's house. She had only been back in Dalton for two days and was still shocked at her mother's frailty. Lila sat in her wheelchair, seemingly not caring about anything. Jenny told Trish that her return to Dalton might just be the event that would catapult their mom into taking more of an interest in life, but it hadn't happened yet. True, Lila did smile when Trish came in the door, but it hadn't really affected her very much.

Trish, her head full of memories from her walk home, was quiet. This was so unlike her that Jenny frowned. Something must have happened at the grocery store. She followed Trish into the kitchen. Trish was putting the candy in the cupboard. Even though she had been dying for some chocolate an hour ago, it was the last thing that she wanted now.

Jenny quietly asked her, "Trish, did something happen at the grocery store? You seem so quiet and sad."

Trish looked at her with sad eyes and said, "I ran into Shaun and Mary. They were buying candy prior to going to the movies. Mary was glad to see me and gave me a big hug. Shaun only said 'hello' because it would have been rude to ignore me after I said 'hi' to him. He looked at me as if he couldn't stand the sight of me. You know that I wanted to see him sometime and ask him for an explanation. I now know that I should have done that before leaving the way I did. However, I can't undo the things I did. I just hope that he will someday allow me to ask him for forgiveness and his explanation. Maybe then I will be able to forget him and move on with my life."

Jenny put her hand on Trish's arm in support. "I'm sorry that you had to run into him that way. He was very likely shocked to see you. You know how stubborn he is. He is probably just giving you a taste of your own medicine. It's not very nice, but you must agree that he has his pride. Why don't you give it some more time? Maybe there will be a chance to talk with him in a few days or next week. You never know, maybe he just didn't want to talk in front of Mary or in a public place."

Trish agreed, and they stopped talking about it. They went into the living room to talk some more with Josh about the mural that Trish promised to paint on his basement bedroom wall. He had moved down there a few months ago to have a little more privacy. At twelve years old, he was starting to think like a teenager.

Trish hadn't painted in a long time. She missed the way painting made her feel. Her sketchbook and colored pencils were all that she brought with her to Brazil. The anticipation of painting Josh's mural brought back that excitement. This project would consume her until it was done perfectly.

Josh was into baseball in a big way and couldn't wait until he was in high school, so he could play on the schools' team. He already played on the town's local team. They were not very good, but he was an excited member of the team. The older men fondly worked with Josh on his batting and fielding. He already was a very fast runner.

A quiet week passed. Lila got a little stronger, but she was still so listless and uninterested in life. Trish tried everything she could think of to get her mom interested in something. She also spent quite a lot of time in Josh's bedroom, sketching the baseball scene on his gray cement walls. Now she just needed some paint.

The plan was that Jenny would drive their mother to Mason City for her doctor's appointment. Josh wanted to go along and help her buy the paint that Trish needed for his bedroom. Trish planned to stay at home and start painting the wall with the paint that she already had.

That morning, before her family left for Mason City, Trish had gone out to the small hardware store in town and bought new painting supplies and a beautiful green paint for the outfield. She had already decided on the colors of paint that she would need for the mural. The hardware store did not stock most of those colors in small cans. It was not like she needed a whole gallon of each color. She did need quite a lot of the green paint, though.

Hank, the owner, had been a good friend to her father, and Trish always loved talking with him. He regaled her with anecdotes of her dad. She always came away from his store with a smile on her face. He used to give her chocolate when she came in to buy anything. Her father laughingly told old Hank about her love for it. It was a standing joke among all of them for years.

As usual, Hank had some tales to tell Trish. He had heard that she was back in town, so he stocked up on her favorite chocolates. When she paid for her items, he produced the candy with a flourish. She suspiciously asked him if it was three years old. He bellowed with laughter and told her he had just purchased it a few days ago after he heard that she was in town.

She gave him a big hug and happily accepted it. When he heard that she would be alone in the house later today, he gave her a few extra pieces—comfort candy, he called it. Trish waved as she walked back home. In some ways it felt really good to be back home. She had grown up here, and she knew just about everyone.

Trish showed her green paint to Josh and got his excited approval. If she could get the outfield painted, she could start with another color tomorrow. It would take her at least a week to allow one layer of paint to dry before adding a new color.

She hugged her family goodbye. They planned to eat supper in town and be home in the late evening. Trish was not scared of being in the house by herself. She had grown up here. There was nothing to frighten her in the town.

After lunch, Trish took her green paint and painting supplies to Josh's bedroom. Their CD player belted out music as Trish happily painted the green outfield. She took a few breaks but doggedly kept going. She thought that she could finish the outfield before Josh came home. He would be excited to see part of the baseball mural done.

* * *

While in Mason City, Jenny heard about the tornadoes that were developing over the surrounding area. One was moving in the direction of Dalton. She tried to reach Trish multiple times to tell her to take shelter. Every home in the Dalton area had a storm shelter, given the high rate of tornado occurrences.

Trish never heard the telephone ring. Her favorite music was playing loudly from the CD player. The basement swallowed up all sounds from above.

Jenny realized that Trish was very likely busy painting in the basement and couldn't hear the phone ringing. She wondered who could help Trish, so she called a few of their neighbors, but she didn't get anyone at home.

In desperation, she called the Healys. She hoped Mrs. Healy could get one of their neighbors to check in with Trish. She explained to Mrs. Healy that Trish was at the house but not answering the phone. Jenny believed that the tornado might come right through Dalton.

Mrs. Healy grasped the situation immediately. She was concerned about Trish but didn't think that she wanted to tell Shaun. He had been very grim-faced for a week since he had seen Trish at the grocery store. Not that he told her about it—she had to hear it from Mary's mother. The two women were good friends. Their farms were only a few miles from each other.

Mrs. Healy was on the phone calling some neighbors to go and check on Trish when Shaun strode in. His face was set. "There is a tornado coming, Mom. Get the backpacks and head to the shelter. I'll bring Dad with me," he said.

He heard her talking to the neighbors on the phone. He rushed further into the kitchen as soon as she hung up the phone.

He said urgently, "What was that all about, Mom? What is going on with Trish?"

She told him the situation. He grabbed one of the backpacks that they always had ready to go in case of a tornado. There was water, food, and a lightweight blanket in there, along with other useful supplies.

"Mom, you take Dad to the shelter. Go now. I will go and see what is happening with Trish. You know how frightened she is of these kinds of storms." He wore a determined look.

His mom protested a little, but Shaun cut off her words. "Mom, this is Trish we're talking about. I can't sit in the shelter knowing that she might not be safe. I'm going, no matter what you say. Now, please, get yourself and Dad to the shelter right now. I'll let you know how everything is as soon as I can. Bye."

Shaun rushed out of the house, the backpack over his shoulder. Tearing down the road, the usual five-minute drive took him three minutes. He looked at the sky as he jumped out of the truck. It was black and whirling. This did not look good. Trish Newberg's front door was unlocked, so he ran inside and looked around. He heard the music blasting from the basement, so he ran down the steps as fast as he could.

Trish heard something and looked toward the door. She nearly jumped out of her skin when she saw Shaun in the doorway. Before she could utter a word, Shaun leaped forward and grabbed her arm. As he was pulling her out of the room, he said hurriedly, "Trish, there is a tornado on the way. We need to get into the tornado shelter. Come on, now."

His words were sufficiently urgent to get her moving. She had been totally unaware of the tornado and the danger she was in. They ran for the shelter and pulled the door closed just as a huge wind passed over it. The door rattled, but they were now safe inside.

Shaun pulled the high-powered flashlight from his backpack and turned it on. He then led her to the lumpy couch that was in the far corner of the shelter, pulled the lightweight blanket from his backpack, and wrapped it around her. He could already see the stark fear on her face, so he sat her down on the couch and wrapped his arms tightly around her. She was stiff with fright. Shaun crooned softly to her and slowly caressed her wild hair.

Trish finally started to calm down when they heard a terrible sound. It sounded like the house was being torn apart. She screamed loudly and buried her head in Shaun's shoulder. He kissed the top of her head and said that they were fine. He held her for half an hour until the awful noise ceased.

Shaun told her to stay on the couch while he checked things out. He cautiously opened the door of the shelter and looked out. He could see the black clouds in the distance, but the sky was clear where they were. Pieces of wood and roof shingles were scattered around the yard.

Then he looked at the house. A large corner of the roof had been torn off by the tornado. He thought that the rest of the house looked intact, but he couldn't be sure. His truck had not escaped damage. There was a huge piece of wood sticking out of the windshield. The front end of his truck had been crushed.

Shaun steeled himself to be calm for Trish's sake. He returned to the shelter and sat next to her on the couch. Her eyes still showed a remnant of fear. He took her hands and said, "Trish, we're going to sit here for a while and talk. That horrible noise we heard was the tornado tearing off part of the roof. My truck is damaged, too. We are not going anywhere for a while."

He held her again when she started to cry. It broke his heart to hear her. Shaun knew that she didn't cry easily. Her emotions had to be really stressed for her to start crying. As he held her, his feelings of love returned full blast. Her small body felt so right in his arms. He wanted to kiss her, but this was not the right time.

Suddenly, she sat up straight. "Nolan! Nolan was in the house with me. I forgot about him. Oh, Shaun, what if he is hurt or worse? We've got to find him!"

She struggled to remove the blanket and rise from the couch. Shaun caught her and gently sat her back down. He assured her, "Trish, animals have a way of knowing where to hide in situations like this. I'm sure that he is alright. However, I am not sure if it is safe to go into the house right now. Let's go and open the house door and call for him. If he can hear us, he'll come out to you. Then we can keep him with us outside the house. Bring your blanket with you, okay?"

His very calmness helped Trish pull herself together. They left the shelter. Trish looked around her yard and shuddered. She gasped when she saw the house and Shaun's truck. She had been totally unaware of the impending danger. Shaun may have saved her life, and she hadn't even thanked him, yet. As soon as they found Nolan, she would give him the biggest thank you that she knew how to give.

They opened the house's front door, calling Nolan's name loudly. After five minutes, they heard him bark. Trish called for him to come out. He slowly emerged on shaky legs. The poor dog had been in the house when the roof came off. It must have been terrifying for him. Trish knelt and hugged Nolan. She put the blanket around her shaking dog.

Trish looked at Shaun with a beautiful smile. She quietly said, "Shaun, I can't thank you enough. You may have saved my life. I'm sure that I would have died of fright if I had been in the basement when the roof came off. Thank you for helping me find Nolan, too."

Shaun looked at her grateful face and eyes. He wanted them to have that talk that she had denied him three years ago. Maybe it was not too late to salvage their relationship. The invitation to talk had to come from her. He couldn't just bulldoze over her emotions, especially right now when she was still vulnerable.

People were coming out of their houses and looking around. Shaun nodded at Trish's neighbors. Some of them came over and asked Trish if she was alright. She told everyone that Shaun came over just as the tornado was overhead. He got her safely to the shelter and sat with her while they heard the roof coming off. The neighbors nodded at Shaun and patted him on the back. They were grateful that Trish and Nolan were safe.

Mrs. Rush, who had received a frantic call from Jenny, came over to see how Trish was doing. She heard the story and invited the whole neighborhood to come over to the Dalton Cafe to have some coffee and pie while they discussed what they should do.

Several other homes had been damaged. Mrs. Rush's sister owned the cafe, but she was out of town on vacation. Mrs. Rush had the keys, and she felt it was her duty to help the townspeople after the storm.

As much as Shaun wanted to talk privately with Trish, he was pulled along to the cafe. He was a hero in their eyes. Trish might have been badly hurt alone in the house.

Trish insisted that Nolan come with her. For once, Mrs. Rush turned a blind eye to a dog on the premises. Nolan was an old, tired dog. He sank thankfully under the table near Trish's legs. She gave him a few chunks of her pie. She was not all that hungry, only thirsty.

* * *

Mrs. Rush called Jenny and told her what happened to Trish. Since the house was not livable for the moment, Jenny decided to take her mom and son to a motel for the night. She made up some excuse so that they would not be frightened about Trish's near catastrophe. Mrs. Rush promised that Trish and Nolan could stay overnight at her house.

She also called the Healys. Their house had escaped damage, and they were back inside it by now. Shaun spoke to his mom and explained about his truck. One of Trish's neighbors offered to give him a ride home.

The motel on the other edge of town had also escaped damage. There were ten rooms, all available. Trish quickly booked two of them for her family. A few of the neighbors, whose homes had been damaged, booked their rooms, too.

That important concern taken care of, they talked about companies and contractors that could repair their homes.

As her neighbors sat talking, Trish was aware that she hadn't had the time to talk with Shaun, and this saddened her. *In the shelter, it seemed as if he was ready to talk about our issue*, she thought. *Maybe Shaun is ready to give me an explanation and forgive me.* She was feeling very grateful to him right now.

Since they were no longer engaged, the crowd didn't think that Shaun might want to sit with Trish or talk privately with her. While they thought it was decent of him to come to Trish's rescue, the neighbors were oblivious to the fact that Trish and Shaun wanted to be alone.

Shaun could see that he was not going to get the chance to talk with Trish tonight. She would soon be going to Mrs. Rush's house for the night. He didn't know how he could see her tomorrow, either. He might have to wait until she was staying at the motel. Another problem was that he no longer had a truck.

The crowd at the cafe slowly started to break up as people went home. Those few who couldn't go back into their homes were given beds for the night from kind neighbors. The man giving Shaun a ride home was ready to leave.

Shaun, not wanting to keep him waiting, looked at Trish over their heads. He willed her to look at him, but her face was turned away from him. She was talking to Mrs. Rush and didn't see his look—she only saw the back of him as he walked out the door. It was like a slap in the face. She knew that it would be difficult to talk with him privately, but after all they had just gone through this evening, he could at least have said goodbye.

## CHAPTER

# Four

As Jenny transported her family to Dalton the next day, she calmly related details of the storm.

By the time they arrived, Trish was ready to leave Mrs. Rush's house. That good lady was so kind, but she had a steady stream of visitors and phone calls. Trish wanted to be somewhere quiet. She had so much to think about. Number one on that list was Shaun—she couldn't tell if he still wanted to talk with her or not.

After they left, they went to look at their house. Trish had been advised not to let anyone inside until an inspector went through it. The family stood in the driveway, looking at the partial roof and Jenny's exposed bedroom. It was odd to consider that less than twenty-four hours ago, the house was fine.

Since they were going to have to spend some time in temporary lodging, they decided to go shopping for some clothes and supplies. They first went to the motel and checked in. After they got their keys and looked at their rooms, they called Mary Walsh.

Nolan was not allowed in the motel, so Trish asked Mary to take him for a while. They had done the same for Mary's dog when she went on vacation with her folks for two weeks.

They drove Nolan to Mary's house and made much of him. He seemed to know that they were planning to leave him there because he kept trying to get back into the car. Finally, Trish walked him into the house, talked with Mary for a few minutes and quickly left, closing the door firmly. She heard his mournful howl and almost came back for him, but she knew that Mary would cuddle him and treat him just like her own beloved dog.

Lila's cheeks were pink as they set out for Mason City to buy some clothes. It seemed like she was enjoying their adventure. Each bought a few sets of clothes and some pajamas. It would have to be enough until they could get back into the house for some of their other clothes. They bought some cards and other games to prevent boredom. Trish bought a sketchbook and colored pencils.

They had no idea how long they would be forced to stay at the motel. It would depend on the severity of the damage and how quickly the construction crew could get the work done.

From her motel room, Trish called her coworkers in Brazil to inform them of recent events. Ted told her that Senhor Carlos Santos was there and wanted to speak to her.

When Trish's old roommate, Sarah, left Brazil to get married, Carlos was upset because he was infatuated with Sarah. He had even flown to Minnesota before her wedding to ask her to break up with her fiancé and marry him instead.

After Sarah's rejection of his proposal, Carlos returned to his mine and went on a drinking binge. Trish found him one evening, drunk and unhappy. She made pot after pot of coffee for him and talked with him all night. Carlos came to see Trish as more than just a good employee; she became a trusted friend.

Over time, that trust became mutual. She told him about Shaun's apparent unfaithfulness, her quick anger, and subsequent departure. Carlos listened and empathized.

Whenever he flew in to visit his mine, he made a point of spending time with Trish. She was the only one at the mine who knew that he was a widower. He had lost his lovely wife and unborn baby twenty-two years ago. It still hurt him to think about them.

Now, as Trish talked with Carlos on the phone, he told her that she needed to stay with her family. He would not hire anyone in her place until she told him unequivocally that she was not returning to Brazil. He was full of good ideas about the house, too. Besides owning the mine, Carlos owned a construction firm.

Trish enjoyed her chat with Carlos. She felt good about getting advice from him. They needed someone's expert opinion about the house's needs.

The Newbergs spent the first few days at the motel making calls and organizing repairs. Trish hoped to get a call from Shaun but was disappointed at the end of every day when she had not heard from him. She began to think that their chance for reconciliation had passed.

Speaking of Sheila, she was back in town. Most of the townspeople didn't give her the time of day. She had caused enough havoc in the past. There were some who still believed that she and Shaun had an affair, although most of the community believed that she made it up.

Shaun declared his innocence to his family and friends by saying, "I didn't have the affair. I love Trish and would never hurt her." They all believed him.

Meanwhile, Shaun faced the tedious task of finding another truck, which was not easy due to the limited replacement value. Since he used his truck around the farm, he did not want to invest in a brand-new one. The only bright spot in his day was thinking about talking with Trish soon.

* * *

Senhor Carlos Santos drove up to the motel. Trish had told him that Dalton was a sleepy little town with old worn-out buildings. *Still, how could people enjoy staying in such a place?* he wondered. He saw Trish sitting with some other people at the picnic table in the grassy area next to the parking lot. He parked his rented Mercedes Benz in the corner where no one would ding her. Carlos, like many men, thought of his automobile as a fine lady.

Trish looked up and grinned in amazement as Carlos approached. In her excitement, she ran toward her dear friend. He laughingly pulled her into his arms and gave her a big hug. Then he kissed her cheek and, arm around her shoulders, walked her back to the picnic table. To any onlookers, it looked like a reunion between two people who felt mighty close to each other.

Trish had told her mom and Josh about her job in Brazil the first day they stayed in the motel. She didn't think secrecy was necessary any longer, also telling them about her friends there, primarily Carlos. They teased her that it must be nice to have friends in high places. Trish laughed and said that she would never presume upon Carlos' money or position.

As she walked to the table with him, Carlos said to her, "Olá, doce amiga." Setting aside her curiosity regarding his visit, Trish introduced him to her family.

"Carlos, this is my mother, Lila, my sister, Jenny, and my nephew, Josh. Everyone, this is Senhor Carlos Santos, the owner of the mine," she said.

Carlos bent over Lila Newberg and gently kissed her hand. He knew that she was frail and recovering from a stroke. He looked into her eyes and softly said to her, "Olá, Mamãe Newberg. Estou tão feliz em conhecê-lo."

Trish, who had heard that phrase before, quietly told her mother, "He is saying hello and that he is happy to meet you."

Carlos looked approvingly at Trish and said, "That's right. Very good, Trish. I see that you have picked up some Portuguese over the years that you have been with us." He smiled warmly at her. She grinned back at him.

Lila Newberg sat up straight. Here was something new and interesting. This handsome man looked like he cared about Trish. On the other hand, he would be perfect for poor Jenny. Jenny needed someone strong in her life to take some of the weight off her shoulders. She was too young to have so many burdens. *Now she must worry about me, too,* Lila thought with great sadness. Lila nodded and smiled at Senhor Santos—she liked it when a handsome man kissed her hand.

Carlos studied each of them intently. Trish looked a little bit like her mother but nothing like her sister. His heart pounded when he looked at Jenny. She was the type of woman to whom he was attracted. Her sweet face was graced by big blue eyes and a wide pink mouth, and her long hair was pale gold. She was average height and slim, and she looked like an angel to him. He already knew that she was a widow. Trish had told him all about her family during one of their many talks in Brazil.

Carlos knew that Jenny was independent and aloof. While he preferred women to be demure, he understood that she was alone, trying to take care of an ailing mother and a pre-teen son. He felt a sudden wish to take the weight from her shoulders and see what she looked like when she was cosseted and worry-free. He just bet that she would be so beautiful.

Jenny was surprised by her reaction to Carlos. Whenever Trish talked about him, Jenny always had to reign in her negative comments. In her mind, Senhor Carlos Santos was a big shot, with too much money and property. She thought that he was probably arrogant and unable to relate to regular people like herself.

When he softly said hello to her and stooped to kiss her hand, she became flustered. Somewhere, deep in her gut, she felt the beginnings of a fire start. He was so handsome and charming, and he treated her as if she was someone very special. She had not felt special in such a long time. Jack used to make her feel that way, but he had been gone for more than seven years.

Carlos' soft words, "Olá, anjo bonito," made Jenny want to run to a computer to find out what he said to her. It was different from the words she heard him say to Trish.

After Trish left for Brazil, Jenny filled the vacancy at the Dalton Library. She had been working part time for the last three years. There were plenty of computers she could use to find out exactly what Senhor Santos was saying. She said the phrase over and over in her head so she wouldn't forget it.

Carlos extended his hand to Josh, who took it and gave Carlos a firm handshake in return. They grinned at each other. "Hello, Josh. Your Aunt Trish said that you were a tall good-looking young man. That looks like you," Carlos said genially.

Josh nodded and said, "Aunt Trish never described you other than to say that you were good friends and that you were a very fair man to work for."

Carlos looked over his shoulder at Trish and smiled at her. "Muito obrigado por suas belas palavras, meu amigo."

Trish understood that he was thanking her for her words, so she jauntily said, "Você é bem-vindo, Carlos."

The others were impressed that Trish understood and could speak some Portuguese. Jenny wished that she knew what they were saying and wondered if there were some romantic feelings between her little sister and this handsome charming man. She had thought that Trish still loved Shaun, but now she was not so sure. Carlos and Trish seemed very close. She would have to have a private talk with Trish. Of course, that would be difficult with her mom and Josh always around.

After talking with Trish and her family for half an hour, Carlos invited them to dine with him.

They informed him that the only place to eat in Dalton was the Dalton Cafe. Accustomed to more options, he asked if there were other restaurants within an hour's drive.

After a brief discussion, they chose the Northwestern Steakhouse in Mason City. This pleased Carlos, who wanted to experience a typical American restaurant.

At the steakhouse, Carlos helped Lila out of the car and into her wheelchair. Her cheeks were flushed with excitement. She was enjoying the attention of a handsome younger man.

Carlos perused the menu and asked the Newbergs what they recommended. He liked steak, and there were some mouthwatering dishes displayed on the menu. After considering their suggestions, he made his selection and urged them to order anything they wanted. The meal was his treat. He grinned inwardly when he saw their happy smiles.

Carlos ordered a delicious wine, which only Trish and Jenny drank. Because of her medication, Lila could not have alcohol, and Carlos was driving, so they both drank soda water. When their water arrived, Carlos rose to make a toast in Lila's honor. Her daughters gave an appreciative nod toward the author of their feast.

Jenny and Trish were feeling quite mellow and in great spirits by the time they left the restaurant. For both, it was a welcome departure from their daily challenges. Carlos dropped them off at their doors and then went to inquire if there was a room for him. Happily, the motel had a room available.

His was the last one in the row. Carlos looked at his home away from home and shuddered a little. It was so drab and old that he didn't think that he would enjoy staying there. However, he wanted to talk with Trish to see how he could help her and her family. He counted Trish as one of his closest friends, and he would do just about anything to help her in her time of need. Besides, he wanted to spend more time getting to know sweet Jenny.

* * *

By the time Shaun could finally get away from the farm, Trish and her family had been at the Dalton Motel for ten days. Still without a truck, his parents gladly allowed him to borrow their car. He drove to the motel, hoping that Trish would be there and willing to take a ride with him.

Shaun pulled into the crowded motel parking lot. Scanning the lot for Jenny's or Lila's vehicle, he wondered who owned the gleaming black Mercedes Benz. *Wow! I don't see many of them around Dalton.* Shaun loved cars and wished he could afford something like that black Mercedes. His truck was a functional workhorse. He didn't lead the kind of life in which he needed a fancy car.

*Still, a Mercedes!* he thought with a tiny bit of jealousy. Then he saw the license plates. It was a rental from Mason City. That made more sense. *Someone in town must have relatives with deep pockets.*

Shaun parked and entered the motel to inquire about Trish's room. The motel clerk, Glen, was an old classmate of Shaun's. They chatted for a while before Glen told Shaun that Trish and her mom were in Room 102, and Jenny and Josh were in Room 103.

After thanking Glen, Shaun set out to find Trish. He knocked on her door several times. Finally, the door to Room 103 opened. Josh peeked out. When he saw Shaun, he smiled and opened the door the rest of the way.

"Hi, Shaun," Josh said with a grin. "Are you looking for my Aunt Trish?"

"Hi, Josh," Shaun replied with a smile. "Yes, I wanted to talk with her for a few minutes, but it seems as if she is not here."

"Oh, she and Grandma went out with Senhor Santos. They took Grandma's car to see how it was running after it was damaged a little in the tornado. They've been gone for a few hours, but Aunt Trish said they would be back for supper. They're bringing supper back with them. I didn't want to go with them, so Mom said that I could stay here while she is at her job at the library. I'm old enough to stay by myself you know," asserted Josh.

"Sure, you are, Josh. You're growing so big and tall. Please tell me, who is Senhor Santos?" Shaun asked.

Josh, feeling that his explanation might take a while, invited Shaun to come into their motel room. Shaun nodded and went inside.

He sat on one of the chairs while Josh pulled a few bottles of water out of the small fridge. They got comfortable, and Shaun waited for Josh to talk.

"Well, Senhor Santos is the owner of the mine. He and Aunt Trish are really good friends. He gave her a great big hug and kiss the day he came here. Grandma thinks that maybe they are in love or something." Josh spoke plainly yet could not avoid a slight roll of his eyes.

Shaun was confused and immediately jealous. "The mine? What mine? I don't know what you are talking about, Josh," he said quietly.

"Oh, I forgot. You don't know about Aunt Trish living in Brazil and working at a mine," Josh said.

"Brazil—as in the country in South America?" asked Shaun, flabbergasted.

"Yup, Brazil in South America," said Josh with a nod.

"Josh, will you please start at the beginning? I'm confused right now," said Shaun in frustration.

"Okay, I'll tell you what I know," said Josh, trying to be helpful.

"When Aunt Trish left Dalton three years ago, you know, after you had that affair, she went to Brazil to work at a mine. Only my mom knew where she was. Anyway, Senhor Santos is the owner of the mine. He's a multi-millionaire. He's a really cool guy, and he's helped all of us ever since he's been here." Josh dropped the bomb on Shaun so casually.

Shaun was reeling from this newly learned information. He wanted to protest when Josh said that bit about the affair, but there was so much more he needed to know. There was no reason to get Josh defensive or uncomfortable.

"What else do you know about Senhor Santos, Josh? He sounds like a great guy." Shaun was still trying to wrap his head around the idea that Trish had been living and working in Brazil!

"Well, he talks to me about baseball, which I like. He likes baseball, too, but he doesn't know that much about American baseball. He said that he would take me to see the Burlington Bees or maybe even drive to Minnesota to watch the Minnesota Twins if my mom agrees. His car is awesome—a Mercedes Benz. Sometimes he takes me for rides in it." Josh smiled widely when he thought about Senhor Santos.

"How long has Senhor Santos been here, Josh?" Shaun was almost afraid of the answer.

"Let me think . . . I guess he came four days after we moved into the motel. Aunt Trish called him the first night we were here, and he got on the first plane he could. He said that he needed to be here to help his dear Trish. He's staying here, too, in Room 110. I don't think he likes it very much, but he said that he wants to stay close to us. Grandma really likes him. Mom said that he was just what we needed to give Grandma an interest in living again. All I know is that Grandma smiles a lot again. After her stroke, she just sat in her wheelchair and looked unhappy." Josh abruptly stopped talking. He wasn't sure if he should be telling Shaun about their family business.

Shaun recognized that Josh was wondering if he should be as forthcoming as he was. After all, Shaun was not going to be part of their family anymore. He and Josh had talked quite a lot when he was engaged to Trish, but he didn't know what Trish's family thought about him anymore. Did they still believe that he had that affair with Sheila, or had they finally rid themselves of that nonsense? He certainly had not spoken to any of them much in the last three years.

In the brief uncomfortable silence, each wondered what to say next. Josh looked at Shaun with trepidation. Meanwhile, Shaun regained his composure and spoke.

"Thank you so much for the information, Josh. I don't have time to wait for Trish to return because I still have a bunch of chores to do at home. You don't need to say that I was here. I'll try again, when I have some free time. If you do mention it to her, just tell her that I said hello, okay?" Shaun remained outwardly upbeat, even though he was crushed.

Josh looked at Shaun and saw his friendly grin and felt better. He nodded back at Shaun and stuck out his hand. He saw Senhor Santos do that when he was done talking with other men.

Shaun shook his hand, grinned once more at Josh, and left the room. As he drove back home, he thought about everything that he learned today. Trish had moved to Brazil. She was close friends with a millionaire who seemed to be enamored with her. Maybe it really was too late to think that they could reconcile. That thought made him so sad.

Shaun had dreamt of the day that Trish would come back, ready to forgive him and ask him what had really happened. Even though he had been so upset with her, he forgave her. Now that he had seen her again and held her in his arms, he wanted them to get back together. She was the only woman for him. He loved her so much. That had never changed.

* * *

Lila watched Carlos gently teasing Trish. That they were close was obvious for everyone to see. *Just how close are they?* she wondered. Sometimes they seemed like good friends, but other times, one of them would say or do something that seemed so loving. She didn't know his age or his life story, but it was obvious that he was much older than Trish. He seemed better suited to be with Jenny.

Lila had also noticed his tender care of Jenny. The poor girl didn't know what to do about him. Carlos never said or did anything inappropriate, but he seemed very careful about his interactions with her. He was terrific with Josh, though. He seemed to know exactly what to say to Josh, to bring him out of his shell. That boy was way too quiet for a twelve-year-old boy, in her opinion.

Carlos was driving her car. It had been scratched and dented a bit in the garage during the tornado. He had also talked with the insurance people for her. They were bringing it into the auto shop in Mason City today to be looked at. Before it was to be checked over, Carlos dropped Trish and her off at a nearby mall, so they could shop a little. He stayed with the car in case the mechanics had any questions. She was grateful for his help.

At the mall, Trish pushed her mom's wheelchair around their favorite stores. Trish encouraged her mom to pick out something new to wear. They were all mightily tired of the few clothes they had at the motel. Although the construction firm was currently working on their house, they had not yet been allowed to go inside to get more clothes or other supplies. Trish was going to buy something new, too, if she saw something she liked.

"Mom, look at this pretty blouse. It looks like it is your size. Do you like it? If so, you could try it on. It matches your pants wonderfully, and it would be an extra outfit for you."

Now that Carlos was here, they went out more frequently than she anticipated. She had envisioned them sitting in their motel room day after day until the construction company was done with their house.

Lila's blue eyes twinkled when she looked at the blouse. "Yes, I like this one. I think that I *will* try it on. Will you come into the fitting room and help me? I still have so much trouble with my left arm."

"Sure, Mom. Let's hang onto it and look around for a few minutes first. That way we can take everything into the fitting room all at once."

Trish beamed. Her mom was slowly coming out of her depressed funk. Carlos was directly responsible for her recovery. Trish owed him so much!

Finding several items of clothes that each liked, they took everything into a large fitting room to try on. Getting Lila into one of the blouses was a cumbersome undertaking, but they were both giggling by the time they accomplished it. She looked wonderful in the new blouse.

Lila's cheeks were glowing, and the same wavy brown hair that Trish inherited stuck out because of the static in it. Trish tried to tame her mom's hair the same way she often tried to tame her own.

It was an impossible task without a scrunchy, so Trish ran out to get a pretty cotton one for her mom. Once the scrunchy was in Lila's hair, Trish looked critically at her mom.

"Mom, you look beautiful." Trish was gratified when Lila grinned at her.

Lila also complimented Trish on her finds, as well. The new green patterned sundress was so cute, and it matched her personality and coloring perfectly. The new striped cotton top was flirty and fun, too. Trish had not lost her tan, and the top showed it off quite nicely.

Well satisfied with their purchases, they set out to find the Food Court. Wanting a long cool drink before Carlos came to get them, they purchased pink lemonade and sat comfortably, talking about their new clothes.

Carlos called them on the new cell phone that he had given to Trish. He didn't want her to be limited by landlines at the motel or their house. Jenny had a cell phone, but she was not always around when Trish might need one.

"Ola, Trish. The repairs to the car are nearly finished. I should be at your mall in fifteen minutes or so. Are you finished with your shopping, or do you need more time? It is not a problem if you do because I can wait in the car until you are completely satisfied with your shopping." Carlos' voice was friendly and tolerant. He remembered how long it took his wife to complete her clothes shopping.

"Carlos, thank you, but we're done shopping. Right now, we are in the Food Court enjoying a glass of lemonade. We'll meet you in fifteen minutes where you dropped us off," Trish told him.

Trish leisurely pushed the wheelchair back to the entrance. They window shopped as they walked past the stores. Lila's eyes were bright, and her cheeks were pink.

Carlos picked them up right on time. He explained what had been done to Lila's car. They decided what they should bring home for supper. Both Josh and Jenny would be hungry and looking forward to something good to eat.

Carlos liked to try new American food. He discovered that Americans liked their bread because it seemed to come with every meal. While he preferred the meat and vegetables of his own country, he didn't find them in very many restaurants in Iowa.

They wanted deli sandwiches, so Trish guided him to a submarine sandwich shop. Carlos bought enough sandwiches for two days. Whatever they did not eat tonight could be eaten tomorrow.

Trish smiled when he added a large bag full of chips, cookies, and bottles of soda pop to their order. Carlos knew that the Newberg family liked cookies, especially chocolate chip cookies. They had no way to make them at the motel, so he wanted them to have a stash of them for subsequent days.

Trish had never known quite how kind and generous Carlos was before now. He went out of his way to do and get things for the Newberg family that they liked. It made him seem like one of the family.

Carlos enjoyed doing nice things for Trish and her family. He had been alone for so long that he had forgotten how good it felt to do something for people he cared about—and he did care about this family. Trish was a dear friend. She asked for so little in life. He felt that she deserved every good thing that she could get.

Carlos also found that he cared about Lila and Josh, too. He realized quite soon after his arrival that he was falling in love with Jenny, not that she ever said or did anything to encourage him. She was aloof toward him, although she blushed so prettily a few times when he said something personal to her. He found it much easier to talk to her in Portuguese. Even though he knew that she didn't understand his words, they came so much easier to his lips. They came from his heart.

Josh forgot all about telling Trish that Shaun had dropped by. He was too intent on eating his way through sandwiches, cookies, and chips. This was a meal that he really enjoyed. Carlos stayed around talking with all of them for an hour after supper. When he left to go to his own room, he put an arm around Trish's shoulders and asked her to go for a walk with him. He had something that he wanted to discuss with her.

Trish agreed at once, and they left together. Lila and Jenny just looked at each other with their eyebrows raised. *What could that be about?* they both wondered.

Jenny secretly felt bad that she was starting to have some romantic feelings about Carlos. She found out from the library computer that he had called her a beautiful angel the first time they met. *Was he always that sweet to someone he just met? What if he was in love with Trish?* she wondered.

She would never encourage him if Trish was who Carlos wanted to be with. Jenny was so conflicted. Sometimes Carlos looked at her like he was truly interested in her, but other times he acted so close to Trish.

Jenny never had the time or opportunity to get Trish by herself and ask her about Carlos. Also, knowing Trish the way she did, she knew that Trish might just tell her that it was not any of her business. Trish had always been a little difficult to read. She sure kept poor Shaun guessing for more than a year before they got engaged.

CHAPTER

# Five

As Carlos gently guided Trish into the motel parking lot, he was immediately unsatisfied with their prospects for a private chat. There were too many people within earshot. Trish was a bit surprised when he suddenly asked her if they could talk in his car, but she had no reason to question his motives and quickly agreed. Still, her curiosity was piqued.

Carlos turned in his seat and looked at Trish. He took her small hands in his. He felt very close to this good friend.

"Trish, there are some things that I have been thinking about since I have been here. I hope you will listen and understand what I am about to say," he said with a quiet voice.

"Yes, Carlos, I'm ready. You can say anything to me. We are good friends, and I owe you so much. Go ahead." Trish studied him intently.

"I have been here for a week. I am so happy that I could help you and your family. It has been a wonderful feeling for me, to be helpful to my friends. I talked with the construction crew at your house this morning. It will still be a week to ten days before you can move back in. Knowing that, I want to know if you would come back to Brazil with me for five or six days. You deserve to have a little time away from all of this. Everyone back at the mine would love to see you, too," he said gently.

Trish was very surprised and asked, "Why do you want me to come with you, Carlos? I understand if you need to return. Your businesses are there, but why do you want me to come with you?"

"Trish, I know that you look every day for your Shaun to come and see you. When he does not come, you are disappointed. Your dear mother told me that you cry at night. Perhaps you think that she is asleep and cannot hear you." Trish averted her eyes from his gaze.

Carlos continued, "You will be refreshed after your little holiday. I need to check on some business for a few days, but I will be around to take you sightseeing and out to nice restaurants."

"Oh, Carlos, I don't know what to say. That is an extremely nice offer. Let me think about it for a bit, okay?" Trish said.

"É um problema, caro amigo. Preciso estar no Brasil em dois dias. Preciso da sua resposta esta noite." Carlos spoke in his native language because he knew that Trish understood quite a lot of Portuguese. He missed speaking his own language. He was not disappointed, because she answered him as if she understood him.

"Oh, Carlos, I need a little more time. May I think about it tonight and tell you my answer early tomorrow morning? That would still give you time to call the airlines and book a ticket for Brazil," she promised.

Carlos nodded and squeezed her hands in friendship, hoping that she would agree to go with him. He missed their talks. It seemed as if her whole family was around most of the time. He wanted to discuss his emerging feelings for Jenny, and in the process, learn more about her from her sister.

*Perhaps Trish's insight will improve my chances as Jenny's suitor,* he thought. *Maybe I can help her in some way with this Shaun of hers, too.*

As the owner of the mine and construction company, he needed to check in occasionally. He had good people in place to take care of the daily needs of his companies. Once he checked in with them, he would be available to go back to Dalton with Trish and try to help her as much as he could. He had long ago realized that it was no good to have money if he didn't have anyone to spend it on. He had no children to leave his fortune to, so he may as well spend it helping people he cared about.

Carlos knew from their many talks that Trish was an artist, who longed to do something creative again. She did quite a bit of knitting when she was in Brazil. She had told him that her long-term goal was to open a yarn shop in Dalton or Mason City. She had all kinds of ideas about creative activities that her customers might enjoy. She wanted a corner of her shop to be dedicated to other art, as well. Not returning to work in Brazil could jeopardize her dream.

Carlos knew Trish well enough to know that she would never accept charity. He wanted to find a way to help her open that shop without making her angry with him. Dalton certainly needed new shops and ways for the community members to make a living. It was something that he thought about quite a bit. He helped a few businesses open in Brazil. They were places that his extended family and friends wanted to run. In each case, the businesses greatly benefited the surrounding community.

Upon his return to Dalton with Trish, he intended to talk with a commercial realtor about buying some land on which to build a small strip mall. His observations of the town led him to the conclusion that this investment would benefit everyone.

People could petition to have their store in the mall. He wanted to give Trish the first choice of retail space. That was one of the things that he wanted to discuss with her in greater detail in Brazil.

Josh happened to be looking out of his motel window just as Carlos and Trish walked to her door. His arm was around Trish, and he hugged her and kissed her cheek as they said goodnight. Josh watched Trish wave at Carlos before she went into her motel room.

Josh turned to his mom, who was flipping through the channels on the television. "Mom, Aunt Trish is back."

The little reporter continued, "Senhor Santos hugged and kissed her before she went in. Do you think he loves her and wants to marry her? He would be a nice uncle. I liked Shaun, too, but he made her so sad that she had to go away. Maybe Senhor Santos will make her happy again."

Jenny looked at him and nodded. She smiled at Josh. "You like Senhor Santos a lot, don't you, Josh? He would be a good uncle to you, I think. Now, close the curtain and get yourself ready for bed, okay, honey? I want the lights out in thirty minutes."

Josh closed the curtains, locked the door, and did as she asked. He wondered why his mom seemed so sad tonight. Whenever he asked her about her sadness, she always smiled at him and said she was fine. He wished that she would meet someone whom she could love. She was way too young to spend the rest of her life alone. He loved his dad but thought that Dad would want Jenny to move on and be happy again. Josh wouldn't mind having a stepfather that he could learn to love, too.

Trish talked with her mom about Carlos' invitation to visit Brazil with him. She said that it would only be for five or six days. The monotony of the motel was wearing thin, and she would love to go back and see her friends at the mine.

Lila was supportive and told Trish that she should go if she wanted to. There was not much happening in Dalton right now. The work on the house would not be done for at least a week. At least Jenny got to go to the library every other day, so she had a change in scenery. They had relied on Carlos to take them out and about. While he was gone, there would be no trips, but that was only for a week.

Trish wanted to run it past Jenny. Someone would have to stay with their mom if she left. She was unsure if Jenny could do that for five or six days. Her mom was much stronger now, so that was a good thing. She would decide what to do after her talk with Jenny.

Jenny answered the phone right away. She knew that it would be Trish. She was the only one who ever called her in the evening.

"Hi, Jenny. Do you have five or ten minutes to talk? I have something that I want to run past you tonight. Can you meet me at the picnic table outside in five minutes?" she asked her sister.

"Yes, I'll see you in a few minutes, Trish. Is Mom already in bed?" Jenny asked.

"No, but I'm about to help her into it. She said she is tired and will sleep well tonight. See you in a few minutes." Trish was glad that Jenny was still up and willing to talk with her.

Five minutes later both sisters were sitting at the picnic table. No one else was out of their motel rooms roaming around. If they had been, Trish would have asked Jenny to sit in the car to talk.

"Thanks for coming out here to talk with me. I want your honest opinion about something, okay, Jenny?" Trish asked.

Jenny nodded and told her to go ahead and start talking.

"Jenny, Carlos asked me if I would go with him to Brazil for five or six days. He thinks that it would be good for me to get away from here for a little while. I left so quickly that I didn't have the chance to say goodbye to my friends in Brazil. Some personal belongings are still in my little cottage at the mine. I don't think that I will go back there to work, so I need to bring everything home." Trish looked intently at her sister as she spoke.

"Do you want to go with him, Trish?" Jenny asked quietly.

"Yes, but what about Mom? She can't stay by herself, especially at night. You're at the library every other day. That would leave only Josh to be with her during those days. Oh, maybe I shouldn't even think about it. It will be too much for you and Josh to take care of Mom all the time." Trish frowned and looked candidly at Jenny.

Jenny felt her heart ache a little when she thought about Trish leaving with Carlos. It really seemed as if Carlos loved her little sister. Still, if Trish wanted to go, Jenny was not going to stand in her way. Trish had had too many disappointments in her young life. Jenny never gave a thought about her own situation. If she did, she would just get depressed.

"Trish, if you want to go, we'll make it work out. When would you be leaving?" she asked.

"That's just it, Carlos wants to catch a plane tomorrow sometime. I told him that I would let him know early tomorrow morning, so he could still get a flight. It's all happening so fast. There is barely time to make any plans," Trish said frustratedly.

"Okay, tomorrow is Thursday. I don't work tomorrow. I have lots of vacation time saved up. I could take Friday off. I know I can get someone to cover for me. I don't work on Saturday or Sunday, so that's fine. I could also take Monday off, and I don't work on Tuesday. Do you think that you would be back by Tuesday night or Wednesday morning? If you're not back right away, Josh can stay with Mom for a day, you know. So, you see, it's no problem. You should go, Trish," Jenny told her firmly.

"But what about at night? Someone should be with Mom at night. If you came over to my room, Josh would be alone," Trish said worriedly.

"We can open the connecting door between our two rooms. I can sleep in your bed, and Josh can stay in his bed. He is old enough to sleep alone. I'll be right next door, five feet away from him. It's no problem, Trish. I want you to go with Carlos. Have some fun with your friends. We'll be just fine here." Jenny smiled with confidence. She would think about the situation more in bed tonight. Right now, she just needed to be supportive of her little sister.

"Thank you so much, Jenny. Are you sure that it is okay with you? I won't go if you have any problem with it," Trish said.

Jenny told her that they would be fine. They talked for another two minutes before getting up to walk back to their rooms. Trish gave Jenny a big hug before they went inside.

Trish decided to call Carlos tonight with her answer. Maybe the extra few hours would be helpful to him. He answered after the first ring.

“Carlos? I didn’t wake you, did I?” asked Trish.

“Olá, meu amigo. No, you didn’t wake me. I was still working on the plan for going to Brazil. What do you need, Trish?” he asked her.

“I talked with Mom and Jenny. Both said that I should go to Brazil with you, so I guess that I’m going. I wanted to tell you right away, just in case you can get anything done yet tonight.” Trish’s voice was upbeat.

“Oh, thank you, Trish. I found out that there is a flight leaving Mason City tomorrow afternoon at 4:29 p.m. Will that be okay for you? I can still order the tickets tonight if you are agreeable to that.” Carlos sounded pleased.

“Yes, that’s fine. I think that if we leave here by 1:00 p.m., we should be fine. That will give me all morning to hang out with Mom, Jenny, and Josh. Do you want to meet us for lunch at noon? We still have those submarine sandwiches to eat. We’ll be at the picnic tables. Come if you can, okay?”

Carlos agreed, and they hung up. He called the airlines, purchased their tickets, and packed. Now for some shut eye. He knew that he would likely not get enough sleep tomorrow night. The flight from Mason City to Brazil would be a long and tiring one, and he wanted to be prepared for anything.

* * *

Shaun walked into the Dalton Library on Friday because he knew that Jenny would be there, and he wanted to have a candid conversation with her about Trish. Jenny originally believed that he had that affair with Sheila, but he hoped that she had changed her mind over the last three years.

He remembered the hurt and anger he felt when Jenny gave him back Trish's engagement ring. Jenny, who he had always thought of as such a sweet woman, was cold and hard that day. They hadn't really spoken to each other since, but lately she sometimes had a small smile for him when they saw each other in church or somewhere in the community.

Inside the library, he saw Marcia, who worked on Tuesday, Thursday, and Saturday. She smiled and asked how she could help him.

"Is Jenny sick today?" Shaun asked Marcia.

"Oh, no, she's fine. She's just taking a few vacation days. Did you want to talk with her? Is there something I can help you with?" asked Marcia brightly. She wondered why Shaun would want to see Jenny. She knew that he was no longer engaged to Trish Newberg.

"I wanted to ask her something. I don't need anything from the library. Is she vacationing somewhere or staying at the motel?" he asked quietly.

"Oh, she's at the motel taking care of her mom while her sister is in Brazil. It seems that Trish went back to Brazil with Senhor Santos who has been staying here. I think they are coming back next week sometime. Jenny said that she will be back at work next Wednesday." Marcia didn't know that her words sent Shaun into a spiral of despair.

Shaun smiled to mask his feelings, thanked her, and left the library. Now he really wanted to talk to Jenny. He drove to the motel and wondered what Jenny would have to say—if she would even talk with him.

He drove into the parking lot and noticed that the Mercedes was gone. He parked next to Jenny's car and looked around. It was a nice day, and most people would have already had lunch. He saw Jenny, Josh, and Lila sitting at the picnic table by the parking lot. He slowly went over to them. Josh saw him first and said, "Hi, Shaun. I guess you don't have much luck. Aunt Trish is not here, again."

Shaun nodded slightly and smiled at him. Jenny and Lila looked at him with surprise. Shaun Healy was the last person they expected to see. They both wanted to thank him for helping Trish on the night of the tornado.

Jenny quietly said, "Hello, Shaun. What brings you out here? We're glad to see you, though. Both Mom and I wanted to thank you for coming to Trish's aid during the tornado. We are so grateful. Sorry we didn't tell you that sooner. I heard that your truck was damaged. Did you get a replacement for it yet?"

Lila nodded at her daughter's words and looked at Shaun. She had never quite believed that he cheated on Trish. She remembered the many times she watched him watching Trish with so much love on his face. She always felt bad about that whole situation.

She smiled at him and said, "Yes, thank you, Shaun, for rescuing Trish. She told me that she might have died from fright if she had been in the house when the tornado hit. You were so brave. I hope that Trish thanked you for your help."

Shaun smiled at Lila and nodded. He was happy to see that she was so much better. Word around town was that she had been very ill.

"Thank you. It was something that I had to do. I know how frightened Trish gets in a storm like that. I just wish that we would have had more time to talk. I came out here a few days ago to talk with her, but Josh told me that you and she were out somewhere for a while. I hoped that she would be here today." Shaun's voice was quiet and sad.

"Jenny, I stopped in the library to ask you something, but Marcia told me that you are taking a few vacation days. I heard that Trish is in Brazil with Senhor Santos. Can we talk privately for a few minutes? It's very important to me. Please?" Shaun asked hopefully.

Jenny noticed his sad expression and thought that Shaun deserved a little kindness. She nodded and said, "Yes, Shaun. We can talk. Since it's so warm outside, let's talk in my motel room, okay?"

She looked at her mom as she spoke. Lila nodded, so Jenny led Shaun to her room.

Jenny opened the tiny fridge in the room and handed Shaun a bottle of water before taking another one for herself. They sat down at the small table in the room, and she looked at him expectantly.

Shaun quietly said, "Thank you, Jenny. I appreciate your willingness to talk with me. I didn't know if you would ever speak to me again after that last time three years ago. I know that it was not easy or pleasant for you to give me Trish's ring."

Jenny looked intently at Shaun and said, just as quietly, "I'm sorry about that, Shaun. I was so upset with you at that moment. I couldn't believe that you could do something so terrible to Trish. I've had a lot of time to think since that day. I hope that Trish and you can talk about it. I've always regretted that she didn't let you tell your side of the story. For the record, I don't believe anymore that you had an affair with Sheila."

Shaun smiled bitterly and said, "Well, I guess that's something. Thank you, Jenny. Let me just say one time that I *did not* have an affair with Sheila. She wanted to, but I told her no because I love Trish with all my heart. That same heart has taken quite a beating, but I still love her, even now. I just want the chance to tell her that I didn't cheat on her. It's probably too late for us, though. It seems as if she has found love with someone else. That's what I wanted to talk with you about."

Jenny smiled for two seconds when she heard him say that he still loved Trish. He could have remained hurt and angry, and his love for Trish might have died. Her face grew sad and resigned after that quick smile. She nodded at Shaun to continue.

"Jenny, when I stopped by a few days ago, Josh told me that Senhor Santos came here from Brazil to see Trish. He told me that Santos was always hugging and kissing her. He also said that Lila thinks they are in love. Will you tell me what you know about this situation? Does Trish love that man? I want to talk with her more than anything, but if she loves that other guy, maybe she doesn't need an explanation from me anymore." Shaun's eyes were very sad when he looked at Jenny.

Jenny put her hand over his and said sadly, "I don't know, Shaun. Mom and I wonder about their relationship, too. Sometimes it seems like they are just friends, but other times it seems like they love each other. Trish has not confided in me about their relationship."

Shaun broke in to say, "When I sat with her in the tornado shelter, I had the feeling that she wanted to talk. I planned on doing just that, but we were pulled along to the Dalton Cafe with everyone, and there was no way that we could talk privately. I have had car issues since then, and only had the chance to come out here to talk to her a few days ago. Now, after what Josh told me, I think it's too late. If she loves Senhor Santos, I don't even know if I should try to talk with her. I guess it's all water under the bridge. I love Trish, but if she has no love left for me, I need to try to move on. It's going to be damn hard to move on if she marries him and stays in this community, though. What do you think I should do, Jenny? I'm willing to listen to any suggestions."

Jenny shook her head and said, "I don't know what to tell you, Shaun. I guess you'll just have to wait until they come back from Brazil. None of us know what is happening right now in Brazil or what will happen when they come back. Trish did tell me that she doesn't plan to go back to that job, and she will be bringing all her possessions home from there."

Suddenly, Jenny remembered something that might cheer him up a bit. "Shaun, I do know that Trish wanted to talk with you. After the tornado, she looked for you every day and was disappointed when you didn't come to see her. Of course, that was before Carlos came out here. She hasn't said anything about it since then."

Shaun was quiet and thoughtful for a few moments. It seemed as if he had come to a big decision. He looked Jenny in the eyes and humbly told her, "Thanks, Jenny, for talking with me. I guess that I will wait to talk with her when she returns."

Shaun stopped because he didn't want to tear up in front of Jenny and her family. He was totally devastated by his talk with Jenny. She had not come right out and said the words, but he could tell that Jenny believed that Trish would marry Carlos Santos.

Shaun had always thought that Trish would come to her senses, move back to Dalton, ask him to explain about Sheila, and they would forgive and forget. He had always prayed that they would reconcile. Never in his wildest dreams did he imagine that she would fall in love with someone else. He walked out to his car, waved at Jenny and her family, and drove home.

Jenny looked like she was going to cry, and Lila wanted to ask her about their talk, but she didn't want Josh to hear it. He was too young to hear about certain things. She could wait until Josh was taking his nightly shower. Then she would have a talk with Jenny.

# CHAPTER Six

When Carlos and Trish drove into the mining camp, her friends rushed out to greet them. Ted and his wife, Mary, had gotten a call from Carlos, telling them that he and Trish were on their way. They told Dave, the doctor, and Angie, Trish's roommate. Everyone was excited about seeing Trish.

Angie had taken Sarah Brewster's place as the mine's secretary one and a half years ago. All of them were quite good friends. Dave and Angie were now a couple and intended to marry in six months. They planned to stay at the mine for another few years to save some money. They would live in Dave's cottage, and Trish's replacement would have the extra cottage.

Trish jumped out of the jeep and rushed to hug her friends. They all talked at once and laughed as they pulled Trish along into the recreation hall. Ted looked at Carlos, said hello, and asked him to join them in the rec hall.

Carlos nodded and followed them, wanting to hear what Trish told them. She had been mighty quiet on the trip so far. He thought that she was upset about something, although she denied it when he asked her.

Trish told them about the tornado and the house, never mentioning Shaun. She said that her mother was much better, thanks to Carlos. Smiling widely at him, she reported how he had taken them out and about most days. Trish cheerfully added how helpful Carlos was with the insurance people and construction company.

Carlos just smiled and nodded. He was still happy that he had been able to help the Newberg family. He would have the chance to talk business with Ted later. He usually made time to see and talk with the miners, as well. For now, he just wanted to share Trish's excitement. She was such a dear friend to him.

After supper, they all relaxed in the recreation hall. A few of the miners were there, as well. There was a fierce competition going on among some of the miners regarding the dart game. Carlos was pulled into it. He was a very good dart player, and they knew it. He laughed and had a good time. He looked over to the couch where Trish was sitting with Angie and Mary. It looked like they were having a nice chat.

The temp that Ted hired to replace Trish was there, looking a little left out. Carlos went over to her and chatted with her. She was a nice woman in her fifties. She was a widow with grown children. She was older than any of the rest of his crew, so she felt a bit uncomfortable playing games with them. He sat with her and asked her how everything was going. She said that she liked the job very much.

He wanted to talk with Ted, Mary, and Angie before he offered her the job permanently. Trish told him on the plane that she would not be coming back to work for him. Now that she was back in Iowa, she wanted to stay there. She told him that she might move to Mason City when her mom was completely well. She wanted to go back to her place in the art world. Of course, he hadn't talked with her yet about opening a yarn store in the strip mall that he wanted to build in or just outside of Dalton. He would talk about that with her in the next few days.

Carlos bunked with the miners that night, happy to see them again. Some of the miners had worked for him for more than ten years, and he was on good terms with them. Mary and Ted offered Trish a bed in their spare room for the night.

The next morning at breakfast, Carlos told everyone that he was taking Trish to see his house and meet his mother. She would stay with his mother for a few days, just relaxing and doing vacation-type things. He would bring her back to the mine in three days. They would be there for one day before heading back to Iowa. Trish's friends were happy about that. They were a little curious about Carlos' relationship with Trish, though. Was Carlos interested in Trish as a mate?

Only Angie, Trish's former roommate, knew that Carlos and Trish were simply good friends. Trish had confided to Angie that she still loved Shaun, her ex-fiancé, and hoped they would reconcile when she went back to Dalton.

Carlos drove Trish in the mine's jeep to his home in Barbacena. It took about two hours to get there from the mine. The terrain was mountainous, which is why Carlos usually liked to fly his small plane from Barbacena to the camp. It took him less than an hour when he flew. He wanted the jeep, though, so he chose to drive today.

His home was a palatial building. It was not a warm cozy place. He had servants keeping it ready for the moment he returned to it. He was gone quite often, and they never knew when he would suddenly show up. If he had the time, he called them to give them advance notice.

Carlos didn't have any love for his home. It was the family home of his wife, Sofia. Her father had given it to them as a wedding gift. They had only lived in it together for less than a year before she was killed in that plane crash.

Sofia's father and Carlos' father were partners and co-owned the mine. Because of his poor health, Sofia's father chose to sell his half of the mine to his partner right before Carlos and Sofia married. He and his wife then moved to a sunny villa in France.

Carlos was a few years older than Sofia, but he had loved her since she was eighteen. Her father refused to let them get married until she was twenty-two and out of college. She hadn't really wanted to go to college, but her parents pulled all the strings and forced her to go. She barely graduated with a degree in marketing. She was never interested in working in that field, though. She and Carlos had been in love for a long time. She just wanted to be his wife and mother to their children.

They had a huge wedding and moved into the family home. Five months after their marriage, Sofia found out that she was pregnant. Carlos and she were ecstatic. He couldn't wait for their child to be born. Sofia was three months pregnant when her first cousin asked her to fly to Rio de Janeiro for her wedding.

Carlos planned to go with her, but at the last minute, his father asked him to stay and work through a serious issue at the mine. So, Carlos had taken Sofia to the airport, kissed her, and sent her on her way. It was a stormy afternoon, and the plane crashed, killing everyone on board.

His grief was intense and immeasurable. Nothing else mattered as much as his budding family, now tragically removed from him.

The cruelest cut was not knowing the gender of his unborn child since they had planned to discover this after returning from her cousin's wedding.

Carlos' father ran the mine, with Carlos' help, until his death ten years ago. Sofia's parents died while they were in France. They were both sickly and never got over the shock and pain of Sofia's death.

His mother still lived in the home that he lived in as a boy. He loved that house and knew that his mother planned to leave it to him upon her death. At that point, he planned to sell his house and move into his former home. There were happy memories there.

Carlos and his mother had a good relationship. He visited her many times whenever he was in town. She understood that he traveled quite a lot and was happy when he stopped by to see her.

Her son knew that she hoped he would remarry and have some children. Carlos was never motivated to remarry until he met Sarah Brewster a year and a half ago. He was more infatuated with her than anything. Part of it could have been that he was very aware of the years passing. If he ever wanted to have a loving relationship with a woman and have any children, he would have to find her soon. Even though he barely knew Sarah, he told his mother about her before he flew to Minnesota to ask her to leave her fiancé. He was pulled out of his brief depression that followed Sarah's refusal by Trish.

Carlos always wished that he would fall in love with Trish, but he was not attracted to her in that way. They were just very good friends. Besides, he knew that she still loved Shaun. He trusted her because she didn't care about his position and money. Although she respected him as her boss, her honest and matter of fact way of speaking was refreshing. He could see her deeply caring heart.

She was an amazingly outspoken young woman, but as honest and loving as the day was long. *Shaun would be lucky to get her back,* he thought.

Now that he had met Jenny, he wondered if they could ever get together. He was extremely attracted to her and felt kinship with her because they both lost their spouses. Even though he thought he liked demure women, he was impressed with the way Jenny took care of everything around her. She was a strong woman, and that made her unapproachable at times.

If he could just take some of the burden from her shoulders, he would be happy. Under that strong haughty exterior, he believed there was a sweet and gentle heart. She demonstrated that attribute in the way she took care of her family. He wanted to see her completely at ease and totally happy. *She would be astoundingly beautiful, then*, he thought.

Carlos hadn't shown Sofia's picture to anyone other than his family. He decided to show his wedding picture to Trish. It was one of two pictures that he had of his wife. After Sofia's death, he gave all the rest of the pictures to her family. The only other photo that he kept of Sofia was her college graduation portrait. It was formally done, and it showed how beautiful she was. Both pictures sat in their antique silver frames on his dresser in his bedroom.

"Oh, Carlos, she was so lovely," Trish said softly. She quickly observed his face. It was expressionless, but his eyes looked sad. She put her hand on his arm and lightly squeezed it. She smiled gently at him. "You certainly were a dashing young man, too, Carlos," she said with a small laugh. He nodded and smiled.

"Thank you, Trish. Those days are long gone, I'm afraid. I try to keep in good health, though. Even though I'm now forty-seven, I still feel like I'm in my thirties. May I ask you something, Trish? I want an honest answer, too. I know that I can trust you to tell me the truth." Carlos took her by the arm and sat her down on the couch. He held her hands in his.

Trish regarded him with wide eyes. Carlos seemed intense. She nodded at him to proceed.

"Do you think that I am too old for your sister, Jenny? I am very attracted to her and want to get to know her better. I wonder if you would tell me more about her." Carlos gave her a straight look in the eyes. There was no time like the present to get the information he wanted about Jenny.

Trish looked startled and then began to smile happily. She had wondered if Carlos liked Jenny. She noticed how careful he was with her sister.

"Carlos, I wondered if you liked her. I'm very happy about it. If you and Jenny got together, it would make so many people happy. Jenny is a stubborn and strong woman. She has had to be ever since Jack died. If you could have known her before he died, you would have seen a different woman. She was always smiling and happy. Beneath her tough exterior, she has a very gentle soul." Trish sat forward with her enthusiasm for this subject.

"I think that I knew that," Carlos said quietly. "Please go on, Trish," he encouraged.

"My impulsive nature sometimes caused problems. Jenny always had my back, though. She tried to take the blame for some things so I would not get into trouble. My mom and dad saw through her, though, and shook their heads. They knew us both well and loved us for who we were."

Trish laughed a little at that. Her dad tried to be tough on them, but he really was a big marshmallow. He loved his two wonderful daughters. Her mom was a softy, too. Trish loved her parents very much.

She continued her look back into the past. "Jenny was always interested in interior design. She went to college in Mason City to earn a degree in that field. She was dating Jack during that time. They were so in love that she married him a month after she finished her degree. As a farmer's wife, she had little time to do any interior decorating, but she did decorate their old small house as much as she could, despite limited money. They had Josh a year after they got married. She was such a good mother."

Trish paused momentarily to gauge Carlos' interest. He was listening intently.

"Their little place was not good for farming, so Jack hired himself out to one of the big commercial farms about twenty miles from Dalton. One day there was a big barn fire. Jack went back inside to get some cattle out. Shaun's father was there that day because the owner and he were good friends. When they heard the roof falling in, Mr. Healy rushed in to warn Jack. His leg was crushed by falling wood from the ceiling. They pulled him out alive, but Jack was not so lucky. A falling beam broke his back, killing him instantly.

I was living at home at the time because my dad had just died a few months earlier. My mom insisted that Jenny and Josh move in with us. Jenny needed help with Josh. He was going through some terrible times—not sleeping, crying and screaming all the time. Jenny stopped smiling after Jack's death. She is still a great mom, daughter, and sister, though. We all want her to find happiness again." Reliving those memories put Trish in a somber mood.

Carlos looked sad. He was thinking of the young Jenny Horton, a mother and widow at age twenty-eight. Of course, he was only twenty-five when he lost Sofia and their baby. *Life can be so cruel sometimes,* he thought.

"Trish, do you think that Jenny still thinks about interior decorating? I have a wonderful idea that I want to talk with you about. Before I do, please finish your story about Jenny. My heart hurts for her and the things that she went through. I know how she feels because I went through the same things." Carlos' voice was soft and quiet.

"Well, there is not much more to tell you. Jenny and Josh have lived with mom for seven years. They've kept her safe and happy. When Mom had the stroke, Jenny was so strong and brave, taking care of everything. She only called me home because she wanted me to be able to spend time with Mom. I think the world of my big sister. I would do anything to make her happy," Trish said emphatically.

Carlos nodded. He knew that about Trish. He knew that Jenny would say the same about Trish if she were asked. It made him long for a brother or sister. At times, it was difficult being the only child. *Well, a wife and children would make up for the lack of siblings,* he thought.

He glanced at his watch. They had another hour before he would take her to meet his mother. She knew about their visit and had already invited them to supper. He wanted to discuss the strip mall idea with Trish. Maybe both Trish and Jenny would like to have a store in his mall.

Carlos went to get them some beverages. Trish took that time to look around the living room. The decorations were ornate, and it was filled with heavy dark furniture. It reminded her of an old Victorian house that she once saw in a movie. There was a sweeping wood staircase that led to the upper floors. It looked like it would take a posse of servants to keep it clean. She smilingly wondered what Jenny would think if she ever saw this house. She imagined that Jenny could fix it up so that it was more comfortable and homier.

Carlos gave Trish her drink and then sat next to her again. He proceeded to lay out his vision for the Dalton shopping mall, including his sole purpose of revitalizing the town's economy. Carlos would be happy to simply cover his construction costs. Trish readily saw the joy return to Carlos' eyes and heard the eagerness in his voice. She shared his enthusiasm.

Then he dropped the bomb. How would she like to be one of the store owners? She could have first choice of retail space, opening her own yarn shop. Maybe Jenny could also have a small storefront, displaying her interior decorating skills.

Trish was speechless. It was like a dream come true. She could have her own business and still live close to her family. Artful and creative ideas culled from years of dreaming came rushing in as her mind suddenly raced with possibilities.

Amid her reverie, Trish's subconscious rained on her parade with a simple question, *What about Shaun?* It was like one of those Iowa thunderstorms. Trish could not avoid the very real possibility that Shaun and she might continue to live in the same small town, and that could be problematic if they were still not talking.

Carlos saw her face fall and asked her what was wrong. She shared her feelings. She had not lost her love for Shaun, but he might not want anything more to do with her. She didn't think that she could live in the same community and see him with his wife and family. Carlos held her hands in sympathy. He could understand her dilemma.

"What if I built the mall ten or fifteen miles outside of Dalton? You could live ten miles away on the other side of the mall. Then you would be twenty or twenty-five miles away from Dalton. If you made sure that you did your shopping and entertainment closer to Mason City, you would rarely see him. I doubt that he would have much use coming to the mall to shop at a yarn store." Carlos was sincere and kind. He wanted Trish to say yes to having a yarn store in his mall.

"Let me think about it for a while, please, Carlos," Trish said.

"Okay, but I want to get started on the mall when we get back to Dalton. I just think that it is such a good thing for the community to have some new stores," he said.

Trish nodded and said that she would let him know before they stepped off the plane in Iowa.

Carlos took her to his mother's house. They had a lovely time talking and eating supper. Carlos told his mother, Maria, about his plans for a strip mall. Maria was happy for him, but she hoped that he wouldn't spend all his time in Dalton because of it. He reassured her that he could easily fly back and forth from Brazil to Iowa.

Carlos left by 9:00 p.m. He kissed his mother and told Trish that he would pick her up by 10:00 a.m. the next day. He wanted to take her sightseeing.

Trish and Maria talked some more after he left. She searchingly asked Trish if she and Carlos were dating. Maybe her son decided to marry his best friend, never mind that he was not in love with her. Trish smilingly shook her head no.

Since she expressed interest, Trish told Maria about Shaun. Then, encouraged by their fast friendship, she also shared that Carlos was attracted to Jenny.

Maria was visibly excited at that news and stated that at least he was attracted to someone. It was a big improvement over all those years when he wanted nothing to do with young women. He had been so devastated by Sofia's death that he wanted to avoid any relationship that might result in pain.

They spoke briefly of Sarah Brewster. Trish, who kept in contact with Sarah, told Maria that she was happily married with a six-month-old son. Maria nodded and said that she was glad that Sarah was happy. Carlos had gone through a few bad months because of Sarah, but he said that he was now totally over her.

He had been more in love with the idea of being in love than anything else. Sarah was just the woman who shook him out of his apathy towards women. Now that he knew that he could feel love (or infatuation) for a woman again, he could move on to happier circumstances.

Trish slept comfortably in Maria's home. She really liked Maria. She had given Trish more insight into Carlos' hopes and dreams. Trish just wished that Jenny could have been the one to talk with Maria. If Jenny liked Carlos at all, she would be interested in knowing everything about him.

They spent two more days sightseeing, taking Maria out to eat, and relaxing. Carlos looked so peaceful sitting back in his mother's comfortable chair. He looked at Trish and grinned. "It has been wonderful having this mini vacation. Thank you for coming to Brazil with me, Trish. If I had been by myself, I know that I would have spent most of the time doing business. Sometimes you just need to relax."

He looked fondly at his mother. "Obrigado, mamãe, por sua hospitalidade. Você tem sido tão gentil com minha amiga, Trish."

Maria looked at Carlos with love and softly said, "Você é bem-vindo, meu filho. Da próxima vez que eu te ver, talvez tenha boas notícias para mim. Eu quero que você seja feliz."

Trish, who understood quite a lot of Portuguese by now, smiled. Maria was telling Carlos that she was happy to have Trish stay with her and that she hoped that Carlos would have good news for her the next time they met. She wanted her son to be happy.

Trish hugged Maria goodbye. She would be a wonderful mother-in-law. Maybe she would tell Jenny how incredible Maria was.

They drove back to the mine and spent the rest of the day with their friends. Everyone went to bed a little early since Carlos and Trish had to leave by 6:00 a.m. They wanted to see them off.

The return trip to Iowa was long and tiring. By the time they landed in Mason City, Trish had decided to accept Carlos' offer of a store in his strip mall. She was just going to have to deal with the issue of seeing Shaun occasionally. Maybe she would be so successful and busy that she wouldn't have time to think about him or go anywhere that she might run into him. She told Carlos that before they disembarked, as promised. He hugged her warmly, happy with her decision.

# CHAPTER Seven

Jenny was home by the time Carlos and Trish drove up to the Dalton Motel. She could see that Trish was very excited about something. She wondered if Carlos and Trish had gotten engaged while they were in Brazil. *Well, Trish deserves happiness*, Jenny figured. She contrived a smile and went to greet them.

"Welcome back, world travelers. You look like you could go for a long cool drink. Sit down at the picnic table, and I will bring you something. I'll just get Mom and Josh. Hold on, okay?" Jenny said brightly.

She took off, and Trish took Carlos' hand and pulled him over to the table. He was carrying the three colorfully wrapped souvenirs for Jenny, Josh, and Lila. He was genuinely happy to be back in Dalton. He looked forward to telling Jenny about his plans for the mall.

They bought Josh a blue, green, and yellow National Baseball Team of Brazil cap since he loved baseball. Carlos picked out Jenny's gift. It was a lovely glass angel with a flowing gold and pale blue skirt. For Lila, they bought a traditional figurine of a dancer. She was wearing a full skirt that was covered in beautiful flowers. Barbacena, Carlos' hometown, was nicknamed the "City of Roses". Trish had a figurine resembling that of Lila's. Carlos bought it for her when she was admiring them as a gift for her mom.

Everyone admired their gifts and thanked Trish and Carlos. He enjoyed the kisses on his cheek from Jenny and Lila. Josh shook his hand like a man. Carlos joked around with them. He told them that ironically, his hometown's "sister city" was Burlington, Iowa USA. He said that for sure he needed to make a trip there. Since he was going there, he may as well take Josh and visit the home of the Burlington Bees. Josh grinned widely at that. Jenny looked at Josh's happy face and nodded her agreement. She trusted Carlos enough to keep Josh safe.

When there was a quiet moment, Carlos told them about his plan to build a strip mall near Dalton. He prompted Trish to speak up about the yarn store. Jenny and Lila knew that Trish had always dreamed of having her own little store. Then Carlos looked directly at Jenny and told her that there would be space available if she wanted to open an interior decoration showroom. He confided, "Trish revealed your interest in that field."

Jenny couldn't believe it. She had a little money saved up, but she was saving that for Josh's college education. She had dreamt long ago, while she was still in college, about having a small showroom to advertise her services. She gave that dream up when she married Jack. She never regretted that, though. Her marriage to Jack meant more to her than any interior design job.

Now that she was alone, it might be a good idea to have her own business. Lately, she had been giving considerable thought to her future. Since Josh would likely be living with her for only another six to eight years, she would find herself with ample time for such an undertaking.

"I don't know what to say, Carlos. I never expected to have the opportunity to open a showroom. Do you need an answer right away?" Jenny asked quietly.

Carlos gently smiled and said, "No, think about it for a while. It will be quite a long time before I will need to know. I was thinking that six stores would be the right amount for the mall. I told Trish that she got the first pick. She can have whichever location and size of store that she wants. If you want to be a part of it, I will give you the second choice. Once I have the planning permission, I will advertise. People can come to me and talk about what kind of store they want. If it fits with the theme of the mall, I'll get their specifications, so I can have the mall built to accommodate everyone's dream store."

They talked excitedly about Trish's yarn/art store for half an hour. Jenny was quiet as she contemplated the showroom. She also thought that Trish must not plan to marry Carlos. *Trish wouldn't go through the trouble of building a yarn store if she was going back to Brazil to live with Carlos, would she?* Jenny wondered. Concluding that he did not plan to relocate permanently in Dalton, Iowa, Jenny felt that he would get the mall started and then return to Brazil. He could conduct the mall business over the phone or internet.

Jenny allowed herself to begin having feelings for this dynamic man whose kindness toward so many had already begun to change the town for better. She wondered if he helped this many people in Brazil but quickly decided that this was unique to the Newbergs. She would miss him when he left.

As she listened to them talk, Jenny studied the glass angel in her hands. She pondered its intended meaning, recalling that Carlos had greeted her with "Hello, beautiful angel" when he met her. *Does he think I am an angel?* She grinned inwardly because she had some very un-angelic thoughts at times. He had never gotten the sharp side of her tongue. Of course, he never did anything to make her angry, either.

* * *

Shaun passed his lonely hours at home with ceaseless thoughts of Trish. One moment, he was taking her to their favorite park bench at the scenic site and kissing the stuffing out of her. Other times, he fantasized about her coming out to his house, dragging him to their underground shelter or cow shed, and initiating some fantastic kisses on him. He would set her straight regarding Sheila, and she would ask him for forgiveness for running away. They would participate in some magical kissing, he would put her ring back on her finger, and they would be engaged again.

It was difficult to do his chores with these wishful thoughts running through his head. Jenny said that Trish and Senhor Santos would possibly be back on Wednesday. He would wait to see if anyone in town talked about Trish's engagement to Senhor Santos.

He spent most of his free time with Mary. She understood how he felt and never bugged him with questions about it. When they went out, they talked about general things, never about relationships or love. Meanwhile, he heard the rumors in town. People were speculating whether he and Mary were seriously dating. Shaun was nonplussed. "People are stupid," he told her. "Disregard all of that nonsense."

* * *

The Newbergs moved back into their home twenty-five days after the tornado. They were excited to see Jenny's new room. Due to extensive water damage in her room, as well as in the kitchen, the construction crew had to remove everything. Many of her personal belongings were broken or ruined at the time of the tornado. Jenny didn't mind the loss of her clothes, but cherished mementos—such as gifts from Jack and photos from her wedding and Josh's birth— were irreplaceable. Only memories of them remained now.

They planned a big shopping trip to Mason City to buy new items. Besides all of Jenny's things, each family member had a few things to replace. When the tornado struck the house, many things fell off the shelves in each room and broke.

Lila loved the look of her new kitchen. The appliances were all white, while the walls were painted a very soft blue. The tiled floor was a marbled dark gray and white, as were the countertops. Her renewed interest in life was buoyed by her improved surroundings. Something good had come from something so traumatic.

Lila planned to buy towels, rugs, and other kitchen essentials in a deep blue color with dashes of bright red. She had always wanted a blue and white kitchen. It was so much nicer than that old dusty gold and orange kitchen that were part of the original decorations of the house. Her new kitchen looked so crisp and neat.

Since Carlos hated living in the Dalton Motel, Lila invited Carlos to stay with them while he was in town. He made several quick trips back to Brazil to look after his other businesses, but he always returned after four or five days. Since there were no extra rooms available in the house, Carlos moved into the basement with Josh. They shared the downstairs living room, bathroom, and Josh's large bedroom.

The baseball field mural on Josh's wall was only partially done since Trish had to leave it during the tornado. While Carlos was there, they decided to put off painting any more. Trish shook her head every time she went into Josh's room. That wall looked strange, but Josh was okay with it for now.

Carlos announced that he was going to build a house about ten miles east of the mall. Now that he was going to build the mall, he would be a regular visitor to the Dalton area and needed a home base. The Newbergs were all glad to hear that.

He asked Jenny to design the interior of the new house. It wouldn't be finished for a few months, but he was impressed by the pictures she had taken of her past work. He wanted the house to look modern but very warm and cozy. He drolly described his home in Brazil, and he said that he wanted it to be the opposite of that. Trish added her own comments about Carlos' home. They all laughed about her vivid description of his cold and palatial home.

Jenny happily accepted his request. It required Carlos and she to spend quite a lot of time together, perusing wall and floor colors, window treatments, and furniture. Carlos enjoyed those times with Jenny. He lovingly looked at her fair bent head with longing in his eyes. Trish and Lila could readily see his affection for Jenny, while she remained oblivious.

By now Lila and Jenny knew that Carlos and Trish were not in love and had no intention of marrying. It was a huge relief to Jenny, who was fast falling in love with Carlos.

Carlos already knew that he was in love with the strong, pretty Jenny. He was getting to know Josh quite well, too. He would be so proud to be this young boy's stepfather. They talked about baseball all the time. Carlos was planning a trip to Burlington with Josh to see Iowa's minor league baseball team play.

Both Carlos and Josh arose early on the day of their eagerly anticipated baseball excursion. While Jenny elected to not take the day off work, she nonetheless sent them off with her blessing.

Seeing the Burlington Bees play was a wonderful treat for Josh, who harbored dreams of playing in the big leagues. Carlos enjoyed his time with Josh, even imagining a new role as his stepfather. Since it went so well, Carlos secretly started planning a trip with Josh and Jenny to see a Minnesota Twins game.

* * *

The night the Newbergs moved back to their house, Trish wrote a long letter to her good friend, Sarah Brewster Thompson. They had remained friends in the one and a half years since Sarah moved back to Litton, Minnesota, from her stay in Brazil.

Sarah called Trish immediately after receiving the letter. Now that Trish was back in Iowa, Sarah wanted to bring her husband and young son to visit. She said that they would be in Dalton in a week's time. Trish made reservations for them at the Dalton Motel. She would have liked to have them stay at the house, but there was so much going on, and many pieces of furniture needed to be replaced to make it comfortable.

Sarah, Paul, and six-month-old Christopher arrived around 1:00 p.m. on a beautiful July day. The friends hugged tightly before settling in for a long conversation. Trish recognized Paul from the photo that Sarah had kept near her bed when she lived in Brazil. Chris was exclaimed over and held by everyone. Being such a sweet little boy, everyone fell in love with him.

Carlos was at the Newberg house when the Thompsons arrived. He was eager to talk with them and make amends for his behavior nearly two years ago. Carlos shook Paul's hand firmly and apologized for his actions and words that day in Litton.

"Paul, it's nice to formally meet you. I want to apologize for my crazy behavior the day I came to see Sarah before your wedding. I wasn't thinking clearly. Sarah was right to tell me to go home. I only thought I loved her because she was the first woman to interest me in twenty years since my wife's death. I hope you will forgive me."

"Yes, of course I forgive you, Carlos. It caused a brief hiccup in my relationship with Sarah, but everything worked out fine in the end. I didn't know about your wife. I'm so sorry to hear about it," Paul said compassionately.

"Thank you, Paul. No one except Trish knew about Sophia. Sarah didn't even know. But thank you for your forgiveness. When I get a moment, I will apologize to Sarah, too. I see that you have a young son. You are a blessed man, Paul," Carlos said quietly.

Carlos smiled at Paul before he walked toward Trish, who was talking animatedly to Sarah. He gently touched Sarah's arm. She turned to him and smiled; all awkwardness forgotten.

Carlos smiled genuinely at Sarah and asked, "May I give you a hug, Sarah?"

Sarah nodded and Carlos pulled her into a light hug. He wanted her to forgive him for asking her to break her engagement to Paul.

"Sarah, you look wonderful. I see that your hair has grown long again. You look very happy. Marriage to Paul obviously agrees with you. Your son is a real cutie."

He let her go, but he looked intently at her before speaking again. He sincerely apologized to her for showing up in Litton and asking her to break up with Paul. Sarah touched his arm and said that she forgave him. They talked generally for a few more minutes before Carlos moved away to talk with the rest of the Newberg family.

Carlos and Trish took the Thompsons to the mall site. Since Paul was a businessman, he was intensely interested in the whole mall project. He and Carlos walked away still talking about the site.

Sarah, with Christopher in her arms, looked avidly around the spot where Trish's yarn shop would be. The two friends had often talked in Brazil about Trish's dream to have a yarn store when she came back to Dalton. Sarah also quietly asked Trish about Shaun. Trish had to say that they had not yet talked. At that point, Trish was still hopeful that Shaun would talk with her, tell her what happened with Sheila, and they would reunite.

Sarah put her arm around Trish, who was looking a little sad and downhearted.

"Well, Trish, I will pray that you guys talk and work things out. Remember that I will want to hear about it and come to your wedding one day." With that positive statement, Sarah hugged her friend and kissed her cheek.

Trish appreciated Sarah's positive words and her friendship so much.

The Thompsons had a wonderful mini vacation in Dalton. Trish and her family made them feel so welcome. Carlos went out of his way to be helpful and show them around town and Mason City, which he was becoming quite fond of. The only thing Sarah regretted was that she didn't have the chance to meet Shaun.

After the Thompsons left to go back to Minnesota, life started getting busier. The groundbreaking at the mall was very exciting. Carlos and Trish visited the mall site nearly every day.

* * *

Jenny had to admit that it was fun to consider her creative bent regarding interior design. For the first time in years, she would lie awake with ideas buzzing in her head instead of the weary task of figuring out a way to pay her bills. She had to admit that Carlos' attention had affected her as well. In the end, she agreed to have tasteful pictures of her work posted along the wall that led to the Food Court. Hopefully, people would look at her work and call her to schedule a consultation.

It was an excellent solution. This way her name and photos of her work would be out there, and she could manage her part time library schedule in a way that made availability for her mother and son possible.

Carlos was happy with Jenny's decision because he wanted to eventually marry her and live in Brazil. Since he caught her watchful gaze quite often, he was hopeful that Jenny was captivated by him as well.

With planning permission granted, Carlos advertised the space in the mall for five more shops. He decided to call the strip mall Hancock Towne Center since the mall was in Hancock County. It was located twelve miles east of Dalton, along the main road to Mason City. Because of the frequency of tornadoes in the area, it was going to be a long and low building, with a large basement underground for everyone's safety.

The colors of the building would be Carlos' favorite combination—cobalt blue, terracotta, and creamy white. Trish thought that the color scheme was beautiful. Her artistic side appreciated Carlos' good taste. She had the best time designing her yarn/art store.

Carlos convinced Trish to have a 3000 square foot store, so she would have enough room to showcase the different kinds of art that she wanted. It sounded huge to her, but when she started designing the store, it was almost difficult to squeeze everything she wanted into it.

She was going to maintain the mall's color scheme within her store, so she planned to have the wall with the large windows overlooking the tasteful parking lot painted a soft creamy white.

There would be window seats under each large window so her customers could sit comfortably while they decided what to buy. The cushions on the window seats would be cobalt blue and terracotta. On the same wall would be built-in white shelving with hundreds of small cubicles for her multitudes of colored yarn.

On another creamy white wall, Trish planned to have four wooden hutches painted cobalt blue. These would be sectioned inside to accommodate more yarn, other knitting supplies, and other art supplies such as paintbrushes, canvas, and such.

The face of the third wall would be made of terracotta brick. She planned to have a variety of mannequins showing off handmade sweaters and shawls, hats and scarves, and gloves and socks. A wide wooden shelf against the wall would have huge shallow wicker bowls filled with balls of yarn and other art items. In the center of the room would be a few large wooden tables with comfortable chairs where customers could work together. The floor would be warm medium-colored wood.

Trish eventually wanted to host some classes for knitting, drawing, painting, and even working with metals and other mediums. She thought that in a country mall, her classes would likely be quite small. The tables and chairs could accommodate up to twelve people at one time.

The last wall would be a showcase for other kinds of art. There would be room for handmade rugs and wall hangings, paintings, and sculptures. Her sales counter and a small stockroom with a bathroom would be at the back of the store. That way she could see the entire store from her counter. White twinkle lights would be woven into the ceiling and along the tops of the walls. She had always loved the look of white twinkle lights in a bedroom or a store.

The theme of the mall was "homemade goods". The other shops included a honey/jam and other baked or canned goods shop, a furniture store that made unique wooden furniture to order, a clothing boutique, a handmade jewelry store, and a landscape and garden store.

The Food Court would have a central location and would offer typical American shopping mall fare.

Once groundbreaking started, Carlos and Trish drove to the site nearly every day to watch the mall start to take shape. Carlos was very familiar with construction sites and took the building of the mall in stride. Trish, however, was astounded at how quickly the construction crew finished each section. She paid very close attention to her store. Townspeople often came out to watch, as well.

# CHAPTER
# Eight

Unbeknownst to Jenny and her son, Carlos had been doing his homework. In the interest of mutual friendship, he planned a mini vacation for the three of them in Minneapolis, Minnesota. This would include a Minnesota Twins game experience.

Carlos broached the topic one night at the supper table.

"Jenny, how would you feel about going to Minnesota with Josh and me? I sort of promised him that we would go to a Minnesota Twins game this summer. It could be fun to take a few days off and have a mini vacation. Trish got away for a few days when we went to Brazil. Now it's your turn to get away and have some fun. What do you say, Jenny? Will you and Josh go to Minnesota with me? I've never been there, and I would love to experience the state. I've read about it, and I'd really like to go with you two."

Jenny's heart started beating fast when she thought about spending some time alone with Carlos. Well, not exactly alone because Josh would be there. But still, better than having the rest of her family always around them. Her shyness and practicality won out. She stammered and stalled when she told him that it wouldn't be a good idea. She had to work, for one thing. Also, she did not want Trish to have to do everything for their mom without help.

Lila interjected and said that she was nearly well and would not be too much for Trish to handle. Trish also said the same thing. She wanted Jenny to get away for a few days, too. Everyone made their objections to Jenny's excuses, and she finally caved in with a small laugh. If everyone thought that it was a good idea, she guessed that she should go.

Jenny arranged to take two days off from work for their vacation. They would be gone for about three and a half days, starting Wednesday, July 23rd. They would leave early in the morning and drive to their hotel before getting to the stadium before the 12:10 p.m. game.

The trip from Dalton to Minneapolis was approximately two hundred miles, and it would take them about three and a half hours to drive there. Luckily, it was freeway driving for most of the way. Carlos loved to drive the Mercedes and was looking forward to the trip.

In the meantime, Jenny looked up the cost of hotels near Target Field, where the Twins played their games. She was shocked at how much even one hotel room cost, much less two. Carlos assured them that he intended to pay for everything.

Jenny would not let Carlos spend more than $140 per room per night, so they decided to stay at Towne Place in downtown Minneapolis. Carlos protested at first because he wanted to treat them to a pure luxury hotel stay. They may not have another chance to stay in such a place in Minnesota again. However, Jenny refused to even consider going on the trip if he spent that kind of money on them. Carlos acquiesced after he finally understood Jenny's need to be somewhat frugal.

Towne Place had excellent ratings and was only a nine-minute walk to Target Field. It was a hassle to park at the stadium, so Jenny thought that they could walk to see the game. Josh and Carlos agreed with her. They were just happy that Jenny was agreeable to staying in that great hotel. Besides, it was only an eleven-minute walk to Nicollet Mall, which they wanted to explore.

Wednesday, July 23rd, dawned beautiful and clear. Jenny was up extra early, going through her suitcase once again. She did not have very stylish clothes, but she took the best of them with her. Carlos told them to bring their swimsuits, casual clothes for the game and walking around, and something dressier for their evening meals.

They all met in the kitchen to eat the wonderful hot breakfast that Lila and Trish made for them. After hugs and kisses all around, Carlos finally ushered his traveling companions into the Mercedes. They all waved to Trish and Lila who stood in the driveway watching them leave.

Even though the trip was long, time passed quickly. True to his nature, Carlos studied the route, and his preparation allowed him to drive calmly and confidently. Jenny noted this and was impressed, both by his attention to detail and his embrace of new experiences. She was not so sure of her own ability to do the same. Meanwhile, she sat back in the luxurious front seat and enjoyed the ride while Josh peppered Carlos with dozens of questions about everything from baseball to international travel.

The happy trio arrived at their hotel by 11:00 a.m. It was too early for them to check into the hotel, but Carlos was given permission to leave his car in the parking lot while they attended the Twins game.

After making sure everything was locked in the trunk, Carlos took Jenny's arm, and they all walked to Target Field. He had already purchased their tickets online, so they just had to pick them up and enter the stadium. Before they got to their seats, Carlos took them to the Twins Pro Shop and bought them all a tee shirt and cap. They used the still clean restrooms to change into their new tee shirts.

Carlos smiled when he saw Jenny decked out in her Twins shirt and hat. She had pulled her long blonde ponytail through the back of the cap, and her slim body, long hair, and youthful face made her look like a lovely teenager. He felt quite old next to her. He wondered if people would think that he was the father to these two young people. That momentarily made him sad.

Carlos intended to immerse himself completely in the game experience. He joined his companions in devouring hotdogs, nachos, and a frosty malted cup. Nearly three hours after it began, his first Minnesota Twins game ended with the hometown team victorious over the Cleveland Indians by a score of 3-1.

They walked slowly back to Towne Place, their high spirits obvious to the delighted staff. Josh related the highlights of the game to the hotel clerk who checked them in.

After opening the connecting door between their rooms, they chatted for a while. Carlos asked them to each pick a place in the Minneapolis/St. Paul area that they wanted to visit. He had somewhere in mind, as well.

He stunned them with his offer to purchase a special souvenir, insisting that it be something they wouldn't normally buy for themselves because it was too expensive. Jenny protested, but Carlos was gently firm about it, setting the limit at $200 each. She could readily see that Carlos truly enjoyed using his wealth to bring joy to others.

Carlos wanted to visit Nicollet Mall, checking out each of its shops. Following that, he intended to go to the top of the IDS Center. He instructed them to start looking for their souvenirs while also considering something for Lila and Trish.

They had a great time. After looking at so many wonderful shops, they trudged their tired feet back to the hotel to sit around the outdoor pool for a while. While both the pool and the weather were glorious, the pool was packed with hotel guests, so they decided to wait until tomorrow morning to go swimming.

At 7:00 p.m., they drove to J.D Hoyt's Supper Club. Carlos had made their reservations earlier that afternoon.

As they walked to Carlos' car, the sun glinted along the length of the thick 14 K gold chain that graced the column of Jenny's pretty neck. Carlos thought that Jenny looked so beautiful, even in her simple dress. Unlike other women of his acquaintance, Jenny didn't need haute couture clothing to enhance her natural beauty. Her slim shapely figure and calm sweet face were enough to make him see how beautiful she really was. He was so attracted to her specific kind of beauty.

They all ordered steaks and salads at the restaurant. This restaurant was known throughout Minnesota for their sumptuous steaks. It was a nice end to their wonderful day.

When they got back to their hotel, Josh said that he was tired and just wanted to relax in his room. If he chose to watch television, there were a hundred channels from which to choose.

Carlos was not accustomed to going to bed so early, and he did not feel like going into the bar alone, so he invited Jenny to join him in the now vacant pool area. He asked the waiter who came by to bring them a fine white wine to sip as they talked.

For the first time in a long while, Jenny found herself in an intimate setting with an attractive man, and she was acutely aware of him. He smelled great—very masculine and a little spicy. He had changed into casual dress pants and a nice button-down shirt. He left the top two buttons unbuttoned, and she could see a hint of his brown chest. *He is such a fit man for being in his forties,* she ruminated.

Meanwhile, Carlos was thinking that Jenny was lovely, even in her old dress and sandals. He would love to see her wearing something beautiful and stylish. She would turn all heads wearing something like that. How he wished that he could buy her something new and pretty to wear, no strings attached.

Carlos idly took her small capable hand in his while they talked. Because he wanted her to feel comfortable with him, he discussed Dalton, the Newbergs, the strip mall, and his home in Brazil. Tomorrow, he planned to tell Jenny and Josh about his wife and child since he was sure that they did not have a clue that he was a widower.

After more than an hour of gentle chat, Jenny said that she should go inside and check on Josh. She suspected that he had likely eaten everything in the mini fridge in their room. He might have even called room service for some snacks. Carlos laughed out loud and said, "I'm okay with that. Josh is a growing boy."

They walked up to their rooms. Carlos said goodnight and gently kissed Jenny's cheek. He would knock on their door at 8:00 a.m. to take them to the breakfast buffet. She nodded and looked deeply into his eyes before entering her room. She was struck by the tenderness in Carlos' eyes as he returned her gaze. *Interesting . . .* she thought.

Day two of their vacation dawned beautifully. It was a sunny warm day—perfect for exploring outside. After their breakfast, they decided to go for a morning swim. They dressed in their swimsuits and met at the pool at 9:30 a.m. There were several other guests already there, but there was plenty of room on the loungers for the trio.

Jenny felt a bit conspicuous in her plain navy-blue one-piece swimsuit. She was aware that it was shabby and lacked any kind of glamor, but it was all she had. She hadn't swum for at least five years, so she had not bothered to buy a new one. Josh outgrew everything lately, so he had a brand-new pair of swim trunks.

She saw how tall and slim he was getting. He was starting to look more like Jack every day. It brought a big lump to her throat. Jack would have loved looking at his son, marveling at Josh's growth and wonderful personality.

Carlos could read every expression on Jenny's face. He decided to say nothing. *Let Jenny have her memories,* he thought tenderly. She had lost Jack only seven years ago, while Carlos had come to terms with Sophia's death over the past twenty-two years.

Refreshed after their swim, they planned their day. Jenny was dying to walk through the Como Park Conservatory and Zoo. Josh wanted to go to the Mall of America. He had never been there before, and he was curious about it. It would be a great place to look for souvenirs, too.

They decided to go to Como Park first since it would be cooler in the morning hours. Dressing hurriedly, they met in the hotel lobby at 10:45 a.m. *Perfect—the conservatory shouldn't be too busy right now,* they all thought.

Once at the Como Park Zoo, Carlos insisted that they go for a ride on the beautiful old carousel. Josh thought it was tame, but he respected Carlos and loved his mom, so he acquiesced.

After walking around the zoo for an hour, they went to the Sunken Garden in the Conservatory. Jenny felt her heart lift at the sight of the beautiful flowers and gorgeous plants. Carlos held her hand as they walked. Josh noticed but didn't say anything. His mom did not seem to mind holding Carlos' hand.

In the gift shop, they found a fantastic frame that Carlos wanted. It was a classy brown leather picture frame in the shape of Minnesota, with a cutout of the word 'Minneapolis' on the lower part. There was room for a picture. Since he wanted to get a photo of the three of them at the Mall of America, it would be the perfect souvenir for him.

Noting Jenny's interest in a fragrant bouquet of summer flowers, Carlos purchased an arrangement of them in an exquisite vase and had them sent to her hotel room. Jenny was touched by Carlos' insight and generosity.

Carlos bought Josh a large box of popcorn since he claimed to be hungry. They all drank their cold sodas as they walked around the beautiful place. At last, Jenny said that she was ready to go. Josh cheered, and they all grinned. Off to the Mall of America they went.

Josh and Jenny were awed when they saw MOA's immensity. They could hardly imagine any one place having so many stores, restaurants, and an amusement park all under one roof.

Carlos' first objective was to locate a photo booth, as he was intent on having them take their picture before they forgot all about it. He wanted it to be a nice picture that he could keep in the Minnesota frame he bought earlier. Hilarity ensued as it took several clumsy attempts to achieve a pose that they all liked. Carlos decided that photobooths were not designed for high occupancy. Nonetheless, their laughter was a joy.

When Carlos finally had one that he liked, they moved on to see other stores. While they walked around, they stopped and had a treat at Cinnabon's. They decided that they would have their supper at Bubba Gump's. They all liked seafood, but Josh and Jenny did not have it very often.

They had a blast going into so many unique stores looking for souvenirs. In one of the sports stores, Josh bought the coveted Rawling baseball glove that he had drooled over for a few years. It was a men's glove since Josh was growing so fast. It would not be long before he could use it.

In a watch store, Carlos bought Jenny a dainty gold and silver Timex Carrington bracelet watch. She had been meaning to buy herself an inexpensive watch. Carlos saw her looking at watches and insisted that they go into the store to look at some of them. He steered her away from the very inexpensive ones and showed her some moderately priced pretty watches. She liked the idea of having a watch that was both gold and silver, so she could wear any piece of jewelry with it. He talked her into the Carrington watch. It looked very nice gracing Jenny's slender wrist.

All that remained was to find a souvenir for Lila and Trish. After much debate, they decided on a lovely white picture frame with pastel metal flowers and leaves adorning three corners of the frame. Lila had said that she wanted some new frames for possible future weddings, a not-so-subtle hint intended for both daughters.

In an art gallery, they found a striking painted picture of the Minneapolis skyline for Trish. She loved pictures like that. She was an excellent artist herself, but since she had never seen the Minneapolis skyline at night, it would be difficult for her to paint it, sight unseen.

Spurred on by hunger, they made their way to Bubba Gump's for supper. After a satisfying meal, they went down to the amusement park on the lowest level and played a game of mini golf at Moose Garden Adventure Golf. Carlos blatantly let Jenny win. Josh willingly obliged. Jenny laughed and protested, to no avail.

Once back at the hotel, Josh said he wanted to watch a little TV before going to bed, so Carlos asked Jenny to sit with him outside by the pool. There was no one else around, so they felt free to hold hands and talk. He hadn't had the chance to tell Jenny and Josh about Sophia, but he would do that tomorrow. Today was just for fun, and they certainly had that in abundance.

He enjoyed spending the last hour of the evening with Jenny. It seemed so natural and right to him to end his day with her. He could imagine being married to her. Jenny was a quiet woman, but she was intelligent and asked searching questions. Her laugh, although much too infrequent, was enchanting.

Tomorrow was their last day of their vacation, and they wanted to make the most of it. After breakfast, they would go to the pool again. Jenny agreed with that plan. He kissed her cheek again as he said goodnight.

The next day dawned with a perfect combination of sun and light breeze, so the three amigos elected to remain poolside for a few hours. They were enjoying a lazy day after their feet took a pounding the day before. Jenny had not felt so carefree since before Jack died. It made Carlos' heart rejoice to see Jenny's contentedness.

Jenny realized that Josh needed a father figure. He was missing out on all the things that sons looked forward to doing with their fathers. Josh was a good boy and rarely asked for anything that he knew was beyond her budget. *Carlos is so natural and good with Josh,* she thought.

Following checkout, they decided to have lunch at The Brother's Deli. They ate slowly since they had plenty of time before driving to Dalton.

Before accessing Interstate 35 for the final leg of their homeward journey, they visited a few more scenic places in Minnesota. Once on the freeway, Carlos knew that he would have their undivided attention for three hours, so he decided to tell them about Sophia. He already knew by now that he loved Jenny and wanted her to be his wife. He would love to have a wonderful boy like Josh as his stepson.

*Well, here goes,* he thought with a bit of nervousness.

"I don't know if Trish told you anything about me. I was married quite young—twenty-four, to a lovely young woman. Sophia was the only child of my father's business partner. I fell in love with her when she was eighteen, and I was twenty. Her parents made her go to college to get a degree in business. I was working at the mine, learning everything about it from the bottom up while I was attending college. Once I graduated from college, I went to work full-time at the mine. I was just waiting for Sophia to finish college, so we could get married."

Carlos stopped talking for a few seconds. He was navigating a tricky part of the highway, and it needed his full attention. In another minute, he began to talk again.

"We got married the month after Sophia finished her degree. Her parents gave us their home and moved to the south of France. They were sickly, and they wanted to be in a sunny place with a few trusted servants to take care of them. Well, the house they gave us is hideous, in my opinion. We lived there only to please her parents. Five months after our marriage, we found out that we were going to have a baby. Both of us were so excited because we both wanted a bunch of children."

The next part of his story was still so difficult to talk about, and Carlos had to stop for a moment and collect his thoughts. In a minute or so, he was ready to continue. Jenny and Josh sat as quiet as mice, wanting Carlos to continue his story.

"Sophia's cousin wanted us to be at her wedding in Rio de Janeiro, so we planned to go. When we got back from the wedding, we were supposed to go to the doctor and find out the sex of our baby. The day that we were supposed to fly to Rio de Janeiro, a huge problem came up at the mine. My father insisted that I stay with him to help, so I kissed my beautiful wife goodbye at the airport and drove back to the mine. The weather was bad that day, and the plane crashed, killing everyone on board. I never got to see my wife or child again. I don't even know if we were having a girl or a boy."

Carlos stopped talking because of the huge lump of regret in his throat.

Jenny and Josh were shocked. They had no idea that something so tragic had happened to this wonderfully kind and generous man. Maybe that was why he was so generous to his friends. He didn't have anyone else to spend his millions on.

Jenny gently put her hand on his arm. He turned briefly to look at her. She saw in his eyes the same feelings that she had about Jack. Here was a man who understood her feelings about her late husband. He must have felt some of those same feelings when he lost Sophia and their unborn baby. At least she had Josh—Carlos never got to hold his baby.

The rest of the trip home was somber, each of them thinking their own sad thoughts. Josh wanted to say something comforting to

Carlos, but he didn't have the words. Jenny was thinking about Carlos, Sophia, and their baby. She was also thinking about Jack. She knew that Jack would want her to move on. He would not want her to stay single for the rest of her life.

They stopped for supper at a fast-food place just before driving over the state line into Iowa. They didn't speak much at the restaurant, but it was a comfortable silence. It seemed that everyone respected each other's feelings and just wanted the rest of the trip to be harmonious.

They arrived at the Newberg home around 8:00 p.m., tired and quiet. Trish and Lila looked at them and guessed that something must have happened. They would try to get Jenny alone later to find out the details.

Josh and Carlos went downstairs after Lila and Trish opened their souvenirs. At their urging, Jenny revealed details about Sophia's tragic death. Lila was shocked to hear Carlos' sad story. Trish, of course, already knew everything about it. The three women stayed up for another hour, talking about Carlos. They all wanted to find small ways to show support for Carlos in the morning. He had seemed so sad when he dredged up all those memories today.

Jenny thought so much about Carlos and Sophia when she went to bed that night. *So, Carlos knows how I feel,* she thought. *No one else quite understands the need to hold on to the memories of Jack but also the desire to have another loving relationship and father for Josh.* Carlos was the only man since Jack that Jenny was attracted to and could see herself with in twenty years. He seemed to be attracted to her, as well.

*It's too bad that he is so wealthy,* she thought. *It would be better if he was a poor man, like Jack had been.* If they got together, she wouldn't know how to live as a wealthy man's wife. *Of course, it might be fun trying it,* she thought with an impish grin. She had some of the same impish tendencies as Trish had, but since her marriage, they had been thoroughly stifled.

* * *

After they returned from their vacation, Carlos took every opportunity to spend more time with Jenny. He saw so much of Josh since they were essentially rooming together in the basement.

Jenny now knew that Carlos and she shared the same heart wrenching experience of losing a spouse. In a way, it made it easier to accept her growing affection for him. She still struggled with moving on and marrying again. She had loved Jack with all her heart. If she dated, and then married Carlos, would she forget Jack and all they had meant to each other?

On the way home from her work at the library one day, she stopped at the cemetery and had a long talk to Jack. She sat by his grave and told him everything about her feelings for Carlos and her fear that she might eventually forget Jack. She felt so much better getting her feelings out in the open. Of course, it was a one-sided conversation, but Jenny left the cemetery feeling that Jack would want her to move on with her life.

She was still so young, and Josh was at an age when he would need a father in his life. Jenny stooped to kiss the cold cement cross on Jack's grave, and then she thanked him for listening to her talking.

Her take-away from that visit to the cemetery was that if Carlos loved her and wanted to marry her, she would say "yes". He was such a good, kind, and generous man to everyone he met, especially those he cared about.

Carlos felt Jenny's reserve melting, little by little. He wanted to give her time, but he also wanted their fragile relationship to move forward. He wondered what her family would say if he took her out on some dates. It was important to him that they progress in this relationship properly, building up to the moment at which he would profess his love.

Two weeks after their vacation together, Carlos decided to ask Jenny to accompany him to Mason City to look at some furniture for his new house. He didn't want anyone else to come with them. It would be tricky since the Newberg family seemed to do *everything* together.

After supper one evening in early August, they sat around the table just talking. Carlos looked at Jenny, smiled sweetly at her, and asked, "Jenny, you have the day off tomorrow. Would you go to Mason City with me to that big furniture store? I want your opinion about what furniture would look good in the living and dining rooms of my new house. In appreciation for all your hard work, I will take you to that good steakhouse we went to on my first night in Dalton. What do you think, Jenny?" His black eyes were gleaming and hopeful.

Josh was about to chime in and say that he wanted to go with them, when he felt his aunt's and grandmother's eyes on him. Both were frowning slightly and shaking their heads. Josh was astute enough to know that they were warning him that the invitation was for his mother only. He smiled slightly and gave them both a small nod to let them know that he understood.

Josh sensed lately that Carlos liked his mom. He, for one, would gladly welcome Carlos as his stepfather. That made Josh grin widely. Trish and Lila saw the grin and knew then that Josh was on board if Carlos wanted to date Jenny.

Jenny looked around the table. Seeing nothing but smiles and nods, she knew that she had everyone's blessings if she wanted to go out with Carlos.

Jenny looked directly at Carlos and said, "Yes, I'd like that. The house is coming along nicely. It's about time that we started thinking about some furniture and wall hangings for it. I love that steakhouse and would be happy if you treated me to a good meal. Thank you, Carlos."

Her smile at Carlos was beautiful.

Carlos felt his heart race at her words and her smile. Maybe they would be able to talk seriously at some point on their date.

Trish and Lila got terribly in the way the next morning when they badgered Jenny about what she should wear.

In the back of her closet was a dress from days gone by. Trish pulled out the pretty, silky short-sleeved sky-blue dress. It had to be at least eight years old, but it was one of those classic dresses that never went out of style. The color was perfect for Jenny's long light blonde hair, pale skin, and large blue eyes. It still fit her perfectly and showed off her trim arms, slim waist, and long legs. With a pure white soft sweater and comfortable tan sandals, it was the right dress for both daytime and evening.

Jenny laughed at her mom and sister for twittering around her like she was going on her very first date ever. Truth be told, Jenny did have a few butterflies in her stomach when she thought about spending the whole day with Carlos. He was such a handsome and charming man of the world, although he showed his sweet and patient side often enough with her family.

They met up in the kitchen. Carlos looked like his usual smashing self—subtle dark silk tie, white silk shirt, and charcoal gray suit.

He was a man who had his suits made to fit him, and a discerning person could tell that his clothing was of the very best quality. He looked equally handsome in well-cut jeans or slacks and a nice buttoned-down shirt. Right now, he looked exactly what he was—a handsome, wealthy business owner.

Carlos beheld Jenny's beauty and smiled. His dark eyes and face revealed his appreciation of her looks and outfit. Jenny saw his look and felt excited and comforted. *Good, I wore the right clothes,* she thought happily. *Carlos looks mighty nice, himself.*

Carlos said, "Good morning, Jenny. You look lovely—just right for today's events. I think we should eat breakfast before we head out. What do you think?"

Jenny smiled at him and said, "Thank you, Carlos. You look very nice yourself. Yes, Mom made a nice breakfast, so let's eat."

After breakfast, the rest of the family saw them off. Jenny was quietly amused. It was like they were going to be gone for a week, instead of only one day.

Carlos made sure Jenny was comfortable before they drove off. It would take them less than an hour to get there in this wonderful Mercedes. He didn't want Jenny to feel uncomfortable with him all day, so he limited his topics to the strip mall, his new house, and the Newbergs. Jenny was relaxed and enjoyed their conversation.

At the store, they found several furniture sets that would work wonderfully in the new house. Carlos told Jenny not to look at the prices or be influenced by them. He told her to pick whatever pieces she felt would look the best in the house. He trusted her judgment. He found that everything that she picked out was also to his taste.

They had a fun-filled day looking at furniture, wall hangings, and art for the walls and end tables. Both grinned whenever a salesperson assumed that they were a couple looking to furnish their home.

Carlos gently teased Jenny all day, trying to maintain a lighthearted mood. All the years of being the sole provider for Josh and herself had made her a bit single-minded. She had forgotten how to be young and carefree. Carlos was trying to give that back to her. He subtly let her know that he was willing and able to take charge of everything.

All day Carlos quietly asked Jenny about her life. Jenny realized what Carlos was doing and happily supplied the answers. She knew that Carlos was trying to get to know her better. Soon it would be her turn to ask him questions. Carlos and his private life were still a mystery to her.

Happy with Jenny's recommendations, Carlos arranged for payment and delivery. He then drove to the Dalton Mall, where they grabbed a snack. Refreshed, they walked through the mall.

Carlos was curious about American malls and wanted his own strip mall to look somewhat like others. Their wanderings led them past Jenny's favorite clothing store. She tried not to be obvious about looking in the window, but her eyes were drawn to the tempting blouses and dresses on display.

While many men would run screaming from a women's clothing store, Carlos was a perfect gentleman, encouraging Jenny to find new clothes to replace those lost in the storm. He patiently waited and commented only when Jenny asked for his opinion. Later, as she paid for her items, Carlos leaned in and discreetly said, "These clothes will be so delighted to be seen on you, my lovely Jenny."

Jenny, blushing at Carlos' directness, nevertheless smiled with joy at his compliment.

Later that evening, they had a delicious steak dinner, discussing their productive day. On the drive home, Carlos noted that Jenny was mellow and comfortable, and he endeavored to keep her that way. In his estimation, she deserved to have nice, uncomplicated days.

Still, Carlos wanted them to move forward with their relationship, so when he saw a rest stop ahead, he pulled into it. Jenny raised her eyebrows and looked at him.

He took her hand gently in his and quietly said, "I pulled in here, Jenny, so we could talk without any interruptions. It is too difficult to do that when I am driving. Is that okay with you?"

Jenny nodded, wondering what they would talk about.

"Jenny, I want to tell you a few things. First, I want you to know that I think you are a lovely lady. I am very attracted to you. I haven't been attracted to many women since Sophia died. I used to think I was better off alone. But now I wonder if I've been missing something all these years.

I've always wanted a family, even a ready-made one. I'm lonely sometimes. Trish and I used to talk about that. She's been so lonely without Shaun, too. As much as I wished I could fall in love with Trish, we only remained friends. She only feels friendship for me, too. I am a wealthy man. I like to share my good fortune with my family and friends. I don't have much family left, but I do have some great friends—like Trish and the rest of you Newbergs.

I know that you might not have moved on since losing Jack, and I can respect that. However, I would like for us to start dating, if you are agreeable to that. It feels like you and I are in sync and that we both enjoy each other's company. You are a beautiful woman, and I would like to see you going out and enjoying yourself—especially with me. I promise to take things as slow as you need me to do. I know that I want you in my life—more than we have previously been.

I'm a go-getter. I go and get what I want. I want us to spend more time together—just us. If you don't want that or if I'm going too fast, please tell me now. I will not pressure you to go out with me, but I think that we could have many happy times together. What do you think, Jenny?"

Jenny was not altogether shocked at Carlos' words. He had been sending off those kinds of vibes toward her for a while. As for herself, she now felt ready to pursue a new loving relationship.

Jenny gave Carlos a direct, albeit shy, look. "Carlos, thank you. I am attracted to you, too. I would enjoy going on some more dates with you and finding out where this attraction leads us."

Carlos smiled tenderly at her before sliding over and putting his arms around her. He bent forward and gave her their first kiss. It was tentative and sweet, and Jenny accepted it. She pressed her lips back on his, and he immediately deepened the kiss. They clung together in a long lingering kiss. When Jenny gently pulled away, her cheeks were flushed but so were Carlos'. He gently chuckled as he touched her silky hair.

"I'd say that we are quite compatible—kissing wise. You kissed me very sweetly, Jenny. I enjoyed our kiss very much."

Jenny, whose cheeks were just returning to normal, nodded and smiled at him. She enjoyed that kiss very much. She could hardly wait until their next kiss.

Carlos smiled at her and drove the rest of the way home. They would both have sweet dreams that night.

The next day, Jenny gave her family a rundown on her date with Carlos before she took herself off to work at the library. The rest of the family went to Carlos' house site to see how it was progressing. The exterior was done, and the builders were finishing the interior rooms.

The Newbergs could really start to see what the finished house would look like. It was a beautiful four-bedroom home with a huge kitchen and pantry. There were several other large rooms that could be used as a living room or den/study. There were two full bathrooms and a good-sized laundry room. The attic was large enough for a small suite of rooms. The house also boasted an attached three-car garage.

Carlos described the furniture and wall hangings that Jenny and he bought yesterday. Everything would be sent to the house in ten days. The Newbergs promised to come to the house the day the furniture arrived and help him place everything in the correct rooms. The delivery van was supposed to arrive at the house on a Saturday, so Jenny could participate in the fun of decorating the house.

Trish promised to make a colorful Brazilian wool and stone wall hanging for the large wall in the living room, adjacent to the stone fireplace. Carlos and she discussed the wall hanging while the others wandered around through the other rooms. Lila had a few great ideas about how to decorate the kitchen and dining area.

Carlos took the happy crowd out for lunch. He had the staff at the restaurant prepare a package of food for Jenny. He drove to the library, so her family could say hello. Jenny was tickled pink that they remembered her and brought her a nice lunch. She had only taken an apple and granola bar from home for her lunch today.

Carlos intently watched Jenny the entire time she chatted with her family. When she turned to him and shyly thanked him for bringing her a beautiful lunch, he smiled sweetly at her. The rest of her family said a quick goodbye to Jenny and told Carlos that they would wait for him in the car. He nodded and tossed the keys to Josh. He wanted a few minutes alone with Jenny.

Jenny leaned over and gave Carlos' cheek a delicate kiss. Carlos grinned and said, "I think we can do better than that, Jenny." Then he pulled her into his arms and gave her a quick burning kiss on her lips. He wanted to stay and talk with her longer, but he knew the others were outside waiting for him.

Jenny's cheeks were a deep pink when she said goodbye to Carlos. He smiled at her and waved as he walked out the door. Thinking that he would bear the brunt of endless teasing from the Newbergs, he was pleasantly surprised to see only happy grins. Their blessing, especially that of Josh, was very important to him.

Later that day, Carlos and Trish took Lila's grocery list and walked to the store. They immediately saw Shaun and his mom buying a few items. It was awkward for Trish to see Shaun after all this time. After a long silent look at Shaun, she took Carlos' arm and dragged him around the aisle, out of Shaun's sight.

Despite each wanting to talk, Trish and Shaun's bravery quickly disappeared. She did not want to have an audience for their conversation. His misapprehension of Trish's friendship with Carlos only worsened when he saw them together. Even though Shaun had not met Carlos before, he believed the town gossip that predicted Carlos' marriage to Trish.

Shaun had stopped by Trish's house several times in recent weeks, but each time the house was vacant. He assumed the worst.

Now, seeing the man for the first time, Shaun's insecurity only grew. He noted with regret that Carlos was a handsome man. No wonder Trish was in love with him.

Shaun looked down at his dusty work clothes and thought, *I could never compete with Carlos. He has more of everything than I have—money, exotic good looks, clothes, car . . .*

Trish's heart was racing when Carlos and she walked around the store, picking up everything on Lila's grocery list. Trish had nearly given up hope that Shaun would come over to have that talk. In the tornado shelter he had made her believe that they would have that talk, but he never came to see her. She knew that word would have gotten to him that they were staying at the Dalton Motel, and now they were back in the Newberg house.

Shaun wondered if Jenny had told Trish that he tried to see her when she was in Brazil. If so, shouldn't Trish initiate their talk? He was still so unsure of Trish. He supposed that, now that Carlos was here, Trish decided to put her old relationship with Shaun in the trash. Maybe she no longer wanted them to talk about the incident with Sheila Warrant.

Jenny had decided to say nothing to Trish about Shaun's visit, and she honored Shaun's request to say nothing about his profession of love for Trish.

When Carlos and Trish arrived home with the groceries, he could see that she was upset and sad. He deduced that it was because they had seen Shaun. He wanted to talk with her about it, but she abruptly told everyone that she wanted to be alone to think. With that, she went to get Nolan to go for a walk. They went in the opposite direction from Shaun's home because she didn't want to run into him again today.

By the time Trish and Nolan returned home almost two hours later, she had regained her composure. While she was gone, Carlos had instructed the others not to mention Shaun's name. The evening passed uneventfully.

On her walk, Trish decided once and for all, not to seek Shaun out. He apparently decided not to tell her about the incident. While she now thought that he was innocent of any wrong-doing, he must have put it out of his mind. Besides, she had been hearing lately that he went out exclusively with Mary. He likely thought that Trish was not worth any more thought and concentrated on wooing Mary. After all, Mary was a sweet and pretty lady.

Shaun declined any of his mom's urging to talk about Trish and the handsome man whose company she was keeping. She supposed it was Carlos Santos. She wondered out loud where Carlos was staying when he was in Dalton.

Shaun tersely told her that the word in town was that Senhor Santos was staying at the Newberg home. People saw his Mercedes parked in their driveway all day and every day.

Seeing them together made Shaun clench his hands and teeth. Hearing her distinctive laugh in the store made him think that she was happy. *How can she be happy while I am miserable?* he wondered. *She's moved on. She doesn't want or love me anymore.*

Shaun encountered Trish in town a few more times during the next two months. She was always accompanied by a family member or Carlos. Sometimes Shaun was with Mary and sometimes with his family. Even though they looked intently at each other, there was never the opportunity for Shaun and Trish to talk privately. Both were trying their best to move on without the other. However, the green-eyed monster was alive and well in Dalton. Both Trish and Shaun grew increasingly reticent to talk with each other if Carlos or Mary was present.

Trish hadn't talked privately with Mary for months. *Since Shaun doesn't love me anymore, I'm glad that he has Mary,* she told herself, untruthfully. Both Shaun and Mary were dear to Trish, and even in her sadness, she wanted them to be happy. Of course, she didn't want to see them together after they were married. She would have to move away from Dalton when that happened.

Meanwhile, Jenny was a good older sister. Had Trish confided in her that she still loved Shaun, Jenny would have insisted that she tell him. Instead, Trish was stubborn and seemed more focused on opening her yarn store. Jenny erroneously concluded that her sister no longer loved Shaun, not realizing that Trish's pride supported her facade.

No one knew that Trish cried into her pillow some nights about the futility of her relationship with Shaun.

Shaun became terser and quieter as the months went past. He was only himself around Mary. She was such a good friend that he poured out all his feelings to her. Mary understood Shaun very well. She sometimes wished that Shaun and she could fall in love and let go of Trish and James. That would be so convenient. Shaun was the sweetest and nicest man that Mary had ever known. She knew he would be a loving husband and father, just as she would be a good wife and mother.

* * *

Jenny and Carlos continued to date during these next few months. They always went to Mason City or other larger towns on their dates, so the people of Dalton never saw them together or guessed that they were a couple.

Carlos' new house was nearly finished, and the strip mall was nearing completion, too. Trish spent a lot of time ordering materials for her store and then putting them in place once she was allowed inside.

The town was excited about an upcoming wedding. Shaun's first cousin, Bill, was marrying Cheri Bond, another resident of Dalton. The wedding date was set for October 10th, which was exactly three years from Shaun and Trish's originally planned wedding date. Trish thought it was terribly ironic. Cheri, a lifelong friend from school, invited Trish to attend with a guest.

Since Carlos was going to be in town on that date, Trish invited him to be her guest. Josh would accompany them with Cheri's permission. Jenny wasn't friends with either Bill or Cheri. Therefore, she decided to stay at home with Lila, who didn't want to go either.

CHAPTER

# Nine

James Regan did not hesitate to act. Not for one second. Only minutes ago, his mother, Norah, alerted him that his father was having difficulty breathing. Keith had relied on his son to keep the farm successful, and now father was relying on son to get medical help.

It wasn't easy for Keith to ask James to forego his dreams of being an agriculture lawyer when poor health threatened his ability to run the forty-acre family farm ten years ago. Even with the Black Angus cattle grazing on the thirty-five acres of pastureland, there was plenty of work involved, as any Iowa farmer understood.

James enjoyed working on the farm when he was a youngster. In high school, he became very interested in agricultural law. He was aware of the troubles that small farms sometimes had with government regulations. He wanted to live in Dalton near his parents and help his neighbors navigate the increasingly challenging government oversight in farming.

Then, in his last year at college, his father had a stroke. James left college five months short of getting his degree and moved back in with his parents to take over the farm. His father was unable to do any more of the physical work on the farm.

The farm had been in the Regan family for five generations. Now, faced with the possibility of having to sell the farm, James adamantly stated that he was willing to take over. He knew that his parents couldn't bear the thought of selling, especially to strangers. If he took over, his parents could remain, and the farm would not be sold.

James, a quiet and honorable young man, never spoke about his squashed dream. He felt that, above everything, his duty was to his parents. However, there was another dream that he equally cherished. James hoped that one day he would meet a girl and settle down. He wanted a family life and a son to someday take over the farm.

Keith Regan had been getting grayer in the face recently. His doctor advised the Regan family that there was a possibility of another stroke if Keith didn't take all precautions. James made sure that Keith didn't have any stress regarding the farm.

Norah tried to make sure that the family ate plenty of fresh and healthy food. James and she were strong and bursting with good health. Now in his early sixties, Keith had never quite recovered from his severe stroke when he was fifty-two.

It was sixty miles to the Mason City Hospital, and James put his foot down. He didn't mind if the local sheriff caught him speeding. That way he would have a police escort to the hospital. However, he did not get stopped. It only took him forty-four minutes to go the sixty miles.

He pulled into the Emergency entrance. Within seconds, a team of doctors and nurses rushed to the truck. James quickly explained, and they wheeled Keith into the hospital. Norah followed them in.

James parked the truck and raced inside. He found his mom in the Emergency waiting room. After what seemed to be an eternity, a doctor approached them with his diagnosis. Keith had suffered another small stroke. He was going to have to remain in the hospital for several days.

James left his mom for an hour to rent motel rooms near the hospital. After that, he telephoned his good neighbor, Charlie, and explained the situation to him. Charlie had two teenage sons who could tend to the Regan cattle for a day or two.

James and Norah stayed near Keith for two days. Keith was doing okay, but the doctors were carefully monitoring him. They said that Keith's heart was weak, and he was overly tired. Norah wanted to stay in Mason City with Keith, but she wanted James to go back to the farm. After hugging and kissing his parents, James reluctantly returned to their farm.

While at the hospital, Norah telephoned a few friends and neighbors. The whole town soon knew that Keith Regan was in the hospital. They also knew that James would be alone on the farm. He worked with the cattle for much of the day and would not have much time to do any cooking or cleaning for himself—not that he even knew how to do those things.

The neighborhood ladies called each other and arranged times for each of them to go to the Regan farm to cook and clean. Most ladies could only come for a few hours at a time because they had their own families to care for.

Mary's mother, Eileen, talked with her about which days she should volunteer to help James. Eileen, like most of the other neighborhood ladies, only planned to go for short chunks of time. The ladies would leave a cold lunch for James and a hot cooked meal for his supper. They would only be able to do some cursory cleaning, as well.

Mary, who was smitten with James, wanted to help, too. Of all the ladies in the neighborhood, she had the most time on her hands because she was not in charge of a family. Her responsibilities included helping her mother with the household cleaning and cooking and her father with the paperwork for the farm.

Eileen told her neighbors that she would take her turn helping James. She said that Mary could fill in for anyone if they found themselves unable to go to the Regan farm during their rotations. Although Mary protested, saying that she could do her own rotation, Eileen wasn't sure if it was proper for Mary to spend that much time in James' company.

Mary exasperatedly told her mother that James and she had been casual friends since high school. She was not in the least nervous about spending time alone in the Regan house. James would be outside most of the day. Eileen was a bit over-protective of her daughter and thought that some of the housework would be too much for Mary to handle with her clubfoot.

Mary longed to be treated as a normal healthy young woman. She knew that she had enough stamina to take care of a whole house and even a family of her own. Moreover, she wanted James to see her in this light—a capable, strong, and desirable woman. They had lightly flirted with each other in the high school art class. Of course, she was only a sophomore and he a senior, so he may have decided that Mary was too young for him at that time.

Ever since Mary returned to Dalton after her college graduation, they frequently saw each other at community events. James was always courteous and pleasant with Mary but no more so than he was with other girls. Since he took over the Regan farm, he didn't seem to go on any dates at all. There were a few local girls who would have gladly gone out with the dark-haired handsome young man.

Mary's parents had taken her for treatment of her severe clubfoot when she was an infant. The doctors treated it the best they could. However, because of the severity of her clubfoot, Mary was left with a slightly turned foot, which caused it to drag a bit when she walked.

She could do just about everything as well as any other girl except run and dance. In fact, she was more aware than other people of her imperfect foot. When she wore pants or a long skirt, no one even saw her slightly turned inward left foot.

Three days after the neighborhood ladies started their rotation, Mary was called to take over for Mrs. Hubers, who had a sick child. Mary dressed carefully in a cute pair of jeans and top. She put her long shiny blonde hair in a loose ponytail and added some pink lip gloss to her nice red lips. She thought that she looked okay, when in fact, she was quite pretty.

She drove her car to James' farm, which was only three miles from her own home. She pulled up in front of his house and knocked loudly on the door. It was only 7:30 a.m. James, fresh from his early morning shower, opened the door, still rubbing the towel over his wet head. His dark curls bounded around his handsome face. Mary, at five-feet-six-inches tall, still had to look up to his six-feet-two-inch height. She smiled sweetly at James and said, "Good morning, James. I'm taking over for Mrs. Huber today. Her youngest is sick. Since I'm here early, I'll make you a hot breakfast. What would you like? I'm a good cook, so ask for anything you want."

James looked at Mary with appreciation and gave her a small smile. He had been having cold cereal for several days in a row. He could go for a hot breakfast. "Well," he drawled, "I won't ask you to make me a steak and egg breakfast, but how about bacon, eggs, and toast? That's probably my second favorite breakfast.

I like my eggs over medium and my bacon crispy without being burnt. I would very much appreciate it if you could make that kind of breakfast for me. Have you eaten? If not, I would enjoy your company at the breakfast table."

Mary, who was secretly amused at James' formal tone, said that she would like to eat with him. Truth be told, she had already had some toast at home, but she wanted to spend more time with James. She could manage an egg and one piece of bacon.

James showed Mary where to find the things she needed to make breakfast. For some men, certain smells elicit quick action on their part. It could be anything from fresh-baked apple pie to engine exhaust. Mary knew this, having keenly watched her father, so she inwardly grinned as James bolted from his bedroom when the bacon was nearly done.

"I absolutely love the smell and taste of crispy bacon," James exclaimed upon sitting down at the kitchen table. As he devoured his breakfast, he idly watched Mary move around the kitchen. Her movements were sure and clear, and her clubfoot was not obvious to him.

While they ate, Mary asked him what he liked to eat for lunch and supper. She said that she would be happy to make anything he fancied for his meals. It didn't matter to her what she made. What did matter is that she was the only one giving him a choice. James was pleased with her logic and gave her a list of his favorites.

He did not tell her that his favorite meal was lasagna with garlic bread and green beans. Most people preferred not to make it because it was so time intensive. Additionally, his mom tried to make lean and healthy meals due to his father's health, so having it at all was a special occasion.

Mary told James to gather his soiled clothes for washing. He went off to put them in the laundry basket that she provided. As he did not want her to wash his underwear, he only put his jeans, tee shirts, and buttoned-down shirts in the basket. He intended to wash and dry his own underwear after she went home.

Mary grinned when she spied the basket's contents. There was not a stitch of his underwear there. Poor man was probably embarrassed. Mary, who had been washing her father's underwear for years, was not embarrassed about washing men's clothing.

The Regans had a very old washing machine and dryer. It took ten minutes for Mary to figure out how to run them. Once she got the washing machine going, she looked around the living room. It was well-ordered, but it showed the dust. Not for long, as she began cleaning. Her purposeful approach meant that high traffic areas were top priority while other areas, especially James' bedroom, were not touched.

Once she was sure that the house was as clean as could be, she found a drawer full of cookbooks and sat at the kitchen table to look at them. Her leg was tired by now, anyway.

Mary found a loose recipe for lasagna shoved into one of the cookbooks and wondered why it was there. James had not mentioned that he liked it. Perhaps Keith or Norah really liked it. She set it aside and looked at other recipes. Finding a recipe for delicious beef stew, she decided to make it for supper. James' freezer was chock-full of vegetables and various meats, including exactly what she needed for stew.

Since James liked meat and cheese sandwiches, Mary creatively arranged several selections on a plate. She gathered ingredients for a salad and sliced a loaf of fresh bread she retrieved from the bread box. Having noted that James liked coffee, she prepared a fresh pot.

At five minutes to twelve, Mary put everything on the table. She added pickles, mayonnaise, mustard, and two types of dressing for the salad. The table looked good. *Any hungry man would be happy with the choices I've offered,* Mary thought with satisfaction.

James came in and went to wash his hands. He had combed his hair before coming inside. *The house looks so clean and neat,* he thought. The smell of coffee and the sight of the food pleased him, too.

"Hi, James. You're right on time for lunch," Mary said in her soft, friendly voice. She was a cheerful person who liked to talk with people. She knew that James was a quiet man, but hopefully, he was more talkative in his own home.

James nodded at Mary, smiling slightly. He realized that he enjoyed coming into his house and finding her there. He had always thought that Mary was a nice girl.

They ate lunch in friendly silence. It was James' habit to remain inside after lunch, either reading the paper or talking with his parents. In this regard, he felt completely at ease with Mary. It was like they were an old married couple.

At 1:30 p.m., James got up and said that he needed to head back outside. He told her that he usually had supper at 6:00 p.m., if that would suit her. Mary nodded and told him to have a good afternoon. Mary tried not to be too chatty, since James did not usually say very much. She didn't want to annoy him.

After he went back outside, she dried his clothes and entered his bedroom to put them away. James' bedroom smelled like him— a mixture of masculine cologne and earthiness. *If I was his wife,*

*I could smell this every day,* she thought with an inner smile. He was everything that she wanted in a mate. He was handsome, kind, loyal, intelligent, and hardworking.

While supper's beef stew was bubbling, Mary made homemade cornbread and a chocolate cake. James hadn't mentioned that he liked dessert, but she thought that most people liked cake. The house smelled heavenly by 5:30 p.m.

Mary had time to go into the bathroom with her purse and brush her hair, leaving it free and flowing over her shoulders in a shining mass. She put on more lip gloss and studied her reflection critically. Her blue eyes were clear and pretty. She didn't wear mascara because her lashes were thick and curled nicely around her eyes. Her pink cheeks gave her pale skin color. The lip gloss made her red lips look shiny and inviting. If James didn't like the way she looked, there was nothing more she could do. *This is about as good as I can look,* she shrugged.

As Mary set the table for supper, she scrutinized her pretty blouse. It was still clean and crisp despite the work that she had done today. She planned to eat supper with James and then clean up before going home, promising her mom that she would arrive shortly after 7:00 p.m.

She hoped that James would talk a little more at the supper table. One whole day with him and she didn't know anything new about him. Maybe she never would. That was a sobering thought.

James came in at 6:00 p.m. sharp. He inhaled deeply. Everything smelled so good, especially the chocolate cake, which was his favorite dessert. Mary was proving to be a very good cook and housewife.

James savored every bit of his supper. Mary had pampered him all day with three luscious meals, a nice clean house, and gentle conversation. He knew that she was only helping today, but he wished that she would be there every day. He liked her and felt comfortable around her.

Mary reminded him that she needed to go home by 7:00 p.m. James nodded. He had the schedule and knew that Mrs. Cohen was coming tomorrow. He was so grateful to the neighborhood ladies for their help and care.

While they ate, James looked often at Mary. Her hair was so shiny and pretty. It reminded him of his horse's fine mane. Both were long, silky, and honey colored. Her sweet face was pink, and her eyes were beautiful. She was a slender to medium-sized girl, and her blouse and jeans looked cute on her.

*Why haven't I previously considered how attractive Mary is?* James used to think of her sometimes when they were in high school. At the time, he thought that she was too young for him. By the time she returned from college, he was so busy working on the farm that he didn't have time for dating. He knew about her clubfoot, but it didn't seem to slow her down today.

Word was that she and Shaun Healy went out quite a bit. Maybe they were in love and going to marry. He had always hoped that Trish Newberg and Shaun would reunite. Having been friends with Shaun his whole life, he knew that Shaun was deeply in love with Trish. *But perhaps now, Mary had taken Trish's place in Shaun's heart,* he thought regretfully.

If Mary had been totally free, James might have asked her for a date. With his parents now staying in Mason City, he no longer needed to remain home to keep them company. James was candid with himself, *I'm getting older, and it's time for me to take dating seriously if I want any chance of finding a wife.* Practicality aside, James desired romance as well. It wasn't enough that certain criteria were met; he wanted to share all his hopes and dreams with a woman who wanted the same. As he considered this last thought, he now wished that he had asked Mary if she and Shaun were a couple.

Mary prepared to leave at 7:00 p.m. She cheerily wished him well and said that she might see him again one of these days. He walked her to her car and smiled at her as he said good night. Then he went back inside to do a load of his underwear, grateful for the other clean clothes in his bedroom closet.

It's human nature to create private fantasies that help us trudge through our daily reality. So, naturally, Mary was frustrated as she drove home. She didn't know what she had expected from James. It's not as if he would suddenly fall in love with her and sweep her into his arms for a long kiss. In her secret fantasy, she had hoped for that, but she needed to be realistic. James seemed to be comfortable with her—that was something, at least. He didn't seem very comfortable with many people when he was out and about at community events.

Mary told her mom all about her day and then quickly added that she wanted to go over some paperwork for her father. She sensed that her mom was uncomfortable about her spending all day at James' house. It wasn't as if anything happened. James could have been her uncle for all the attention he paid her. It would have pleased Mary a great deal to know that James was thinking about her right now.

Keith Regan's doctors recommended that he and his wife move into an apartment always staffed by medical personnel. There were some very nice apartments like that in Mason City.

James drove to Mason City to have a candid talk with his parents. His father now used an oxygen tank all the time. The strokes had damaged his heart, and his doctors were cautious about his prognosis. Still, James tried to be upbeat as he gently teased his parents. Above all, he encouraged them to do whatever they thought best.

Keith was grateful for his son's efforts to keep the farm viable and in the family. Now it was possible for Norah and him to seriously consider an assisted living facility.

Norah liked the idea that she could get medical help for Keith so quickly. She was a friendly person, so she thought that she could easily make friends in Mason City. Her old friends could visit them, too. It only took an hour to drive from Dalton to Mason City.

After a daylong discussion, Keith and Norah decided to make the move into assisted living. James accompanied them as they looked at several apartments. Despite the sobering aspects of their situation, they focused on the positives and chose a very nice two-bedroom apartment. James was welcome to stay overnight at any time. Since the apartment was much smaller than their house, they would have to carefully choose which possessions to bring with them. They also needed to leave sufficient furniture and household items at the farm for James' comfort.

On a subsequent trip back to the farm, James' parents made their selections while he ensured that his dad did nothing more strenuous than point to things from his comfortable chair. After two days, it was obvious that James needed to buy replacement furniture. He airily said that he would enjoy the task.

Within a week's time, parents, furniture, and personal items took residence in their new home in Mason City. James was thrilled to help, although the strangeness of living alone on the farm after living most of his life with his parents began to dawn on him.

He joked, "I guess I need to shop for a wife while I'm looking for some furniture. I wonder if I can get a BOGO offer."

Pleasantly surprised at her son's levity, Norah replied, "I could check my coupon caddy." She flashed Keith a quick look, and he chuckled, shaking his head.

"Norah, I can see where our son gets his sense of humor!"

Even though James never considered himself the wittiest of people, his attempt at humor inserted a few moments of fun into his parents' lives at an appropriate time.

Privately, James kept thinking about Mary. He was quite attracted to her. There were obvious things to admire, like being a good cook, housekeeper, and companion; however, he liked her quiet and gentle ways, too. Somewhere deep inside himself, he appreciated her more forthright ways and speech. She was not a shrinking violet. She had some strong convictions and could give as well as take. He didn't give her clubfoot another thought since it didn't seem to limit her in any way.

Mary worked at James' house several more times. She was always bright and cheerful while in his company. Since nothing seemed to be happening between them, Mary occasionally remarked that she had a date with Shaun. If James liked her at all, that news might make him a little jealous. Then he might do something about it.

James thoroughly enjoyed Mary's meals and company. He thought, now more than ever, that Mary and Shaun were a couple. Everyone in town seemed sure that they would get married before the end of the year. He berated himself for not taking notice of Mary sooner. She had been free for years, not going out with anyone. Now, just when he found that he liked her a lot, Shaun Healy beat him to Mary's door.

Mary had been working at James' house several days in a row since her neighbors were all busy. She continued to wonder about that lasagna recipe she found and decided to make it for supper one evening.

She wore her favorite outfit that day. During the daytime, her hair was confined to that loose ponytail that kept her neat and clean. Before supper, she loosened her hair, brushing it until it shone with good health. It fell, thick and shiny down her back.

Her blouse was a beautiful deep pink one that was embroidered with flowers. Her jeans were snug, flaring at the heel. Cheeks flushed pink and eyes sparkling with anticipation, she came out of the bathroom and looked directly at James, who was already in the house, having finished his chores early.

Lost in her eyes, James was more speechless than usual. Although he lacked the words, every fiber of his being was desirous for the touch of Mary's lips. A full minute went by as he stood mesmerized by her beauty.

Mary was very aware of James, too. Droplets of water clung to his wavy dark hair. After washing away the day's grime, he had hurriedly changed into a clean shirt, and she glanced at his firm chest through undone buttons. The smell of his wonderful cologne competed with supper's aroma.

James couldn't believe his nose. *Lasagna! How did Mary know that it is my favorite?* His senses were overcome with Mary's beauty and the heavenly smell of lasagna.

Mary and James made furtive glances at each other throughout the delicious meal. Several times their eyes met and lingered. James felt his heart race and realized with shock that he was in love with Mary. Fighting the urge to tell her, he recalled that she had told him earlier that she had a date with Shaun later that evening.

By now, Mary was very aware that James was staring at her. *Maybe he does like me a little bit after all.* As for her, the sixteen-year-old's crush was now full-blown love. She could readily imagine herself married to James, living in this house, and having their babies.

James was enchanted by Mary. Yet, above all, he was an honorable man. It was the only way he knew how to be. While he wanted to reveal more about himself to Mary, he would not do so out of respect for the relationship he presumed she now had with Shaun. This was no easy decision as Mary's inviting red lips were but a few feet and one moment away.

When Mary said she had to leave, James walked her to her car. He thanked her profusely for her help and the delicious meal. Just before she closed her car door, James reached down and kissed her cheek. This was the first time that he had ever done that or even touched her. Mary smiled as she drove away.

She told Shaun about it during the drive home from their date. He could tell that Mary was very interested in James. In fact, he had known for years that Mary liked James. She was always willing to go out with Shaun, though, and he appreciated that.

# CHAPTER Ten

Dalton was gearing up for Bill and Cheri's wedding. They were going to have a traditional wedding in an untraditional setting. A local farmer had converted his big old barn into a place where weddings and other community events proudly took place. In this small community, weddings were a very big deal.

The barn had a small, raised stage where the pastor and bridal couple stood in clear view of the guests. There was a beautiful large window looking out over the fields. The main floor was set with rows of hay bales, each covered with a clean pure white linen cloth. A family of gray cats were allowed to walk around as if they owned the place. Well, it had been their home before it was repurposed.

White twinkle lights descended from the lofty ceiling. The pleasant familiar smell of fresh hay filled the wedding service area. Ample seating was provided around the bar located in the back. Since almost everyone in these parts expected to cut a rug at weddings, a sizable dance floor was merely steps away.

Shaun was Bill's Best Man. The groom and his groomsmen wore black dress pants and cowboy boots, white shirts with snap buttons from neck to waist, a bolo tie, and black cowboy hats (not during the ceremony, of course).

The bride wore a tea length frothy white lace dress with a handkerchief hem and short white cowboy boots with a heel. Her head was graced by an elaborate headband, glittering with simulated diamonds and pearls. Her three bridesmaids wore wine colored knee-length chiffon dresses with full skirts and light brown cowboy boots.

Bill was a farmer, and Cheri worked in a store about fifteen miles from Dalton. They had been a couple for about two years and had many friends and relatives living near the Dalton area. Just about everyone from town and twenty miles in all directions was invited.

Cheri had stopped by the strip mall site to talk with Trish about the wedding. She also wanted to get a look at Carlos Santos, the man the whole town was talking about. Cheri gave Trish a big grin and a thumbs-up sign before she left.

Cheri mentioned that there would be dancing—country music, of course. Trish was to make sure that she was ready to do the two-step. Trish laughed and smiled at that. It was her favorite kind of dance. Shaun and she used to two-step to some of their favorite songs.

Ironically, their favorite song was Randy Travis' "Forever and Ever, Amen". The lyrics poignantly stated that the man would love the girl forever and ever. They had always said how perfect the song was for them. Now, Trish just hoped that the DJ would not play that song at the wedding, although it was a typical wedding dance song.

Trish took Carlos and Josh aside at home to teach them how to do the two-step. She told Josh that he was not too young to learn.

Lots of eleven- and twelve-year-old girls might ask him to dance, and he should be ready and prepared to do so. Josh rolled his eyes, but he agreed to learn.

Surprisingly, Carlos was a quick learner. He was a very good dancer. He explained that there were Brazilian dances similar to the American two-step. They laughed a lot while they danced. Carlos even grabbed Lila and Jenny to dance with him occasionally. He was becoming one of the family.

The beautiful October day dawned—a perfect wedding day for Bill and Cheri. The temperature was a warm seventy degrees, not too hot and not too cold. The wedding party would be able to get some wonderful wedding photos at local scenic spots. The wedding ceremony was set for 2:00 p.m. at The Old Barn. It wasn't a very inventive name, but it accurately described the place. Its rustic nature was charming.

Shaun dressed and drove to Bill's farm where he waited for him. Bill loved Cheri so much and was excited to marry her that day. However, it was bittersweet for Shaun since he was to have married Trish three years ago, today.

The wedding ceremony was lovely. From his place standing next to Bill, Shaun could see everyone in the room. Mary, his date, was sitting near the front. She looked pretty in a long pink dress. Her loose hair was shimmering with light. Shaun gave her a big smile. As for those assembled, they wondered which couple would marry next—Mary and Shaun or Trish and that handsome foreign fellow.

Shaun saw Trish arrive with Josh and Carlos. She looked adorable in knee-length cowboy boots, a short, flared denim skirt, and a red frilly blouse. Her hair was subdued for now in a stylish ponytail. He knew that later she would likely take out the scrunchy and let her wild curls frame her face, which he always loved. Her wild curls gave her such an impish look.

During the reception, Shaun kept Mary's glass filled with champagne and her plate filled with tidbits of food. Because of his position as Best Man, he had to leave her for stretches of time. She said that she didn't mind. So many neighbors and friends came over to talk with her.

Mary saw James Regan come in by himself. She waved and smiled at him when he caught her eye. He acknowledged her with a slight grin and a small wave. He found a place to sit with his neighbor, Charlie, and his family.

Trish kept to her table with Carlos and Josh. Friends and neighbors sometimes came over to say hello. She couldn't help her gaze from straying to Shaun a few times. He looked so handsome in his black pants and white shirt. Form-fitting clothes showed off his nice physique. He wore his black cowboy hat, too.

She had bought that hat for him in the spring after they got engaged. He said that he would wear it for their wedding. Since they had planned an October wedding, it would have been very similar to Cheri and Bill's. As she recalled details of her own wedding plans, she wondered if Shaun remembered the significance of this day.

The dance started at 7:00 p.m. The food and extra tables were cleared. Now, there were small tables surrounded by chairs for the guests. The bales of hay were still in the front of the barn in case guests wanted to get away from the dancers and loud music.

Trish first took to the dance floor with Josh. Afterward, Carlos and she danced quite a few dances together. Trish also danced with friends and neighbors when they asked her. Carlos obliged any lady who requested, as he relished the opportunity to dance. Josh was sought out by two or three pre-teen girls. His big smile was wonderful to see.

James waited for a chance to talk with Mary. Shaun had touched her arm, smiled at her, and left her alone for a few minutes. James was nervous because he was going to ask Mary if she and Shaun were a serious couple.

"Hi, Mary. You look very nice. Pink suits you," James said quietly.

Mary smiled widely and blushed a little. "Thank you, James. You look nice, too. I think that men look nice in cowboy hats."

"You look so happy tonight. May I ask you a personal question?" James asked seriously.

"Go ahead, James. What do you want to know?" Mary asked in surprise.

"The whole town's talking about you and Shaun. Are you a couple? Do you plan to get married?" James asked her very quietly. How he wished that she would deny it. He wanted a chance to date Mary.

Mary looked searchingly at James. She shook her head slowly and said, "No, James, we're not a couple. We're just good friends. I don't get asked out very much, and Shaun is working through his issues with Trish. I know that the town talks about us, but there's nothing like that between Shaun and me. Why did you ask me that, James?" she asked him softly.

James smiled in relief and said, "I wanted to ask you if you would be my date next Saturday at my cousin's wedding in Mason City. I wouldn't have asked you if you were in love with Shaun. I don't do that to friends."

Mary smiled brightly as she said, "Yes, I'd like to go with you to your cousin's wedding. What time do you want to pick me up?

Oh, are you a groomsman in the wedding like Shaun is today? Do you need to get there extra early?"

James shook his head and said with a slight smile, "No, I'm not a groomsman. Ian and I are friends as well as cousins, but he has three brothers who will be the groomsmen. I have the leisure of coming to the wedding without any ties. I will pick you up at 11:00 a.m. The wedding is set for 1:30 p.m., but I want to visit with my family before the wedding. The reception starts at 3:00 p.m. and will go until 7:00 p.m. There will be a dance starting right after the reception. We can go to that if you want to, but I am not much of a dancer. My feet seem to grow ten sizes because I always trip and step on my partner's feet. I'll let you decide if you want to stay for the dance, okay?"

Mary cheerily said, "I'll be ready, James. I'm looking forward to it." James nodded and said, "I am, too. See you next Saturday."

As he walked toward the exit, he turned to look at her one more time, instantly catching her gaze again. They smiled at each other shyly before breaking eye contact.

When Shaun returned to Mary's table, she told him about her date with James the next week. He was very happy for her, especially since he knew how much she longed for a chance to date James.

During a slow song, Trish went up to talk with Mary. She saw Mary's shining eyes and wondered why she looked so happy. Shaun had gone to talk with the bride and groom for a bit, so Trish felt safe going over to talk with Mary.

"Mary, you look lovely—and happy. What's going on, my friend?" Trish asked in a friendly voice.

Mary looked at Trish with an ecstatic smile. "Oh, Trish, I am happy. I'm in love, and I can't stop myself from smiling." She didn't want to say anything about James at the dance. There were too many snoopy people around.

She wanted to have a nice heart-to-heart talk with Trish, anyway. She wanted the scoop on Carlos. She didn't believe what the town was saying about Trish and Carlos. She knew from personal experience that there were a bunch of gossipy women in town with nothing better to do than make up things about people.

Trish's heart sank. Now she knew the answer to the question she kept wondering about. Mary was in love with Shaun. It wasn't hard to understand why—Shaun was amazing. Trish had always wondered how Shaun could love her out of all the girls he knew.

Mary said that she wanted to have a good long talk with Trish sometime soon. Trish invited her to come to the house and see everyone and get introduced to Carlos. She wanted to talk about her yarn shop with Mary, too.

Trish hugged Mary and slowly went over to where Carlos was talking with Josh. Carlos had his long arm around Josh's thin shoulder, and they were laughing about something. When Trish got to their side, Carlos looked at her and immediately put his other arm around her. Trish looked like she had just lost her best friend.

Carlos quietly asked her if she wanted to talk, but Trish shook her head. This was not the time or place. They were standing there talking when the DJ started to play Randy Travis' song, "Forever and Ever, Amen". Trish's head shot up, and she automatically looked for Shaun. He was standing next to Mary, but he was staring at Trish. Their eyes locked across the room. Trish looked away first. Shaun loved Mary now. How ironic . . .

Carlos, who found out last week that this was Trish and Shaun's favorite song, looked straight at Shaun. Since Shaun didn't make a move to invite Trish to dance, Carlos took it upon himself to pull Trish out onto the dance floor. He danced supremely well with Trish, and everyone thought how good they looked together. Some of the older guests thought it was a shame that Shaun and Trish were not together anymore.

It was getting late, and the wedding dance was nearly over. Shaun found himself walking toward the table where Trish was sitting with Carlos and Josh. Just before he reached them, Carlos and Josh were asked to dance. *Good, that means that Trish will be alone,* thought Shaun. He had found it so difficult to not ask Trish to dance to their favorite song. They used to love two-stepping to that song. It had some sweet memories for him.

This was the first time that he had been alone with Trish since that night that he saved her from the tornado. She had been back almost five months, and still they had not talked. Perhaps talking at a wedding dance was not the right time or place, but he just wanted to be next to her for a few minutes.

Trish licked her lips nervously. Shaun followed her tongue with his eyes. How he wanted to kiss Trish! In the past, she always had so much passion in her kisses for him. *Well, I can't do that at a dance, not in front of all these people,* he thought irritably.

Trish looked warily at Shaun. She wanted to still have that talk with Shaun, but it was obviously too late if he loved Mary now. Shaun also wanted that same thing, but he was sick of seeing Trish and Carlos together. Shaun was in love with her and as jealous as hell. *Still, I should say something to her,* he thought.

"Hello, Trish. You're looking very well. I saw you dancing. You've obviously not forgotten how to two-step." Shaun's voice was restrained.

Trish nodded and said, "You look great, too, Shaun. I like the bolo tie and the black hat."

Both stopped because they didn't know how to move on. Finally, in desperation, Shaun said, "Trish, I've waited more than three years to talk to you. I guess it should be obvious to me that it doesn't matter to you anymore. You didn't try to talk to me, and I guess it's too late now. I've had to let it go. You obviously never wanted to find out the truth about what happened between Sheila and me." His voice was belligerent.

Then, brokenly, "Trish, how could you ever believe that of me? I loved you so much. I would never have hurt you that way." He looked away from her, trying to keep tears from welling in his eyes. Even now, with Trish apparently in love with Carlos, Shaun still wanted her to know that he could never hurt someone that he loved so much.

Trish put a hesitant small hand gently on his arm. She quietly asked, "Shaun, do you think that we could still be friends? We have so much history together and like the same things. I would be willing to be friends if you are." Trish's soft voice was so hopeful and sincere.

Shaun was about to tell her that he would like that too, but when he looked up from the perusal of his boots, he saw Senhor Santos watching them. He remembered then that Trish loved Santos and not him. Shaun's quick temper flared to life. He saw red. He moved his arm abruptly so that Trish's hand would fall.

He looked at Trish with hard blue eyes and said through clenched teeth, "No, Trish, I don't think that I could be friends with you. You've proven that you don't trust me. I trust my friends, but I no longer trust you."

He wanted to hurt her at that moment. He cruelly said, "We can be, let me think . . . We can be neighborly. That's the best I can do. Take it or leave it." He couldn't believe he just said something so mean to the woman that he still loved—but he couldn't help himself.

Trish's heart plummeted to her feet. Shaun didn't want to have anything more to do with her. He was still hurt and angry with her. All this time of waiting to talk with him, and this was the result. She was stunned, shocked, and unbelievingly sad. Tears stung her eyes as she turned away from Shaun and looked right at Carlos.

Carlos could see her devastation and quickly said something to Josh. He was at her side within seconds. He put his comforting arm around Trish's now shaking body. He looked Shaun in the face and spoke. "Hello. Shaun, isn't it? It's nice to finally meet you. I'm Carlos Santos."

He squeezed Trish's shoulder and said tenderly, "Trish, if you've finished talking with Shaun, we had better get going. I promised Jenny that we would have Josh back home by 10:00 p.m. You have about ten minutes to say goodbye to your friends before we leave, okay?"

He looked at Shaun again and stuck out his hand and said, "Well, goodbye, Shaun. It was nice to have met you."

Since it would have been very rude for Shaun to ignore the handshake, he begrudgingly shook Carlos' hand. Even though he was as jealous as hell, he wanted to tell Carlos to take good care of Trish and treat her with love and care. All words just stuck in his throat, though, and he nodded dumbly at Carlos as they shook hands.

Shaun wanted to retract his hurtful words to Trish after he saw her sad face and tear-filled eyes, but it was probably better this way. If

Trish and Carlos stayed in or near Dalton, her natural friendliness would cause her to come and talk with him whenever they met. He could not bear that. Now that he told her that he would be neighborly and that was all, Trish would stay away from him in the future.

While he would miss seeing her sweet gamine face and big smile, he would be better off. He might even be able to forget about her since he now had closure and knew that she would never be his bride.

Mary took one look at Shaun's face and put her hand gently on his arm. She had no idea what Shaun said to Trish, but it was obvious that it was something that caused him some pain. She knew his moods so well by now that she could imagine how he was feeling. He needed her friendship now, more than ever.

Shaun's eyes followed Trish as she, Josh, and Carlos said goodbye to friends and neighbors. They left without looking in Shaun's direction again.

*This is it; I don't think that I'll ever see Trish again.* He knew that Trish would try her hardest to stay completely out of his way. He would remember how she looked today, so cute and fresh in her short skirt and cowboy boots. Shaun had always admired Trish's long shapely legs and freckled lean arms and pretty hands. This was the picture of her that he would remember—and he knew that he would think of her and dream of her.

He regretted that they couldn't have danced one last time before he purposely sent her away from his life. He would always remember the feel of her slender small body in his arms. No other girl could ever compare to Trish in his heart and mind. All he had left of her was his dreams . . .

## CHAPTER

# Eleven

On October 14th, Carlos, with a beautiful ring for Jenny in his pocket, made the final arrangements for the next day's special date with her. They were going to a chic new steakhouse for supper. On the way home, he planned to stop at the scenic overlook, which had become their place to stop and kiss since they never encountered anyone else there. They would have found it amusing to learn that it had been Shaun and Trish's kissing place years ago.

Jenny, who was anticipating a memorable night, wore her lovely new purple dress. As Carlos held the car door open for her, his eyes expressed his appreciation of her beauty.

They had a wonderful time at the steakhouse. Now, sated by good food and wine, they were both relaxed and happy. As Carlos pulled into the scenic overlook, Jenny involuntarily smiled. She had known for a while that she loved Carlos and was pretty sure that he loved her, too.

Carlos parked the car and turned sideways to look intently at his beloved. Her calm demeanor was betrayed by the excitement revealed in her eyes. He suspected that she anticipated what was about to happen.

Carlos' heart thudded anxiously as they sat on the bench. He gently took her hands in his and kissed them. He earnestly said, "Jenny, I love you. I think that I fell in love with you the moment I met you. You're everything that I want and will want for the rest of my days."

He stood up suddenly, then went down on one knee. Taking her hands again, he asked, "Will you marry me, my love? I already love Josh and the rest of your family. I know that I can make you happy, my dear." Even if Carlos had not spoken any words, his face and eyes were full of love for her.

Jenny smiled beautifully and nodded. "Yes, Carlos, I will marry you. I love you, too. And so does my family."

They lingered in a long kiss before Carlos asked her if she and Josh could live in Brazil for most of the time. He promised that they could return to Dalton for a long weekend each month.

Jenny was intrigued and excited about that, although she knew that she would miss her mom and sister so much. Carlos saw the conflict in her eyes, kissed her tenderly, and said they could come back as often as she needed to on the weekends. He still had a mine and a construction firm in Brazil to manage during the week, though.

Jenny nodded. She would likely want to come back to Dalton quite a lot to start with, but she would probably work through it and only need to come back once a month after some time had passed. She wanted to be there for her mom, who was still recuperating, and for Trish, who was so sad right now.

Lila and Trish felt something special in the air when Carlos took Jenny out tonight. In the hope that Carlos would propose to Jenny tonight, Lila sent Trish to the liquor store to buy some champagne. Trish did this slyly, so as not to tip off Josh. She didn't know that Carlos already had some very fine champagne in a cooler in his trunk.

Carlos and Jenny arrived home to an expectant audience. Lila took one look at Jenny's ecstatic face and knew that her wishes for her daughter had come true. Jenny was about to start a whole new life with a very wonderful man. This was something Lila had wanted for Jenny for several years now.

Carlos pulled Jenny further into the living room and sat her down on the couch. With his hands firmly holding Jenny's, he regarded Lila and Trish. "Ladies, we have wonderful news for you," he said. Then he looked quickly at Jenny and nodded slightly. He wanted Jenny to tell her family about their engagement.

Jenny smiled sweetly at him and nodded back. She leaned forward, looking at Lila. "Mom, Carlos and I just became engaged. We want to get married soon."

Trish and Lila jumped up and rushed to hug both Jenny and Carlos. There was excited talk for a minute or so, but Carlos asked them to sit back down so they could discuss it. They agreed to talk it out for a while before going down to wake Josh and tell him the good news. If he was too excited to sleep again, they would excuse him from school tomorrow. They would tell him when they had most of their plans made. That way they could answer his questions even before he asked them.

Jenny squeezed Carlos' hands tightly before she resumed talking. "We want to get married in Brazil in Carlos' church, with his mother and all his cousins there. It is going to be a short engagement because the wedding will be on November 20th."

She grinned before saying the next bit.

"Carlos, in anticipation of my agreement to marry him, already set the date with the pastor of his hometown church in Barbacena, Brazil. That only leaves us five weeks, but we can do all the planning in that time. Carlos wants all of you to stay in Brazil for two weeks while we are on our honeymoon. You are all welcome to stay with his mother, Maria."

She looked back at Carlos. "He apparently already asked his mom about that, too. I don't know what he would have done if I would have said no." She laughed gently at him.

He squeezed her hands and laughingly told her, "I would have had to really turn on the charm and change your mind, my love. If that still didn't work, I would have appealed to your mom and sister to see if they could make you change your mind." He leaned forward and kissed her small nose.

Jenny giggled delightedly. They felt that enough details were decided, and they could wake Josh to tell him.

Josh sleepily looked at all the adults who now crowded into his room. He focused on Jenny and Carlos who were holding hands and looking very happy. Suddenly, he sat up straight in bed. *Could Mom finally be engaged to Carlos?* he wondered. He, Trish, and Lila had talked about it often while Jenny and Carlos were out on one of their dates. He would be very happy to welcome Carlos as his stepfather.

Jenny hugged her son and said quietly, "Honey, Carlos and I got engaged to be married tonight. How do you feel about that?" she asked apprehensively.

Josh gave a great shout of happiness and hugged his mom fiercely. He wanted this for himself, but he mostly wanted this for his mom. She needed someone like Carlos to take all the burdens off her shoulders and help her enjoy life again. He still remembered how happy and fun she used to be when his dad was alive. Josh wanted Jenny to find that same kind of happiness again before she was too old to appreciate the fun.

"Congratulations, Mom and Carlos. I am very happy. I think that you make a great couple," Josh said with joy in his voice. Then he looked shyly at Carlos and said, "Carlos, I would be so happy to have you be my stepfather. This is something that I have hoped and prayed for since you and Mom started dating."

Carlos and Jenny hugged Josh tightly. They knew that they would be a happy family.

Jenny sat on Josh's bed and shared everything that had already been decided. Josh was a bit surprised that he would be living in Brazil. He was suddenly afraid to move away from Dalton, knowing that he would miss Lila, Trish, and his friends so much. Carlos placed his strong comforting arm around Josh's shoulder, reassuring him that they could come back for a visit whenever Jenny and Josh wanted.

While Carlos was talking logistics with Josh, Lila and Trish were admiring Jenny's engagement ring. It was a very beautiful solitaire diamond with a bright blue sapphire on each side. Carlos said the blue of Jenny's eyes inspired him to buy this ring for her. Amazingly, it fit her slender finger perfectly. Jenny took that as a good omen.

They all agreed to go to Mason City on Saturday to look for the wedding dress and dresses for Trish and Lila. Trish was asked to be the Maid of Honor. Carlos' cousin, Paulo, would be the Best Man.

Josh wanted to know all about Brazilian schools. Carlos said there were English speaking schools, but Josh would have a special tutor to teach him basic Portuguese and Spanish for a year. Josh was extremely excited but also nervous. Nothing this exciting happened to any of his friends in little old Dalton, Iowa.

Amid the shared revelry, Trish interjected, "I need to return to Dalton early to prepare for the mall opening. Inventory needs to be processed, and I still must paint sections of the store." Trish was now lost in her thoughts, which was a welcome break from thinking about Shaun. She added, "I need to hire and train staff as well. There's just so much to do."

She noted their pitied looks and quickly announced, "Really, I'll be okay. It's just part of owning a business, right Carlos?"

They all discussed it and agreed that Trish should return early. They did worry about her being alone, but she assured them that she would be fine.

When it came time for Josh to get up for school just a few hours later, he blearily pulled the cover over his head and asked his mom to report him as sick. He wanted to be a part of everything his family was doing today, anyway.

Jenny went to work at the library because it was too late to call Marcia to come in for her. Besides, it was often so quiet at the library, she could use the computer there to look up things, sit quietly thinking, and make some lists. She decided not to wear her engagement ring. They didn't plan to tell the Dalton community just yet about the engagement. Carlos would place an engagement announcement in the *Mason City Times* and his hometown newspaper next week.

Shaun saw Carlos, Trish, and Josh at the gas station that morning. They were going out to the mall site and then to Carlos' new house. They all looked so happy and pleased with life. While Carlos pumped the gas, Josh ran inside the store to buy some cold pop and sweet treats for them. Trish was sitting in the front seat of the Mercedes beaming for her sister and Carlos.

Shaun wondered why Josh was out of school for the day. He certainly didn't look sick as he bounced into the gas station, intent on buying goodies for the three of them. Then he wondered if Carlos and Trish had become engaged. Too bad he couldn't see Trish's finger. Shaun and Carlos were only ten feet away from each other as they pumped their gas. Carlos looked at Shaun and nodded courteously to him. Shaun nodded back, just as courteously.

Josh came running out of the gas station clutching a large bag. He saw Shaun and grinned at him. He called out, "Hi, Shaun. How are you doing? I'm having a great . . ."

Before he could finish his sentence, Carlos quickly and kindly told Josh to get into the car because they had to get going. Josh shrugged, waved to Shaun, and got into the car.

Trish looked briefly at Shaun, and her beaming smile melted away. She purposefully looked away, so she could no longer see him. She did not mean to speak to him ever again.

Shaun was frustrated because he sensed that Josh was about to tell him something momentous about his aunt's engagement to Carlos, or so he imagined. He felt sick to his stomach at that prospect. He figured that most of his neighbors would be invited to the wedding, but not the Healy family. It would be too strange and difficult for both families.

Then he thought that if he ever married someone else, he would probably not invite the Newberg family, either. *That's just the way things are now,* he thought sadly.

Shaun left the gas station feeling awful. In his confused mind, he sometimes hoped that if Trish married Carlos, they would move back to Brazil, so he would never have to see her again. Then, thinking like that made Shaun shudder. *No, I can't bear to think that I might never see Trish again. I would rather see her happily married to Carlos than to never see her again.* This was a vicious cycle that went over and over in Shaun's poor head whenever he accidentally ran into Trish in town.

The best thing that could happen would be for Shaun to meet someone else whom he could care about. He would marry this new girl—then he could finally be happy for Trish. He loved her so much that he wanted her to have a happy life. She deserved to be happy, and so did he . . .

On Saturday, Lila, Trish, and Jenny took themselves off to the Mason City Mall. They had all day to find the right wedding clothes. Jenny wanted to wear an elegant misty blue calf-length dress and jacket. She had married Jack in a white satin bridal gown, but she didn't feel right wearing another white dress. Besides, Carlos told her that she looked beautiful in blue and purple. She found just what she wanted in her favorite store.

Trish and Lila found equally beautiful light blue gowns that matched Jenny's dress quite well. They found shoes and hosiery to match and were happy that one big item on their lists could be checked off. Carlos would get his own outfit, but they bought Josh a nice charcoal gray suit, white shirt, and misty blue tie. They ate a celebratory lunch at the mall before taking their precious wedding clothes home.

Josh spent the day at the strip mall with Carlos. Now that Carlos was going to be his stepfather, Josh wanted to get to know everything about him. Carlos was patient and kind with Josh. He already loved that young boy, and he wanted them to become even closer. He would never try to take Jack's place in either Jenny or Josh's hearts, but Carlos wanted the three of them to make their own memories.

## CHAPTER

# Twelve

Meanwhile, James and Mary had their first date at his cousin's wedding in Mason City. Mary smiled at Keith and Norah Regan. The Regans and the Walshes lived only three miles from each other for many years, and the families were friendly with each other. James' parents used to ask him about possibly dating Mary, but he never seemed interested in her. However, now might be the right time for these young people to get together.

James and Mary had a wonderful time at the wedding reception. They felt so comfortable around each other even while they were both madly attracted to each other. Mary was a sociable girl, talking easily with James, his parents, and anyone else she met. James was quite impressed by that.

Prior to their date, each had confided a reluctance to dancing. They had conversed with his extended family and friends all afternoon, so no one would be upset if they left the dance early, which was the plan.

Just as they were about to leave the dance, one of Mary's favorite slow songs started to play. James saw the look on Mary's face. She looked as if she was longing to dance. James sighed inwardly, and then gently steered Mary toward the dance floor. It was so crowded that the dancers could not move very much. This suited Mary just fine.

James put his arms around Mary, and they basically swayed in place. He loved the feel of Mary's soft form in his arms, and Mary loved James' strong arms holding her tightly. The dance was over much too soon for both. For two people who didn't like to dance, they sure loved this one.

James reluctantly let go of Mary when the next song began. It was an energetic and upbeat song—just the kind of song that they both disliked dancing to. They hurried off the dance floor back to their table to retrieve their coats and her purse. After saying goodnight to his parents, they left the hot and stuffy room.

Outside, as the night air cooled their cheeks, they walked slowly to James' car. It was a lovely starry night. Mary looked up at the beautiful night sky and saw a falling star. She immediately made a silent wish on it. Unbeknownst to her, James was doing the same thing. They would have been amazed to learn that they basically wished for the same miracle to come true for themselves.

James, who wanted to kiss Mary very much, sternly suppressed his feelings and talked with her quietly about their day together as they drove back toward Dalton. He intended to kiss her after he found a secluded place to stop the car.

Ironically, James pulled into Jenny and Carlos' and Trish and Shaun's favorite location just outside the Dalton city limits. After he turned into a parking spot, he looked at Mary with gleaming eyes. He didn't want to scare her, but he just had to kiss her and see if her sweet red lips were as soft as he imagined them to be.

He hesitantly asked Mary, "May I kiss you, Mary? You look delightful tonight."

Mary, having waited a lifetime to kiss James, just smiled sweetly and nodded. James put his arms around her, bent his head, and kissed Mary squarely on her lips. Neither one had done much kissing in the past, but this first kiss was magical. They kissed for long minutes until breaking away. Both were breathing fast.

James' eyes were very dark, and his face was flushed. His hands were trembling from his intense emotions. *Kissing Mary has been the best thing I have ever done in my life,* James thought with wonder.

Mary was thinking the same thing. She had never been kissed so well in her life. She wanted it to go on and on, forever. *James has the most tender and exciting lips,* Mary thought with wonder, too.

James knew that they should talk, but he intensely wanted to kiss Mary again. He was like a man dying of thirst. He needed at least one more kiss from Mary to feel sated.

They kissed again, long and tenderly. Both were left with the impression that they shared a mutual passion to be able to kiss like that. Time lost meaning and importance as they sat immersed in the sweet night air and the joy of being in love. Whether Mary's sudden shiver was from the evening chill or from that joy, it was James' cue to take her home.

As he drove home, James wondered if Mary would mind talking with him for a little while at his house. He knew that her parents were at her home, and he wanted privacy to talk without interruptions.

"Mary, I had a wonderful time with you today. Are you okay if we stop off at my house for a little while? It would be difficult to talk at your house, and I don't want to have a serious conversation while I am driving," James asked hopefully.

Mary felt perfectly safe with James, even after the amazing kisses they had just shared. She trusted James and thought that he was a man who respected women, so she nodded her head in assent. She smiled shyly at James, and he smiled gently back at her.

James, seated in his armchair, looked intently at Mary. He chose to sit away from her because he wanted to talk before kissing her again.

He quietly said, "Mary, I've wanted to ask you out for a month, but I thought that you were seriously dating Shaun Healy. The whole town has been talking about you two and speculating when you would become engaged. I didn't dare ask you out because of him. Then, last week at Bill and Cheri's wedding, I was so happy when you told me that you and Shaun were just friends. When you came over to make my meals and clean the house, it seemed like you belonged there. I realized then that I have liked you for a long time—maybe even since art class in high school. I do like you so much, and I'd like to date you exclusively. What do you think, Mary? Will you date me?"

Mary smiled widely and said, "James, I think I had a crush on you since I was in the 10th grade. You used to be more friendly with me, but then you backed off ever since I came home from college. Was it because you had to give up your plans to be a lawyer, and you had to take over the farm from your dad after he had that stroke? All your friends felt bad for you, but you are a good son. We knew that you would do what was best for your family. I think all the kids in and around Dalton hoped that you would find happiness being a farmer instead of a lawyer."

She smiled even deeper and continued, "Yes, I would like to date you exclusively. I enjoy being with you so much. We like many of the same things, and you certainly know how to kiss a girl. Wow! Those were some terrific kisses, James," she said boldly.

Even though James was a quiet man, he admired Mary's confidence and candor. He trusted someone like that not to sugarcoat anything. Mary also had her very sweet and shy side.

James walked over to where Mary was sitting on the couch. There was a lot of space next to her, so he sat down. He patted the cushions and said, "Mary, move toward me a little more. I want to kiss you again. If you liked that last kiss, I think you'll like this next one even better." His normally calm face looked a bit mischievous to Mary.

She excitedly scooched over toward James until she was right next to his warm body. He grinned and put his arms around her. He smiled deeply into her eyes just before his lips descended on hers. It was a good thing that they were sitting down because that kiss could have buckled their knees.

When he finally broke that kiss, Mary was on the verge of melting right into the couch. *Wow!* she thought once again. *When did James learn how to kiss a girl like this? I didn't think he ever took out any girls.*

James noticed that her sweetly pinkish/red lips were now a deep red. She looked thoroughly kissed. He might have to suggest that she comb her hair and put on some lipstick before he took her home because he didn't want her parents to get mad at him for kissing Mary so thoroughly.

He was slightly amused, though, that he could make calm and sweet Mary look that way. He wanted her to look that way all the time. Her eyes were very soft and beautiful while she watched him get ready to leave his house to take her home. She had never had a better date.

As he took her home, James asked Mary if he could pick her up tomorrow to go to the Sunday movie in town. He wanted the town to start seeing them together, so it wouldn't be such a shock when they announced their engagement. Again, he was hoping to ask her to marry him quite soon. He just hoped that she would say yes to his proposal.

Mary's parents stayed up to talk to her about her date. They exchanged knowing smiles when they saw their sweet daughter float through the door with her lips bright red from prolonged kissing. Mary shared some details of her wonderful evening but guardedly withheld James' wish to date her exclusively.

The next day, Shaun Healy called her to see if Mary wanted to go to the movie in town. Mary explained about James and their date for tonight. Shaun was happy that Mary was finally dating James. She had hoped for that possibility for many years. Shaun then told her to have fun with James and that he would take his parents to the movie; he would see her there.

Shaun saw Carlos, Trish, Josh, and Jenny laughing together as they entered the theater. Carlos sat between Trish and Jenny and seemed to talk an equal amount with both. He seemed more intent on Jenny, but Shaun decided that he was imagining things. It never crossed his mind that Carlos could like Jenny as a girlfriend. The town had talked about Trish and Carlos as a couple for so long that Shaun's brain didn't recognize that Carlos was courting Jenny.

Because of his dad's wheelchair, Shaun and his mom sat with him in the front—in the side section. Instead of slightly turning to the right to see the screen, Shaun was often turned slightly to the left, watching the rest of the audience. Mary and James were sitting two rows behind Trish's group, so many of the people watching Shaun couldn't decide if he was looking at Trish or at Mary.

James and Mary caused quite a stir and hushed conversation when they came in together. No one could ever remember James Regan taking anyone to the movies before. It was obvious that James and Mary were on a date. James' arm was around Mary's shoulder, and he was very attentive to her. Those close enough also saw him take her hand and hold it all through the show.

People wondered how poor Shaun was doing. First, he was dumped by Trish, and now Mary had apparently dumped him, too.

Shaun was surprised by the number of neighbors who came to talk with him and pat his arm after the show ended. He guided his parents out of the show behind the Newberg party. They didn't speak, but Jenny gave Shaun and his parents a friendly smile.

Mary and James chatted with Shaun in the theater lobby for a few minutes. The few neighbors who were still in the theater saw the friendly interactions among Shaun, Mary, and James. They were all convinced that there were no hard feelings among the three young people. It didn't look like Shaun was suffering from any jealousy because Mary was out on a date with James. The three of them exited the theater talking and laughing. Mary's hand was firmly held by James Regan.

Trish, who had lingered on the street, saw Mary hanging on to James' hand. Mary's face was filled with happiness and love. Trish was confused. Shaun didn't look in the least bit jealous as he stood talking with James and Mary. *Could I have been mistaken?* Trish wondered. *Was Mary in love with James and not Shaun? Does this change anything for me?* Trish wondered hopefully. *No, Shaun detests me now,* she suddenly recalled. *Even without Mary in the way, he still doesn't like or trust me anymore.*

Trish's shoulders drooped as she followed Carlos, Jenny, and Josh down the street. Neighbors who saw the Newberg crowd wondered if Carlos suddenly transferred his attention and affection to Jenny. Was that why Trish looked so stressed and unhappy?

This was a night of confusion for the people of Dalton. Many planned to talk with neighbors tomorrow to see what others thought. Not much went on in this little town, and any news was worthy of a long conversation.

James called Mary every day to either take her out or just talk on the phone. Her parents were delighted that Mary finally had a boyfriend. She had never had a serious boyfriend before.

Since Mary was such a pretty and dear girl, her parents hoped she would find the right man to marry. Now here was James Regan, who had been right under their noses for so many years. It would be marvelous if the two young people got married. They wanted their sweet girl to be happy. She deserved every good thing that life could give her.

After courting Mary every day for nearly three weeks, James proposed to her. They had just come back to his house after a meal at the Dalton Cafe. The people of Dalton had grown accustomed to seeing the two together. New speculations started regarding James and Mary. Would they get engaged this year? James certainly took Mary out nearly every night.

After a deeply moving kiss, James got on his knee and asked her to marry him. He wanted a very small wedding in a week or two. Mary was so happy that she cried as she said yes. James tenderly kissed her tears away and presented her with his grandmother's beautiful engagement ring. She bequeathed it to him with the expressed desire that he give it to his bride. James told Mary that he would buy her a new ring if she didn't like this one. Being old-fashioned and traditional, Mary loved the ring's story and wanted to keep it.

They set the wedding date for November 15th, which was only a week away. It would be in Mason City, so his parents could more easily attend. They planned to have a small reception at Keith and Norah's new apartment and then go out for a meal at one of the nicest restaurants in town.

Both sets of parents contributed money toward their honeymoon. James asked his neighbors to care for his cattle for three weeks while he was on his honeymoon.

James and Mary decided to start their honeymoon in Rome, Italy, and the Tuscan Valley before traveling to Greece to see the Parthenon and other historical monuments. James had always been interested in those two cultures, and Mary was happy to go anywhere that James wanted to go. She had traveled so infrequently that any new culture was interesting to her. Since they would not likely visit these two places again, they wanted to take their time and immerse themselves in the new cultures.

The newlyweds let Mary's parents tell the Dalton community about their wedding and honeymoon. By the time James and Mary returned to Dalton, they would be an old married couple of three weeks.

* * *

Carlos and Jenny had not yet told anyone in town about their engagement. Their plan was to get married in Brazil and live there. The community frequently had nosy neighbors poking around, trying to find any new information about the Dalton inhabitants. People were still curious about Carlos Santos, the handsome millionaire who stayed with the Newbergs when he was in town.

One day, Mrs. Doughtry, one of Lila's neighbors in town, visited the mall site out of curiosity. The mall was nearly completed, and last-minute touches were being added. Mrs. Doughtry watched as

Carlos stooped to give Jenny a lingering kiss. Jenny appeared to be a very willing participant.

Mrs. Doughtry didn't say anything, but she hurriedly went into Trish's store, where she found Trish and Josh working. She didn't think that Mr. Santos would kiss Jenny that way if he was going to marry Trish. She chatted with Trish and Josh for a few minutes before getting into her car and rushing back to Dalton with her juicy news. *Had Senhor Santos thrown Trish over for Jenny? Were we all mistaken about Carlos and Trish's relationship?* she wondered.

She made haste to go into Rush's Grocery Store to tell anyone there what she saw earlier that day.

The next time Trish went into the store for groceries, Mrs. Rush politely asked her about Jenny and Carlos. Trish was prepared. The Newbergs had agreed to tell the people of Dalton about the upcoming wedding in Brazil should anyone ask. Trish cheerfully related Jenny's happy news.

Being the spokeswoman in town whom everyone trusted, Mrs. Rush passed on that news to her customers. She did not embellish the information, merely repeating the words that Trish had told her.

Shaun could hardly breathe when his mother told him the news. *So, I was wrong about Trish and Carlos Santos all these months,* he thought painfully. *Why do I ever listen to anything that the townspeople say?* he wondered in disgust. He then recalled recently seeing Carlos with Jenny at the movies. They appeared affectionate, but he thought he had imagined it.

Wild hope coursed through his veins for a full minute. Then he stopped short as he remembered his last harsh words to Trish. He would gladly give his right arm to retract those words. By now, Trish was very deliberately avoiding him. *How can I get her alone to tell her that I am so sorry about saying those words out of jealousy?* he wondered feverishly.

Shaun could think of nothing else except how stupid he had been. He found out that the wedding would take place in Brazil and that the whole Newberg family were vacationing there for two weeks after the wedding. They would barely be back in Dalton before the Grand Opening of the mall. He had thought that Trish would want to spend every spare moment in her shop, preparing for opening day.

Maybe, once her store was open for a few weeks, he could find a way to talk with her. They wouldn't have to talk about themselves but just get back on more friendly ground. He would apologize for his harsh words and ask her to be friends again, if she was agreeable. Though, knowing Trish as well as he did, he didn't think that she would be easy to convince. She tended to have a pigheaded nature and might refuse to talk with him. *Well, I will have plenty of time to wear her down,* he thought with a self-deprecating grin.

* * *

Days before her wedding, Mary called Shaun and told him about her quiet upcoming wedding and her three-week honeymoon. Shaun went over to James' house to see them. He took along some champagne and toasted his friends. James and Shaun had always been casual friends and neighbors, but now Shaun knew that the three of them would get even closer.

Shaun told them about Carlos and Jenny. Mary said that she never seriously thought that Trish was in love with Carlos. Trish was the type of person to have deep and meaningful friendships with others. People mistook Trish's loyalty and devotion for something else.

Mary secretly hoped that Shaun would now finally talk with Trish. She knew that Shaun had a lot of pride, and it would be difficult for him to go to Trish, hat in hand, so to speak. Still, if he loved her, it was up to him to try to get her back.

Shaun was amused to think that the people of Dalton would miss out on two weddings. Jenny and Carlos were getting married in Brazil, and James and Mary were having a very quiet wedding in Mason City. The people of Dalton thrived on any celebratory event involving its residents. Now if he and Trish, by some miracle, got back together, he would ask her to plan their wedding in Dalton. All his relatives would be chomping at the bit to attend.

CHAPTER

# Thirteen

Trish, having heard from Mrs. Rush about Mary and James' quiet wedding in Mason City and their three-week honeymoon, was happy for her friend. It had been a quick romance and wedding, but she knew that Mary was overjoyed. Now, if Trish could only find joy. She was happy for Carlos and Jenny, but she couldn't shake her melancholy.

Trish barely ate anything these days, and she had no energy. She tried hard to keep this situation from Carlos, Jenny, and Lila. They were all so focused on the upcoming wedding and trip to Brazil that they didn't question Trish much about her loss of weight and energy.

Trish's pretty, blue bridesmaid dress was getting quite loose on her. She secretly decided to buy the same dress in a smaller size so her weight loss would not be so obvious. She borrowed Jenny's car one day saying that she had a few errands to run.

Trish still did not have her own car. She hadn't needed one in Brazil, and she either walked or got rides from her mom, Jenny, or Carlos since she came back to Dalton. She was planning to buy a small used car so she would have it to traverse back and forth from her home to the mall each day. Now, however, Jenny said that she could have her little car. She would not need a car in Dalton once she was married. Trish liked the small car, which was just her size and so easy to drive.

The new blue dress hung in her closet next to Trish's pretty wedding dress. She had to look at it every day when she pulled clothes to wear from her closet. She planned to move to Carlos' new house near the mall in January. When she packed up all her things, she would get rid of the wedding dress at that time. Right now, it was the only thing that she had left from her defunct romance with Shaun.

The day before they flew to Brazil for the wedding, Trish went for a long walk. Her buddy, Nolan, would not budge from his warm and cozy dog bed, so she had to go alone. She wanted to get away for a few hours from the chaotic cheerful mess that now resided in the Newberg house.

Her feet automatically led her down the road past Shaun's house. She wanted to get a quick glimpse of the shed where their romance started five years ago. Maybe she would walk past the house, too. It depended on how tired she was.

Trish was surprised at how winded and tired she got. She had never had any trouble walking three or four miles before. She stopped at the shed but was reluctant to try the door to see if it was open. The Healys had always welcomed their neighbors to use it if they needed rest, food, or water. She sat down on the hay bale that was outside the shed. The wind was cold, and she shivered as she recalled happier times with Shaun.

Trish looked so small and cold to Ella Healy, Shaun's mom, as she drove her car past, on her way home from the grocery store. She wanted so much to stop and talk with Trish, but something about Trish's slouched shoulders and down bent head made her continue driving past. She didn't have the words to talk with Trish. She liked Trish so much, but Shaun got growly these days whenever he heard Trish's name.

After an hour of thinking, Trish wearily got up and slowly walked home. She didn't like the thoughts that she had during her quiet sojourn at Shaun's shed, but she felt calmer. Being in the house with such happy and excited people was wearing thin. She could not wait for Jenny's wedding to be over, so she could start her new life as a yarn store owner.

Trish knew that she would be lonely, but maybe she and Mary could start doing some things together after she arrived home from her honeymoon. James would be welcome to go out with them, if he wanted that. Of course, she should give the newlyweds a month or two of privacy first.

Once she arrived back at the house, the family hugged her cold frame and suggested that they have supper and an early night. They needed to be up early the next morning. They took Nolan to the neighbor who would keep him for the next several weeks. Nolan's woebegone shaggy face almost made Trish cry. *I cry all too easily these days,* Trish thought impatiently, as she kissed Nolan's head goodbye.

* * *

The flight was uneventful, and the Newbergs enjoyed meeting Carlos' mother, Maria. They all settled in before having a late supper. Tomorrow, they would go to Carlos' home and check out his church, as well. The wedding was in two days.

Maria remembered Trish from earlier that summer and was shocked to see how thin she had become. In a quiet moment together, Maria asked Trish if she was okay. Trish nearly teared up because Maria was so sweet and caring. Trish quietly told Maria that she was fine but could never eat when she was under stress. With the mall opening in a week or so, there was so much to do to be ready for it. Once the mall was open, Trish said that she would get back to normal. Maria gave her a hug and accepted Trish's explanation.

Jenny and Maria became instant friends. Maria recognized that Jenny was the right wife for Carlos. He had waited such a long time to remarry. Jenny could see that Maria loved her son, but she didn't interfere with his life in any way. That was a blessing since Jenny and Josh would now be living in Brazil.

Jenny immediately disliked Carlos' palatial home. Carlos, observing his fiancée closely, could tell that she didn't like it. He had never liked it, either. They discussed selling this home upon returning from their honeymoon and finding one that better suited the three of them. In the meantime, Jenny, Josh, Trish, and Lila were comfortable staying with Maria.

Carlos and Jenny's wedding day dawned clear and warm. Brazil's November weather is warmer than Iowa's. Carlos' beautiful church in Barbacena looked so elegant. The Basilica of St. Joseph the Worker was shaped like a Greek cross, but it was originally supposed to resemble St. Peter's Basilica in the Vatican, Rome. It was a massive church which was situated on a hillside, so everyone in Barbacena could see its stately outline.

The wedding party had decorated the church the night before the wedding. Carlos' cousins were there to help, as well. They all treated Jenny like she was already a part of their extended family. Trish saw Jenny relaxing, little by little, as she met Carlos' entire family.

The wedding ceremony was beautiful. Because both Carlos and Jenny were widowed, the church embraced their marriage. Carlos' priest had met and talked with the couple yesterday and gave his blessing. The music was superb. Trish, being the only bridesmaid, felt a bit overwhelmed by the sheer size of the church.

After the wedding, the congregation dined at a fancy restaurant and enjoyed getting to know each other. Lila, under the sweet guidance of Maria, laughed and smiled all day. Carlos' family was so complimentary and attentive to the Newbergs. Trish and Lila kept an eye on Josh, who was having a wonderful time. Everyone was very kind to the young boy.

Trish enjoyed every part of Jenny's wedding very much. Carlos and Jenny left the reception just after 7:00 p.m. They were going to spend one night at his palatial home before starting on their honeymoon tomorrow. Carlos planned to show Jenny all his businesses and the mine before going to Rio de Janeiro and other famous places in Brazil. After that, they were going on a week-long luxury cruise to Cozumel and Cancun. He had been there several times, and he knew all the best places to show Jenny.

Maria was a lovely hostess, and she showed Trish, Lila, and Josh some sights in Barbacena. Trish, who had already seen some of them with Carlos earlier that year, opted to stay home for some of them. She was preparing to leave for Iowa.

Trish was grateful that she did not have to stay with the cheerful crowd for two whole weeks. She wanted to think quietly about things and slowly-but-surely get everything ready for opening day at the mall. Maria, Lila, and Josh saw her off at the airport after many hugs, kisses, and suggestions to take care of herself.

## CHAPTER

# Fourteen

Three days after Trish returned to Dalton from Brazil, she was coming home from a shopping trip in Mason City. The roads were very slippery on the drive home after the sleet storm had come through the area. Trish was distracted by thoughts of her family coming home, the opening of her store, and Shaun.

He was always in her thoughts. She kept beating herself up about not contacting Shaun as soon as she returned home from Brazil earlier that June. It appeared that he was so upset with her because she had not given him the chance to explain. He said it was too late, and that he was done with her. If she had taken the time to contact him, they might have resolved their differences and be together right now.

He never wanted to see her again. He contemptuously said that he would treat her as courteously as any neighbor. Well, she didn't want any courtesies from him, in that case. She would rather never see him again than to have his cold neighborly courtesy.

Trish was so diverted by her thoughts that she did not see the ice on the dark road. Before she could do anything to protect herself, her little car slid on the ice patch and into the ditch. The ditch was steep, and her car tilted to one side. After shakily turning off the car engine, Trish worked to get herself out of the vehicle. She hadn't seen any other car for at least fifteen minutes. It was early evening, and most of the commuters were already at home enjoying their suppers.

She stood in the ditch looking around her. She knew where she was. There was a small local store less than a mile from her location. She regretted that she left her cell phone at home that morning because it needed to be charged. It would have been easy for her to call a towing service to get her car out of the ditch. Now, she would have to walk to the mini market and call for a tow truck from there.

As she was getting herself out of the steep ditch, she slipped and fell onto some pieces of metal that were in the ditch. The jarring pain in her lower right leg made her catch her breath. Because she was wearing black leggings she could not see if she was bleeding, but the wound hurt quite badly. She shook her head in fury at her stupidity and continued to climb up and out of the ditch. Once she reached the road she fell on the slippery ice. When she pulled herself up, she noticed the blood stain that she left on the road. *So, I am bleeding*, she soberly realized.

She painfully walked very slowly on the shoulder of the road. At this pace, it was going to take her quite a while to get to the mini market. She hoped that one of her neighbors would come along and give her a ride to the store.

After fifteen minutes, she noticed car lights behind her. She could tell that the car slowed down right about where her car sat, tilted in the ditch. She hoped that it was someone she knew. The car crept closer. As it pulled alongside her and stopped, the window rolled down and Shaun Healy's face poked out.

"Trish, are you okay? I saw Jenny's car in the ditch a little way back." Shaun's face showed his genuine concern for her.

*Oh, great! It had to be Shaun who stopped,* Trish thought with irritation.

"I'm okay. Thanks for stopping, but I just have a little bit to go before I get to the mini market up the road. I'll call for a tow truck from there. You don't need to stop." Trish's face was set with a mulish frown.

Shaun realized that Trish wanted nothing to do with him. It was his fault. He should not have been so mean to her at the wedding dance—his words hurt her. Whenever he saw her with her family during the past month, she avoided looking at him and never spoke to him. He needed to respect her feelings. But still, she was limping like she was hurt. Her pride would not let her accept help from him. He was concerned about her, so he tried again.

"Trish, get in, please. You might be hurt. I promise not to say anything to you on the way to the store. I'm just being neighborly. I would do this for anyone—friend, stranger, or neighbor."

Shaun was trying his best to keep his voice friendly, but Trish just got under his skin every time he saw her and spoke to her.

Trish looked at Shaun very briefly and then turned to look at the road again. "No. I am not going to get into your car. Just leave me alone. I can make it to the store by myself." Her tone was flat and adamant.

Shaun knew that she would not accept his help. He would stop in at the store and see if anyone there would go to pick her up. Even in his frustration at Trish, he admired her. She was always one to stick to her principles. Still, concern gripped his heart. *Why is she so thin?* he wondered.

"Fine. Take care of yourself, Trish." Shaun said in a clipped voice. He closed the window and crept forward. Through his rear-view mirror, he could see her walking slowly along the side of the road as he drove carefully toward the store.

Once he got there, he noticed that the store was dark. There was a sign on the front door. He got out of his car and went to read the note. It said that the store would be closed for a few days due to an emergency in the owner's family.

Shaun got in his car and turned around to go back to Trish. If need be, he would physically pick her up, toss her into his car, and take her to the nearest store. This was one of those times that he wished that he had a working cell phone. After he dropped his last one in the cow water tank last month, he had gone without a cell phone. He intended to buy a new one but had not gotten around to doing that yet.

Trish watched the taillights of Shaun's car with regret. She had spurned a ride just because it was Shaun. Her leg was hurting quite badly, and she felt a bit lightheaded. Her strong determination to reach the store kept her on her feet. She wasn't looking where she was going and tripped on the large rock in her path. She went down and cut her head on the gravel. After a few moments of excruciating pain in her leg and head, she passed out in a rumpled heap on the shoulder of that lonely road.

Shaun thought that he saw something on the side of the road as he slowly drove back to the last place that he had seen Trish. He got there, and she was not walking on the shoulder anymore. He knew that she hadn't been picked up by anyone else because no cars had come along since his. He went to where her car was in the ditch, just in case Trish decided to go back to it. He got out and slid down the ditch to look in and around the car. No Trish. That meant that she must still be on the road. How could he have missed her? Then he got very worried. *What if she slipped off the road and is lying in the ditch somewhere?*

He drove slowly back toward the store. On the very edge of the highway, almost in the ditch, he came across Trish.

"Oh, my dear little Trish!" he exclaimed in a shaky voice. "I knew that I should have made you come with me."

Trish was unconscious. Shaun, in a near panic, touched her face and tried to see if she had any other injuries. He noticed a spreading blood spot near her leg. Because it was so dark, he didn't immediately see the blood on her pants, but when he did, he became alarmed. That wound, along with the big goose egg on her forehead must be the reason that she passed out.

He opened his back seat door, very carefully picked her up, cuddled her close for a moment, gently kissed her white cheek, and laid her on the backseat. He knew where the hospital was in Mason City. It would be slow going because of the slippery roads. He silently berated himself for not having a working cell phone.

It took forty-five nerve-racking minutes for Shaun to get to the hospital. He kept looking into the backseat to see if Trish had awakened yet, but she remained unconscious the whole ride there.

Shaun pulled into the Emergency entrance and waited for help. Two people came immediately to the car. Shaun explained what he knew about Trish. They carefully put her onto a gurney and wheeled her inside.

Trish was aware of pain and bright lights. Someone was touching her wounded leg. She stared up into a kindly face

The man said, "Hello, young lady. You're in the hospital getting your leg cleaned up. I'm going to give you a quick shot to take away the pain. I hope that you will relax and sleep for a little bit afterwards."

Trish nodded, her head and whole body feeling sore. She winced a little at the sting of the needle in her arm, and then thankfully sank into oblivion.

When she awoke, she was ensconced in a hospital bed and wearing a gown that was much too big on her. She touched her forehead and found a bandage covering the soreness she felt. Her right leg was wrapped in a huge bandage, too. A few minutes after looking around the room and wondering how she got there, a nurse entered.

"Hello, Trish. I'm glad that you are awake. My name is Caroline. I can answer a few questions for you, and I will need to ask you a few, too. So, ask away," Caroline said in a friendly voice.

"How did I get here? And what is wrong with my leg?" Trish asked weakly. She still felt quite sore everywhere.

Caroline smiled. "A man found you on the side of the road where you had collapsed. He brought you here. He's waiting to see you when you feel up to it. Somehow, you scraped your right leg on something sharp, and you have a five inch deep cut on your lower calf."

Trish nodded. It was just as she had expected. She remembered scraping her leg on those metal pieces in the ditch and falling on the road and hitting her forehead. She was curious to see her rescuer. Maybe it was one of her neighbors or friends.

Caroline continued, "Please tell me about your accident and how you received these injuries."

Trish told her about her car sliding off the road, how she scraped her leg on metal pieces in the ditch, and her lonely walk alongside the highway until she slipped and banged her head. After that, she did not know anything else.

Caroline smiled slightly and nodded. It matched the story that Trish's rescuer told the hospital staff.

Caroline said concernedly, "Besides your injuries, you look woefully underweight. I need to check your weight as soon as you feel up to getting out of your bed. Have you always been this thin, or has something caused you to lose so much weight? I'd like you to talk with the hospital psychologist, if you would. She will listen to you and try to help you with any issues that you may have. Are you okay with this plan, Trish?"

Trish looked down at her hands that were resting on the cover. She knew that she had not been eating much since before Jenny's wedding and especially not since coming back to Dalton. It was almost too much work to make herself a meal. She had been in a depressed funk since Cheri's wedding when Shaun basically said that he couldn't trust her and wanted nothing more to do with her. As she thought about it, tears welled in her eyes. Caroline saw them and came over to gently take Trish's hands in hers. She waited for Trish to say something.

Trish shyly looked up and nodded. "I guess that I would like to talk with someone. Yes, something happened recently in my life to make me depressed."

Caroline tightened her hands on Trish's and quietly said, "We'll wait until tomorrow. You may feel better by then—less stiff and sore, anyway. I'm going to bring you a light lunch, and I would like you to eat all of it, please." Her smile was kind as she looked at Trish before turning to leave.

Trish sat back and closed her eyes. This whole situation had been sobering. She probably would not have gone off the road if she had not been so distracted. Her family would be coming home from Brazil in six days. She had hoped to have all her inventory inside the yarn shop and be ready for Opening Day in two weeks. Now, if she had to sit in the hospital for a while, she would never get everything done.

Her mind was working feverishly to arrive at a solution. She would be a model patient and hope that the hospital would release her tomorrow. It might be difficult to do much of the physical work with her leg wound, but she might be okay just supervising someone else from a chair.

She fell asleep for an hour or so. When she opened her eyes, they were immediately drawn toward the man sitting in the chair by the window. He was reading the newspaper. She was astounded to see Shaun's face as he lowered the newspaper to look at her. Their eyes met and clung for a good minute. She could see the concern in his eyes.

*Oh, no! Don't let Shaun be the person who brought me into the hospital. But why else would he be here?* Trish wondered.

Shaun spoke first. "Hello, Trish. I hope that you are feeling better. I was very worried about you when I found you unconscious on the side of the road."

Trish licked her dry lips and nodded. "How did you find me, Shaun? You had already driven away, back toward Dalton."

Shaun leaned forward in his chair, staring intently at her. He slowly said, "I went past the mini market that you mentioned. It was closed for an emergency, so I turned around to tell you. I was going to insist that you get into my car, but I found you unconscious on the road. Why didn't you tell me that you were hurt, Trish? It was a shock to see how much blood you lost lying on the road. Do you hate me so much that you were willing to continue walking injured instead of getting a ride from me?" His face was contorted with strong feelings of sadness and remorse.

Trish looked at him for a moment before speaking. Shaun was acting as if he cared about her physical pain. Maybe, even if all his love for her was gone, he still cared about her well-being. She was grateful that he stopped and brought her to the hospital. Anything could have happened to her lying alone for a long time on that road.

She finally looked him in the eyes. Her face showed her sorrow. She cleared her throat before slowly saying. "I don't hate you, Shaun. I could never hate you. It's just that you told me that you could never trust me again and that I was only a neighbor to you now. That hurt me very much. I would rather never see or speak to you again than to have that kind of reception from you. So yes, I did not want your help at all."

Trish was always forthright and truthful in her explanations to people. Shaun understood that about her. It was one of the things that he loved most about her. He was grateful that she didn't hate him, though.

He nodded and said, "I understand, Trish. Anyway, I'm glad that I turned around. You could have become seriously hurt laying there for a long period of time. I'm going to stay at the hospital tonight, just to make sure that everything is okay with you. I already called Mom and told her about all of this. She agreed that I should stay to make sure that you are okay. I'll stay and talk with you if you want me to. Otherwise, I'll be elsewhere in the hospital. Take care of yourself and get better, please, Trish."

Trish studied his face. She missed seeing the way his blue eyes sparkled when he was happy, and his thick wavy strawberry blond hair stuck in the air when he was preoccupied and running his hands through it. But most of all, she missed seeing the love for her on his face. He used to look at her with such tenderness. She knew those days were long gone.

"I'm tired, Shaun. I'm grateful to you for coming back for me and bringing me to the hospital. You don't need to stay here and wait for me. I don't want to take up your time. In fact, I'd rather you go home." Trish's eyes were sad but full of determination. She really didn't want to have to see or talk with Shaun again. It was just too difficult to be with him and pretend that she didn't care about him or their lost love.

Shaun sighed deeply. Message received. Still, he wanted a few more chances to see and speak to her. Knowing how Trish felt about him now, this might be the last chance that he would have to spend a little time with her. *Love is hell*, he thought disparagingly.

He lightly said, "Well, Trish, I already made plans to stay. I'll keep out of your way if that's what you want, though. Take care of yourself and get better, okay? Good night." Despite his attempt at lightness, Shaun's face showed his sadness and resignation.

Trish saw it and nearly asked him to remain. She might have told him about her yarn store. She recalled that they had talked a lot about it when they were engaged. He told her that he would help her open the store. She could work in it during the day until they had some babies. Then he wanted her to hire someone to take over the day-to-day business at the store.

Trish looked at him with her heart in her eyes. He saw it and almost begged her to let him stay with her. However, her eyes became distant, and she pursed her lips. She was not going to back down now. Whatever Shaun was feeling for her right now did not change the fact that he no longer loved her and did not want any kind of friendly relationship with her.

"Good night, Shaun," was all Trish could manage to say. It felt like her emotions would erupt any second if he did not leave.

She looked forward to talking with the hospital psychologist tomorrow. She had wanted to talk with someone about Shaun for a few months. She felt unable to talk about her feelings with her mom, Jenny, or even Carlos. Maybe it would be easier to share her thoughts with a kind stranger who knew how to handle it if she fell apart.

Shaun looked searchingly at Trish before he walked out of the room. *Why did I have to say those mean things to the woman I love so much?* he asked himself for the thousandth time. *My infernal temper!* he thought darkly to himself.

Trish's eyes followed Shaun's progress out of the room. Because of what she just said, he likely would leave tomorrow without seeing her again. *Well, there is no time like the present to start forgetting about Shaun!* she thought with so much inner pain. This pain in her heart was almost more than she could bear. She closed her eyes on her tears and tried to fall asleep. After half an hour, exhaustion finally overcame her sorrow.

Caroline came in to see how Trish was doing. She saw her tear-stained cheeks and the lost and unhappy look on Trish's face. Caroline, who was a happy young woman in love with her boyfriend, felt very sorry for this poor sad woman. She vowed to talk with Doctor Peyton, the psychologist, tonight and tell her everything she knew about Trish Newberg.

Later that evening, Trish woke up in pain. She withstood it for as long as she could without calling for a nurse. Finally, when she could barely stand it anymore, an older nurse came in and saw Trish's face. She kindly said that the doctor had ordered pain medication for her if she needed it. She looked quizzically at Trish, who nodded gratefully. The medication started to take effect, and Trish slowly returned to a deep sleep.

Shaun, who sat in an uncomfortable chair outside her room, waited for any news about Trish. The older nurse came out and kindly told him that Ms. Newberg was now asleep and would be expected to sleep until the morning. Shaun, who was very weary by now, took himself off to his nearby motel. Now that Trish was asleep, he could finally get some rest for himself.

After her light breakfast the next morning, Trish was helped out of bed. Her legs were a little shaky. She felt impatient with herself for being so weak. Caroline said that she wanted to weigh Trish now, and then she could rest for an hour before her appointment with the psychologist.

"Trish, you weigh 94 pounds. Even being a petite woman, that really is on the light side. You should be at least 100 pounds. I want you to gain six pounds by the next time you come back for a visit, okay? Please tell Dr. Peyton, our psychologist, all the things that are troubling you. After you do, maybe you will be able to eat normal meals again. I'll be back to take you to see Dr. Peyton in an hour. Rest until then, okay?" Caroline's voice was firm and friendly.

Trish nodded. She had eaten all the breakfast that they brought her. It was difficult because she was not hungry at all. However, she wanted to be released today to get on with her life. She was wondering who she could call to come out and get her. The rest of her family was still in Brazil, and it would have to be someone who was not a gossip. She was dwelling on it when she dropped off into a quick nap.

Caroline came in, woke Trish up, got her into a wheelchair, and took her to Dr. Peyton's office on the next floor. After the introductions were made, Caroline put a friendly hand on Trish's shoulder and said that she would be back in an hour to pick her up.

Dr. Peyton was a kind woman of about fifty years of age. She reminded Trish a little of her aunt, whom she adored. Dr. Peyton looked athletic and fit, just like Trish's Aunt Nellie. Nellie was Trish's mother's younger sister. She had never married and was a high school principal.

After a few minutes of getting to know each other, Dr. Peyton asked Trish to share anything she wanted. She would especially be interested in knowing what Trish was depressed about.

Trish told her a little about her happy life as a child, her college years, Jenny's husband's death, her father's death, and finally about her romantic encounter with Shaun Healy during that bad storm five years ago.

Then, with a few skillful questions from the psychologist, Trish revealed details of her relationship with Shaun, including their happy engagement. Then, she sadly talked about his alleged affair with Sheila Warrant and her impulsive flight to Brazil. Lastly, she told her about coming back to Dalton because of her mother's health and wanting to talk with Shaun to get his explanation. She cried bitterly when she said that she took too long to ask him for that explanation and the subsequent things he said to her at the wedding dance.

Dr. Peyton discovered that the young man who brought Trish to the hospital was that very same Shaun Healy. At some point, she wanted to chat with him and find out his side of the story, too.

Trish felt like a big weight was lifted off her shoulders after she talked with Dr. Peyton. She explained that she had never felt depression before and that her weight had always been stable before this last issue with Shaun. It was just since Bill and Cheri's wedding that Trish felt so lethargic. It became too much work to make and eat a meal.

Dr. Peyton explained that she was feeling lethargic because it was her body's way of telling her that she needed to eat more. Part of it was the depression, as well. They were all a part of each other. Eating better and more regularly would help the lethargy and depression, too.

Trish nodded and promised to eat better now. Dr. Peyton asked if Trish had anyone close to her who would stay with her for a week once she was released from the hospital.

*If she had enough notice, Aunt Nellie would come and stay with me,* Trish thought. She then considered her neighbors and friends. Mary was on her honeymoon; otherwise, she would have stayed with Trish. Trish explained to Dr. Peyton that her family would be home in five days, but Dr. Peyton was adamant that someone needed to be with Trish right away after her hospital release. If there was no one, Trish would have to stay at the hospital.

Trish asked for some time to consider it. Their session was up, anyway. Caroline came to get Trish and cheerfully took her back to her room. She changed the dressing on Trish's leg, too. The wound looked angry and sore. Caroline said that someone would need to change the dressing at least once a day and apply the ointment to keep it from getting infected. She left Trish in a thoughtful mood, trying to think of someone who would do these things for her.

Dr. Peyton sought out Shaun, who was in the waiting room. She asked him if he would mind talking to her in her office. He amicably agreed. She said that she talked with Trish about her depression and lack of eating. Now she would like to hear Shaun's input.

Shaun candidly shared his version of events. Dr. Peyton nodded and understood how the misunderstanding could have happened. Trish had not mentioned Senhor Santos. She must not have thought that he had any bearing on her story, while Shaun thought that Carlos was a huge part of their story. Shaun also did not mention Mary, whereas Trish was sure for a while that Shaun and Mary would get married. Both thought, inaccurately, that the other one would marry someone else. *How interesting*, Dr. Peyton thought.

She thanked Shaun for his time. It was not up to her to tell them what the other had said. If she could get them together long enough to talk, they may finally have that long overdue conversation. If Trish could not think of anyone to look after her for a week, she might just mention to Shaun that he and his parents could have Trish stay with them while she recuperated. Since it was obvious that Shaun still loved Trish very much, he may be agreeable to that plan.

Caroline came in to see Trish before suppertime. She had a dietary sheet made out by the doctor. It had helpful hints regarding how Trish could slowly increase her caloric intake at her meals so that she would gain a little weight. He wanted her to weigh at least one hundred pounds and slowly increase or maintain that weight.

Trish looked it over and nodded. She didn't like the feelings of lethargy and depression that had swamped her for the last few weeks, so if eating better took away those feelings, she planned to do it. She also felt better emotionally after talking candidly with Dr. Peyton.

Trish thought for hours about who could stay with her until her family came home. She did not want to inconvenience any of her friends or neighbors. Her best idea was to ask Mrs. Rush for help. She was a generous and nice lady, but she did have a full-time commitment to her grocery store.

Shaun, who had waited around all day to talk with Trish, was growing impatient. He could not stay in Mason City another full day. One of his neighbors was helping by milking the cows, but he couldn't expect that help for many days. He wanted to get back home tonight, if possible.

Caroline spoke discreetly with Dr. Peyton regarding how they could encourage Shaun to take Trish to his parents' home for her recuperation. An improved relationship between Shaun and Trish would likely benefit her recovery.

Caroline walked past Shaun and pretended to be surprised to see him there.

"Hi, Shaun. What are you still doing here? Did you want a chance to talk with Trish? She is feeling so much better, and we want to release her tomorrow. However, because of her leg injury and nutritional needs, she requires constant care. She must remain here in the hospital if we can't find someone to stay with her."

Caroline briefly perused the chart in her hands, then suddenly added, "You know, her family is coming back from Brazil in five days, but we don't want to keep her here until then. She was talking about Mrs. Rush earlier this afternoon. Do you know Mrs. Rush, and would she be a good person to stay with Trish until her family comes home?"

Caroline's eyes were open and friendly. She had her fingers crossed that Shaun would step up to the plate and say that Trish could go home with him.

Shaun frowned. In his opinion, Mrs. Rush was much too busy to stay with Trish for more than a day. He tried to think which of his neighbors could stay with Trish for a week. The only people he could think of were his own parents. They were retired and had time on their hands.

While Shaun did all the physical work on the farm, his mom kept the house. His dad was disabled and did not do much for the farm except some paperwork. It would be very difficult for Shaun if Trish stayed at their home. He would love to see her every day, but she made it clear that she did not want to see or talk with him anymore. Still, if she was allowed to leave the hospital tomorrow with him, she might agree to that. In Trish's mind, it might be better than having to stay in the hospital until her family could come to get her.

"May I speak with Trish? I might have a suggestion about who she can stay with until her family comes home." Shaun's brow was furrowed, and he spoke slowly, with some trepidation.

"Sure. Trish is awake. I'll just ask her if she would like a visitor and get right back to you." Caroline's face was wreathed with a big smile as she went into Trish's room.

"Hi, Trish. There is someone who wants to talk with you. Are you up for a visitor?" Caroline asked buoyantly.

"Is it Shaun?" Trish asked guardedly. As far as she knew, no one else was aware that she was here.

"Yes, it's Shaun. He asked if he could see you. He has a suggestion as to who you can stay with when you go home. May he come in and talk with you?" Caroline looked intently at Trish, daring her not to refuse to see Shaun.

Trish wondered who Shaun had in mind. She was also glad that he was there to see her one more time. She would try very hard to be kind and respectful to him. He had proven to be a good neighbor over the past few days. Nodding at Caroline, she said, "Yes, let him in."

Caroline went out to get Shaun. When he came in, he gave Trish a searching glance. She looked a little better than she had yesterday. In just a day and a half of regular meals, she seemed to have lost her gaunt look. He smiled right at her.

Trish returned Shaun's gaze. He looked so great. Now he was smiling. *What is going on?* she wondered.

Caroline left them alone. Shaun dragged a lightweight chair over to the bed and sat down, his eyes on a level with hers. After a moment of silence, in which each looked at the other questioningly, Shaun took her hands in his. He used to hold her hands and draw little circles on the back of them. It was difficult for him to resist doing that, but he did. He just held them lightly, like a friend would do.

"Trish, Caroline told me that you can't leave the hospital unless someone dependable comes to get you. How would you feel about staying at my house until your family gets home from Brazil? My mom and dad have time on their hands, and they would be happy to care for you and treat your leg wound. You don't have to worry about me. I'm outside most of the day, so you would only see me at suppertime. I also promise not to speak to you if you don't want me to." Shaun's sincerity was evident.

Trish was shocked at the excitement his words dredged up in her. She had always liked Shaun's parents. Maybe, just maybe, there would be the chance for Shaun and her to work out their issues. It might do no good at all, but she wanted Shaun to have his moment for his explanation about Sheila. She thought that he might feel better getting it off his chest once and for all. If, by some miracle, he retracted his words from Bill's wedding, they might become friends. That was the most she could hope for.

Trish squeezed Shaun's hands. She looked at him candidly and said, "Thank you, Shaun, for that generous offer. If you think that your parents would agree to it, I would be happy to stay with them for a few days until my family can pick me up at your place. I have always liked your parents, and I think that we would get along very well. I would be happy to pay them for my upkeep, too. I would be an extra mouth to feed and all."

"Oh, Trish, we would not expect to get paid for helping you. It's what neighbors do for each other, right?" Shaun was frowning slightly. Her reference to paying them made it seem as if they were a boarding house or something.

Shaun's reference to being a good neighbor made her remember that that was how he thought of her now. Well, his offer was better than having to stay at the hospital for four additional days. She would try to put on her happy face and not give the Healys any reason to regret having her stay with them.

"Okay, then. Why don't you call your parents, and if they agree, go ahead and make the arrangements. And Shaun, thank you for the invitation. It was very neighborly of you." With that said, Trish quickly squeezed his hands once more and released them.

Shaun stared at her for a minute, seeming to make up his mind about saying anything further. Deciding to keep quiet, he nodded and stood up. He excused himself and left the room to call his parents, not wanting to do that in front of Trish in the event they asked any awkward questions.

"Mom, I'm still at the hospital in Mason City. Trish will be released tomorrow if someone dependable will pick her up and stay with her until her family gets back from Brazil. Trish did not ask for this, but I offered to have her stay with us for a few days. I know that you and Trish have always gotten along just fine. She will have to stay in the hospital for four extra days if no one can pick her up and stay with her. She has a nasty wound on her leg that needs to be cleaned and bandaged every day. She is dangerously underweight from not eating much for a month or so, and she needs to gain back some weight. You know that I am outside most of the day, so I won't be the one helping her or talking to her. Are you okay with that, Mom?" Shaun's demeanor remained calm while speaking.

Mrs. Healy was quiet for a few moments before she spoke. "Shaun, we would be happy to help Trish for a few days. I understand that you would not be the person helping her—both because you are so busy and because you are barely speaking to each other these days. It was good of you to offer our home to her. She is still our dear Trish Newberg, even though she is not your fiancée any longer. Please tell Trish that we are happy to have her stay with us for a while."

Shaun was grateful for an understanding mother. "Thanks, Mom. I appreciate you. I'll tell Trish that you want her to stay for a few days. Because she will not be released until tomorrow, I'll keep my motel room for another night, and we'll be home sometime tomorrow. I'll call you from the hospital before we leave so you will have some idea of our arrival. Trish will have her medication, but we will need to stop off at her home to pick up some clothing for her. I love you, Mom. See you tomorrow."

Mrs. Healy quickly added, "Okay, Shaun. I'll talk with you tomorrow. Dad and I love you, too. Have a safe drive home."

Shaun knocked on Trish's door and waited for her permission to come in. He smiled nicely at her and said that his parents were happy and looking forward to having her stay with them until her family came home.

Trish smiled genuinely for the first time in weeks. She felt wanted and was pleased that she would get to see Shaun, even briefly, for the next four or five days.

She invited Shaun to sit down and talk for a few minutes. Shaun asked about Jenny and Carlos' wedding. Trish described it in detail. Her happiness for her sister and her good friend was evident.

Now that Trish's care for the next few days was determined, they each found themselves thinking about the events that brought them to this impasse.

If Shaun had known that Carlos and Trish were just good friends, he would not have snapped at her at Bill's wedding. How he wished that he could atone for his bad behavior. If he could just tell her everything, including the tremendous jealousy that he felt regarding Carlos, Trish might forgive him. But Shaun was a proud and stubborn man. He did not know how to overcome his pride and just tell Trish everything. On the other hand, was he prepared to say goodbye to the love of his life forever just to keep his pride?

Shaun had no idea that Trish had avoided him in the beginning of the summer because she thought that he and Mary planned to get married. Trish's feelings for both were so strong that she would rather keep her distance than cause their breakup. What was now painfully obvious is that Shaun and Trish needed to be open and honest with each other for anything to change.

The next morning, Trish asked to see Dr. Peyton, who was free for half an hour. She thanked Dr. Peyton for her help and stated that her depression and lethargy were already lifting. Then, she told her that she was going to stay with Shaun and his parents until her family came home. The excited look on Trish's face made Dr.

Peyton smile. Maybe Shaun and Trish would finally have that talk and everything would work out for them.

Caroline was on hand to push Trish's wheelchair to where Shaun's car waited. He helped her out of the chair and into his car, putting her seatbelt on her before going to his driver's side and getting in. They waved to Caroline, who blew them an airy kiss, and drove away. They didn't talk very much, but it was a friendly silence.

Shaun asked her if she wanted anything to eat before they got to her home to pick up some more clothes for her. She said that she had breakfast and could wait until lunch to eat. He had skipped breakfast in order to be at the hospital in time to check her out. He just nodded and decided that he could wait until lunch, too.

They arrived at Trish's house by 11:00 a.m. Shaun had not been inside since it was redone after the tornado. He liked the newly remodeled rooms. He accompanied Trish to her bedroom to help pack her things. He told her to sit on her bed while he got whatever she wanted and put it in a suitcase for her. She felt strange about it, but Shaun was so nonplussed about getting her clothes out of her dressers and closet that she relaxed.

The only uncomfortable moment was when he opened her closet and saw the wedding gown that she had bought more than three years ago. Shaun pulled it out and stared at it before putting it back in the closet. His mouth was tight and grim. The huge lump in his throat threatened to choke him.

Trish wished with all her heart that she had carefully put it in a box at the bottom of her closet. She never planned to marry now, and it was just a sad reminder of the wedding day that she would never have. She had thought lately that she should either give it away or sell it because she didn't want that continual reminder of what could have been.

Shaun looked at Trish with a frown, and he saw her pink embarrassed face. He decided to say nothing even though he was very surprised. He hadn't known that she had bought it before she fled to Brazil. He was sure that she didn't buy it after she got back. *Why did she keep it?* he wondered. He decided that some things were better left unsaid.

He asked her, "Now, what things do you want out of your closet? Describe them so I know which ones to pull out."

Trish described a few articles of clothing that would be easy to pull on over the large bandage on her leg. It was November now, and chilly in Iowa. She didn't need to dress up, so she mostly wanted to wear sweatpants and long-sleeved tops. Warm socks, slippers, a flannel nightgown, dressing robe, and a jacket rounded off the clothes she wanted to take with her. Toothbrush, toothpaste, facial soap, deodorant, and hairbrush were added to the suitcase. Oh, and she didn't want to forget her cell phone and charger. Carlos and Jenny might want to call her before they came back to Dalton with Josh and Lila.

Trish debated taking her sketchbook and colored pencils with her. She finally decided to take them because there would be times when Mrs. Healy would be busy, and Trish did not want to be bored. There were so many new things to draw at the Healy farm that she doubted that would happen.

Since she did not want to worry her family, she left them a note in the kitchen telling them that she was at the Healy farm recuperating from a little accident. She made it sound as if it was just a neighborly thing, so they wouldn't think that Shaun and she were back together.

Shaun read the note over her shoulder, and the grimace returned to his face. It couldn't be any clearer that Trish did not want them to reconcile, which was something Shaun wanted very much, despite what he said to his mom or Trish. Despair overcame him when he contemplated her unworn wedding dress and her declaration on the note that the Healys were just being neighborly.

He helped Trish to his car and then went back for her suitcase. Silence reigned during the five-minute drive to his home. Both seemed perturbed by the same thing. Prior to Shaun's discovery of the wedding dress, their communication had been improving. *Why did the sight of my wedding dress bother Shaun so much?* she wondered. His grim mouth and stern look made it very hard for her to resume conversation with him.

Shaun tooted the horn lightly when he pulled up to his house. His mom came out to help Trish out of the car and into the house. Shaun followed with her suitcase. He had been in the same clothes for several days. Even though he showered at his motel each day, he felt uncomfortable wearing the same clothes. Once inside, he immediately went to his own bedroom to change.

His mom was talking cheerfully to Trish in the kitchen. He looked in on them, said hello to his dad, and announced that he had chores to do outside. He was starting as he meant to go on—leaving Trish alone with his parents. He wanted some quiet time to think, anyway.

He went out to the shed where his three sweet Jersey cows lived. After their large barn was destroyed in a barn fire about ten years ago, they converted a large shed into a makeshift barn. Since he just kept the three cows nowadays, it was large enough for them and their hay. It was Shaun's very favorite place on the farm.

Shaun loved his cows and often talked with them like they were people. He rubbed their ears and patted their backs as he talked with them. Their honey-brown bodies and large brown eyes looked at him with total trust because he took good care of them. They were serviced every other year from the neighbor's bull. Shaun sold their beautiful calves to another neighbor for extra money. He often half-seriously asked the cows how they felt about losing their calves as soon as they could be separated from their mothers.

It was Trish's favorite place on the farm, too. There was a bale of hay in the back of the shed, out of the way of everything else. The times they had sat on that bale, holding hands and kissing were not to be counted. Shaun disliked kissing her in front of an audience, and this had been their favorite place to get away from everyone. Trish understood his feelings for his three amigas. The cows' names were Daisy, Rose, and Buttercup.

Trish loved the fact that Shaun loved his cows. She used to lightly laugh and come over to be hugged and kissed by Shaun after he milked them. She once asked him how he could tell them apart since they looked so alike. He just laughed gently at her and said that after milking them every day for years, he would know each of them in the dark.

Now he sat on a stool next to Daisy, who was his favorite, and said, "Daisy, your friend Trish is back in the house, even though I didn't think that would ever happen. She's hurt and needs someone to care for her and her wounds. I promised to stay away from her. We're not friends anymore, even though I wish we were. Even better, I wish that we were still engaged." He paused to get a handful of feed to give Daisy. He stroked her bony head and continued.

"I can't believe that she would think that I had an affair with Sheila Warrant. Why couldn't she trust me and ask me about it instead of running away? Oh, I know that I told you all this before. I'm sorry about bringing it up again. It's just that I am having such a hard time letting her go. Today, I was helping her get some clothes out of her closet, and I saw the wedding dress that she bought for our wedding. It's still hanging there, even though *she* broke our engagement. What does that mean? I love her just as much as I ever did. I think that I might just go crazy with her living temporarily in my house but being as far apart as we can be. I might need your help to get through this, dear friend."

Shaun was all talked out, so he just sat there in the near dark, thinking sad thoughts.

After an hour, he got up to go.

He put on a heavy jacket that was hanging in the shed and walked around his fields for a few hours until extreme hunger brought him to the shed in the far field. He had eaten nothing today, and he couldn't wait until supper, so he found the granola bars and bottled water that were kept in the storm shelter.

As he sat on the rough bench to eat his meager snack, he remembered kissing Trish for the first time on that very bench. His love for her had begun on that same eventful day. Every word they said that evening replayed in his head. Her courage in the face of her fear was amazing.

He looked at his watch and saw that it was nearly time for supper. Good. He was still very hungry. He had just enough time to walk home before his mom would put the food on the table.

While Mrs. Healy made supper, she and Trish talked about Jenny's wedding and Lila's recuperation from her stroke. They were comfortable with each other. After Trish called her Mrs. Healy a few times, Shaun's mother stopped her.

"Trish, when you and Shaun were engaged, I asked you to call me Ella, and you agreed. Even though things have changed, I still want you to call us Ella and Andrew. We call you Trish, so it makes everything all right."

"Thank you, Ella. I did not want to be disrespectful to you or Andrew. Like you said, things have changed," Trish said.

"Oh, you couldn't be disrespectful if you tried," Ella chuckled.

Trish laughed and said, "Oh, you have no idea. I can remember being very disrespectful to my elders when I was young. I didn't take redirection or corrections very kindly. I am happy to say that I finally grew out of that phase."

"Well, now you are a perfectly respectful person, my dear. Both you and Jenny seem to be such nice women. Your mom and dad did a good job raising you."

Trish thanked her, and they continued to talk about Jenny's wedding. Trish described Brazil and Carlos' home. She explained that Josh and Lila were staying with Carlos' mother, Maria, while Carlos and Jenny toured the country.

While the meal was cooking, Ella took Trish into the spare bedroom and helped her put away her clothes. She cleaned Trish's wound and put the healing lotion on the sore before putting a new dressing on it. She was a little sickened by the ugly sore she saw on Trish's nice little leg. It would likely leave a big scar. Trish also might not want to wear shorts or skirts anymore. It was a shame, because Trish had nice legs.

Trish thanked Ella for her care, and they went back into the kitchen. The good smell of their supper made Trish hungry for the first time in a month or so. Shaun had told his mom that Trish needed to gain at least six pounds before her next visit to the doctor in three weeks. Ella took that as a challenge to fatten up this sweet girl.

Andrew wheeled himself into the dining room from the study where he had been doing some paperwork and then the daily crossword puzzle in the *Mason City Times*. Ella set the table and asked Trish to sit on the chair next to hers. That would leave Shaun to sit across the table next to his father. They sat at the table awaiting Shaun. He was usually quite punctual because they tried to have supper at 6:00 p.m. sharp every night.

Sure enough, the door opened at 5:58 p.m. Shaun came in and went to the sink to wash his hands before sitting down. He looked cold and windblown as he nodded at everyone and took a seat next to his dad. They bowed their heads and said grace before Ella passed the dishes around the table. There was not much conversation as they ate. Trish was used to all kinds of chatter at the meals in her house, and she had to get used to the silence.

When Shaun was done eating, he quietly thanked his mom and asked his dad if he wanted to watch television in the family room. After a quick look at his wife, who nodded approval, Andrew said that he would like to do that. Shaun took a quick glance at Trish and then grabbed his dad's wheelchair and pushed him out of the room. He had not said a word to Trish since he brought her home at noon.

Trish was ready to help Ella with the cleaning up and dishes but was told to stay where she was. Ella liked to do the cleaning up by herself, but she would welcome some conversation while she was doing it. Trish sat on her comfortable chair at the table and conversed with Ella about the meal and other meals that she found to be delicious.

When the dishes were done, Ella led Trish to the living room. They sat on the couch with a TV tray in front of each of them and did Word Finds and Sudoku. Trish enjoyed doing them while chatting on and off with Ella. It seemed as if Shaun and Andrew would stay in the family room until bedtime.

Trish began to see that Shaun really didn't mean to stay inside and talk with her. He said that he would stay out of her way—and it seemed as if he was going to do just that. Trish was disappointed and told her kind host that she was tired and wanted to go to bed.

Ella helped Trish to bed and said good night. She quietly closed the door and took herself to the family room. Her husband and son were still there talking quietly about the show they were watching. Ella told them that Trish was in bed. Shaun looked relieved and asked his mom how things went today with Trish in the house.

Ella said that she enjoyed Trish's company all day and looked forward to tomorrow. She told them that Trish's wound was big and nasty-looking, and that Trish would likely have a scar there for the rest of her life. She looked at Shaun when she said that, but he did not say anything about it or make any facial expression that denoted disgust or unhappiness. It hadn't seemed to faze him in the least.

Shaun talked generally about the farm and then said that he would go to bed, too. His day started mighty early. He planned to breakfast early and be out of the house before Trish got out of bed. As much as he longed to see her and talk with her, he had promised her that he would be away from the house all day until suppertime.

He didn't know what he was going to do for all those hours. His cornfields were empty now and his three cows did not take much time. If Trish wasn't here, he would spend some time in the house, chatting with his parents, or he would maybe use the car to go into town and see friends or something like that.

Trish woke early. She was accustomed to getting up and taking Nolan for a leisurely walk. He was so old now that he didn't enjoy the walks anymore, but she cuddled and coddled him while they walked. She hoped that her neighbors were treating him well while the Newbergs were away. Jenny would pick him up when they got home from Brazil.

*I would make a good farmer's wife,* Trish thought, *because I enjoy getting up early and watching the sun rise.* Her mom, Jenny, and Josh all liked to sleep in as long as possible.

She got up and silently went to the bathroom. She heard someone quietly moving around in the kitchen. Thinking that it was Ella, she limped into the kitchen. Shaun heard her and whipped around. He was dressed to go outside. His look was guilty. He thought that he woke her up by making too much noise.

Trish smiled shyly at him and said, "Good morning. I always wake up early, so don't feel like you woke me up by making too much noise. Are you getting yourself breakfast? I could make something for you if you want. I'm a fair cook. Do you like bacon and eggs or something like that?"

Shaun smiled back at her. He said, "No, thanks. I was planning to just have cold cereal and toast. I can get it. I've done it many times before. Go ahead and make a hot breakfast for yourself if you want it or join me for some cold cereal and toast. I haven't made coffee yet, so you can do that if you want. What do you say, Trish?"

"I'm never very hungry in the morning, so I'll join you for some cereal. I hope you have Raisin Bran. It's my favorite," Trish said with a sparkle in her eyes.

Shaun pulled out a box of Raisin Bran like a magician pulling a bunny out of a hat. Trish laughed delightedly. Shaun almost melted. This was his enchanting Trish that he remembered so fondly.

He poured them each a bowlful and then made some toast. Trish moved clumsily around him to make the coffee. They worked in silence, but it was a friendly silence. They sat at the kitchen table eating their cereal and toast and drinking their orange juice and coffee.

When he finished, Shaun put his dishes in the sink, shrugged on his heavy coat, smiled at Trish, and told her to have a nice day. Even without much conversation, he felt good when he left the house. Trish had looked so sweet and sleepy. Her lovely curls were quite messed up, just as he liked them. Her flannel nightgown was pretty and pink, and her slippers were frilly and satin. He could get used to seeing her every morning looking so cute. She had been friendly and fun, too.

He whistled as he walked to the shed to milk his three cows. Even if he did not see Trish until supper, he had a pleasant memory of their breakfast together. However, he would keep his distance because he didn't want Trish to think that he was going back on his promise. *Maybe Trish enjoyed breakfast, too, and will join me tomorrow,* he hoped.

Trish smiled as she got dressed for the day. Shaun had been so pleasant this morning. It almost felt like they were an old married couple getting breakfast in the morning. She should have felt uncomfortable sitting with him in her pajamas and slippers and uncombed hair, but she felt very comfortable. Shaun seemed quite comfortable with her, too.

Trish explained to Ella that she already ate cold cereal with Shaun, who was up early, too. Ella smiled and said that was fine. She made a hot breakfast for her husband and herself. She was planning to do some laundry in the morning, so she sent Trish into the living room and told her to do anything she wanted. Trish took out her sketchbook and colored pencils. She wanted to draw Shaun's face as he had looked while he ate breakfast this morning.

She worked hard on Shaun's picture all morning. Ella came in to see what Trish was doing. She stood over Trish's shoulder, gazing at the picture. It was almost done. Ella exclaimed, "I had no idea that you were so talented, my dear!"

Trish wanted to keep the picture for herself, but Ella was so complimentary about it that she felt compelled to offer it as a gift. After all, they were feeding her and taking care of her for a few days.

"Here you go, Ella," Trish said warmly as she handed it to the older woman.

Ella took it from her with gladness. "My, this is good enough to frame," Ella declared.

Trish was happy that she had made such a good impression on Ella. Tomorrow she would draw a picture of Ella and then Andrew. That way they would have the whole family to hang on the wall.

Trish ate a good lunch. She wondered what Shaun did for his lunch. He didn't come to lunch yesterday, either. Just after they finished lunch, she heard the car start and saw Shaun drive away from the house. Apparently, he planned to have lunch in town. *Does he always skip lunch?* she wondered.

Andrew and Ella didn't seem too concerned that Shaun did not come in for lunch. It must be a regular thing for him to miss lunch with them.

That afternoon, Ella and Trish talked about how to make homemade bread. Trish was anxious to learn how to do it. Her family loved homemade bread, and none of them knew how to make it.

Ella found Trish to be an eager and quick learner. It made her feel like she was working with her own daughter or at least a daughter-in-law. She enjoyed Trish's company so much. If Trish had married Shaun, they would all have lived in this house together until Ella and Andrew moved into a retirement home. By then there would be children, and the old house would be too full for the oldest generation.

Ella felt cheated out of a daughter-in-law. She wished that Trish and Shaun would make up their differences and get engaged again. Sometimes it seemed as if both wanted that. She was hesitant to talk about it with Shaun. He was a grown man, and she didn't want to pry. She didn't know Trish well enough to ask her either. She just hoped that one of them would voluntarily talk with her about their problems. Once she was asked for her advice, she would be only too happy to hand it out.

The house smelled amazing when Shaun came in for supper that night. He arrived a few minutes before 6:00 p.m., washed his hands, smoothed down his unruly hair, and sat down at the table. They were having warm homemade bread slathered with real butter and chili, corn, and peach cobbler for dessert.

It was the kind of meal that Trish loved. She ate a healthy serving of everything. Her mouth was curved in a big smile while she ate. Shaun tried not to look at Trish, but he was captivated by her big smile. He was so happy that she was eating a healthy meal. If she kept this up, she might just gain back those six pounds by her next doctor's visit. He was happy that she was getting better at his home. He knew that most of the credit had to go to his mom.

When he finished eating, he once again thanked his mom. When she said that Trish helped to make a lot of the meal, he turned his attention to Trish and thanked her, too. His smile made her smile broaden. He looked at his dad and asked him if he wanted to watch TV while Mom did the dishes. His dad said "Yes", and away they went.

Trish, who thought that the evening would be like last night, went into the living room and set up the TV trays and found the Word Finds and Sudoku books. She talked with Ella as she did it.

Ella was soon done with her chores and came into the living room. She got out a basket of yarn and some knitting needles. They had talked during the day about Trish's yarn shop. Ella offered to help Trish get the shop ready for Opening Day.

Trish found out that Ella was an accomplished knitter just like she was. Trish offered to sell in her yarn shop some of the things Ella knitted. Ella was tickled pink. She loved to knit warm winter hats, gloves, scarves, and colorful sweaters for children. Trish couldn't wait to see the finished products.

They both sat down in comfortable chairs and knitted for a few hours, talking about their products and Trish's store. It was so much fun for them both. Ella felt very close to Trish by now. Trish thought of Ella as another mother. It was going to be hard to leave this wonderful house in a few days.

At 10:00 p.m., the men came into the living room to see what the ladies were doing. They saw how excited the ladies were and let them talk about the yarn store and the products that would be on sale there. Shaun didn't talk much, but his eyes kept straying back to Trish. Her gamine face was excited and gently flushed. He could hear the enthusiasm for her future yarn store in her voice.

Trish made a few mistakes with her knitting because she could feel Shaun's eyes on herself. It made her nervous. Finally, after half an hour, she smiled at all of them and said that she was going to bed.

Ella packed up her own knitting and went into Trish's room with her. She cleaned and applied ointment to Trish's wound and put a new bandage on it. In a few days, Trish would be able to leave the wound uncovered while she slept. It was starting to look a little better after the two days of care from Ella. They said goodnight and Ella quietly left Trish's room.

Shaun and Andrew once again asked Ella about her day with Trish. Ella spoke highly of Trish and brought out the picture she had drawn of Shaun. They all exclaimed over it. Shaun had seen Trish's work before, but he was astounded by the accuracy and detail she had in that simple pencil-colored picture. She had given his likeness energy and emotion, too. He thought that it was the nicest picture of himself that had ever been drawn or photographed.

He hoped that Trish would get up early tomorrow morning and have breakfast with him again. They only had two more days together before she would leave his home and probably never try to see him again. He was hoping that a miracle would happen in those two days.

The next day was a carbon copy of Trish's second day at the Healy farm. Trish got up early to have breakfast with Shaun. They didn't talk much, but their silence was friendly and companionable.

Shaun continued to keep out of Trish's way for most of the day. After supper, he took care to spend his time in another room with his father.

Ella took every opportunity to talk with Trish. She left Trish alone in the forenoon with her sketchbook and colored pencils. Trish perfectly captured Ella in her kitchen and Andrew sitting comfortably watching TV in the family room. Ella loved each of Trish's pictures and enthused about where she would hang them when she had found the perfect frames for them. She insisted that Trish sign and date each of them. Trish smiled at Ella's pleasure in them.

Trish had missed drawing and creating different kinds of art. Well, in two weeks, her yarn store would be open, and she could be as creative as she wanted. She was going to be quite busy, and she was looking forward to that. Hopefully, she would be so busy that she would fall into bed each night, without one single second to think about Shaun. So far, that had never worked for her. Even in Brazil, Trish had thought of Shaun every day.

Trish secretly made additional sketches of the Healy family. In one, she had drawn herself inside the family circle. She had drawn Shaun looking tenderly down at her as she beamed at the person looking at the picture. Another was a drawing of Shaun in his shed, milking his beloved cows. She had to search her memory for that one since she hadn't been in the shed for more than three years. The third picture showed Ella and Andrew sitting next to each other in the family room. It conveyed the loving feelings that they portrayed about the other.

These would be her keepsakes—remembrances of the care and love she felt in the Healy home. When she was alone, as she would be after she moved away, she could bring them out and look at them. She hoped that she would feel comforted, instead of sad and lonely.

Ella and Trish made quite a pile of knitted articles to sell in the yarn stop. By now, Ella was hooked, and she promised to visit Trish in the yarn shop as much as possible. This was bittersweet for Trish. She would see Ella, but she was sure that Shaun would never darken the door to her shop. *If only we could have that talk!* Trish thought in desperation. *Why won't Shaun talk to me?*

CHAPTER

# Fifteen

During Trish's last afternoon at the Healy farm, Shaun silently came into his house to clean a large cut on his left hand. He had been sharpening a scythe, which he used in the spring to cut down tall grass and weeds. He had needed to find jobs to keep him busy outside all day. Not usually prone to accidents, Shaun was distracted by thoughts of Trish's impending departure.

He was so quiet that neither Ella nor Trish was aware that he was in the house. He heard the quiet drone of their conversation from the kitchen. He went to stand in the doorway of the living room, about to announce his presence, when he heard his mother's questions to Trish. He wanted to hear what was said, so he continued to stand quietly, just out of sight.

Ella, who quite fiercely wanted Trish for her daughter-in-law, finally brought up the issues between Shaun and Trish.

"Trish, you fit in here with us so well. I don't want you to leave tomorrow. You can't begin to understand how wonderful it is for me to have another woman to talk to. I love my husband and my son, but I can't talk with them about cooking or knitting or other things that I enjoy. Isn't there any way that you and Shaun can talk about your problems? You would be the perfect daughter for me." Ella's eyes were brimming with tears.

Trish looked sadly at Ella. She would have loved to be a part of this family. She loved Shaun and already cared very much for Ella and Andrew. They had been kindness itself to her.

Trish said slowly, "Ella, too much time has passed. Shaun told me that he doesn't trust me anymore and that we could only ever be neighbors now. I think that he is still very angry and upset with me for running away three years ago. If we could have talked about it right away when I came home, we may have found some middle ground. As it is, I think that he is having a difficult time having me in the house this week. He never talks with me. I know that he is avoiding me. He stays outside all day, even through lunch, so he doesn't have to see me."

Trish stopped talking and looked down at her hands. They were clenched in her lap. She felt like crying herself. Ella's face and tear-filled eyes cut Trish to the quick. She was so grateful to the Healys for their kindness and caring, but she didn't want to hurt Shaun any more than she had to.

Ella leaned forward and hurriedly said, "But what about your breakfasts together? You even said that you seemed to feel comfortable with each other."

"Ella, I can't explain that. It's true that I have felt comfortable with him at breakfast. We eat at the table and don't say anything. Maybe it's because we were once engaged and knew each other so well. But when he comes in for supper, Shaun is once again quiet and refuses to say anything to me. He can't get out of the room fast enough, can he? It's obvious that he has nothing to say to me. He's behaving as if we are strangers—new neighbors. No, it's time that I moved back to my own house. Once I'm out of this house, it is unlikely that I will see anything more of him."

Trish looked at Ella with a brave face and said, "Ella, I'm glad that we will continue to keep in touch, though. I'll look forward to seeing you when you visit me at my store. You can tell me how Shaun and Andrew are getting on with life."

Trish deliberately changed topics. Ella took one look at Trish's face and went along with the new conversation.

Trish's next words shocked Shaun, still standing in the doorway out of sight. His mom inquired about Trish's plan to stay with her mother since Jenny and Josh would be going to live with Carlos. They would live most of the time in Brazil, with visits to Dalton once a month.

Trish flatly replied, "My Aunt Nellie is going to come and live with Mom in the house in Dalton. She will be retiring from her job as a high school principal in January. She's looking forward to living in a small town again. She's tired of the rat race of living in a large city. She and Mom have always been close."

Ella's eyes grew wide as she asked, "Where will you live, Trish?"

Trish looked steadily at Ella as she said, "I'll stay with Mom until Aunt Nellie moves in. Then I will be moving into the house that Carlos built about ten miles east of the strip mall. It's a large house, with room enough for me and Carlos, Jenny, and Josh when they are in Iowa. I'll only be ten miles away from my store, so I won't have a long commute."

Ella was shocked. "You're moving away from Dalton? I never knew that. Your mom is going to miss you two girls."

"Yes, but I'll be close enough to visit her a few times a week. And Jenny, Josh, and Carlos promised to come and visit one weekend a month. She'll be fine with Aunt Nellie." Trish was hanging on to her calm by a thread. She really did not want to talk about this anymore.

"Well, at least I'll still see you at the yarn store, Trish. How I wish that you would have gotten back together with Shaun. I would so much have liked for you to continue living here with us. I'll miss you, Trish. You are so exactly right for my son," Ella said emphatically, looking tearful again.

Trish looked back down at her hands. They were quietly pulling the knitting apart. She would have to start again on this winter cap. It was unrecognizable right now.

"It's probably for the best that I'll be moving. That way Shaun and I won't run into each other. That may make him feel better." Trish stopped talking. It was too painful to keep hashing it out, over and over. What was done was done. No more talk . . .

Ella saw Trish's face and started talking about the meal they would make for supper in a few hours.

Shaun quietly let himself back outside. He was shaken by Trish's words. With her moving away, he might *never* see Trish again. He thought that was what he wanted when he was under the impression that Trish was going to marry Carlos. Now with Carlos safely married to Jenny, Trish would be alone. He didn't want to think of her being alone. He could have borne the fact that Trish was happily married to Carlos, but now that she was apparently a free woman again, why couldn't they finally talk?

He didn't know about Trish's feelings, but he still loved her as much as ever. He thought about that pretty, white wedding dress that still hung in her closet. Did she regret running away and breaking their engagement? Since they had never had that talk, he didn't know what to think. But if she still loved him and wanted to be with him, why did she seem so eager to move away from him? There were so many questions, and he had no idea of the answers.

He went into the shed to think some more. He didn't know how he would be able to go to supper tonight and sit there as if nothing was wrong . . .

Shaun sat in the shed, totally numb, for more than two hours. Impossible scenarios ran through his weary head. He tried to think of ways that he could get Trish to stay at his house. In his confused mind, he even thought of contacting Jenny and Carlos to stop them from coming to get Trish tomorrow. They didn't even know about her accident yet. It never occurred to him that he could stop her from leaving if he would just sit her down, apologize, and tell her that he loved her too much to let her leave him again.

He sat there, so deep in thought, that he missed going in for supper. It got quite dark outside, although it was light and cozy inside the shed.

Ella, Andrew, and Trish sat at the supper table waiting for Shaun to come in. When it was 6:30 p.m., Ella put the supper back on the stove. She was getting a little worried about Shaun. If he had a problem with one of the cows, he would have run in to tell them before going back outside. She was concerned that he had hurt himself and was not able to come in and let them know. He was such a considerate son that he would never keep them waiting for supper like this without a very good reason.

Ella addressed Trish and Andrew. "I wonder what is taking Shaun so long tonight. He is usually always on time for supper. Trish, does your leg feel well enough for you to go out to the shed and see what is taking Shaun so long? I can see the light on in the shed, so I think he will be in there. Maybe he is having some trouble with one of the cows. Will you tell him to come in for supper, if possible?"

Trish nodded and stood up. Her leg was getting better every day. It only ached if she stood too long or stretched it too much. She said that she would be happy to go and fetch Shaun. She put on her shoes and jacket and made her way to the shed. It had been their favorite place when Shaun and she were engaged. She blushed when she remembered all the kissing they had done in the corner of the shed. This was the first time that she would visit the shed since she ran away. She quietly opened the shed door so as not to spook the cows or Shaun. She stood just inside the door, looking at Shaun and listening to him talking to the cows.

It seemed as if the only way these two people learned what they wanted to know was by silently eavesdropping on the other's conversations.

"Daisy, my friend, I heard Trish say that she's moving away from Dalton in the New Year. I'll probably never see her again. While she lived in Dalton, I had a slight chance of seeing her in town. It would be too awkward to go to her yarn shop, and she'll probably do her shopping in Mason City."

Shaun restlessly moved around and addressed Buttercup. Even Trish knew the cows apart by now. Shaun had told her about the small differences among the cows.

"Oh, why did she have to believe that nonsense about Sheila and me? Didn't she know that I loved her so much and would never hurt her like that? We only had four months to go until our wedding. I could surely wait that long to have a physical relationship with her. She excites me so much, but I only wanted to do what was right for her. I would have waited for her for however long she wanted me to. We wanted to have some babies to complete our loving circle. Imagine what our babies would look like, Buttercup. They would be too adorable for words—her wild curly hair and maybe my coloring. A small curly-haired strawberry blonde little girl and a tall brown-haired boy with blue eyes . . . I would love them so much. I always hoped that our children would take after Trish—her sense of right and wrong, her strong character, and her sense of fun. Ahh, I can still imagine them, even now. Are they never to be born? Life is so unfair. I didn't do anything wrong, and I am still being punished for some reason." Shaun stopped talking for a little bit. He was obviously in emotional pain and wondering how to handle it.

Now it was Rose's turn to be his confidant. He touched her bony back as he resumed talking.

"Rose, how am I going to sit at supper with her tonight, knowing that I will never get the chance to tell her about Sheila and about how much I love her and need her? My heart feels like it is breaking into a thousand little pieces. I want to tell her about how sorry I am about what I said to her at Bill's wedding. I only said that because I was insanely jealous, thinking that she was going to marry Carlos. It was such a shock last week to find out that they were only friends and that Carlos loved Jenny. I want to tell her all these things, but she is so standoffish that I can't come up with the words to say to her. She didn't want to come here to recuperate. That's why I promised to only see her at suppertime. It's been amazingly sweet but pure hell having breakfast with her in the morning. Instead of eating, I wanted to pick her up, hold her tight, and kiss her until she begged for mercy."

Shaun walked around the stalls until he was standing in front of Daisy again. "Oh, Daisy, you're so lucky that you're a cow, without all these feelings for someone else. I wish that I could just pull her into my arms and tell her that I love her and forgive her for running away from me and breaking my heart." Shaun was finished talking. He gave Daisy a pat on her head and stepped back.

He stopped in his tracks when he saw Trish standing so silently in the shadow of the door. Her face was beautiful with her happiness.

As she started walking toward him, Trish quietly said, "I'm here, now, Shaun. Why don't you say those things to me right now?" Her curly hair stuck out like a shiny brown halo around her sweet and excited face. She stopped a few inches from Shaun.

Shaun looked at her with tremendous hope on his face. He gently grabbed her and enfolded her small slender body into his arms and gave her a fierce hug. He couldn't believe that she was here—with him—in their favorite place on earth. He rained quick kisses all over her face and forehead before settling squarely on her mouth. He kissed her like a starving man who finally got a morsel to eat.

Shaun held her and kissed her for such a long time that Trish's leg began to ache and threatened to buckle under her. Trish broke away just long enough to say, "Shaun, as much as I love your kisses, I'm going to have to sit down. My leg is hurting."

Shaun, whose nice face was flushed and sweating, blinked hard and said, "Oh, Trish, I'm sorry. Let's sit for a while on our old bale of hay, so we can talk."

Trish nodded and limped over to their special place. It brought back so many lovely memories to sit with Shaun on their bale of hay in the darkened corner of the shed. The three cows chewed their cud calmly, waiting for something to happen. They were used to spending time with Shaun and Trish as the humans talked, hugged, held hands, and kissed.

"How much did you hear, Trish?" asked Shaun as he tenderly smoothed her riot of curls. How he had missed smoothing and playing with her wild hair. Her hair was perfect for Trish's personality. It was a little bit wild but soft and sweet, as well.

"I came in when you started talking to Daisy about me moving. How did you know about that? I only told your mother this afternoon. Is your house bugged for security purposes, or what?" Trish grinned her fabulous big grin. Shaun had not seen that same grin for more than three years, and his heart lurched. He crushed her small body to him.

"Oh, Trish, I didn't ever think that I would see that smile again. I love that grin." Then his face got serious as he said, "No silly, I cut my hand and went inside to clean it up and get some ointment. You and Mom were talking in the kitchen, and I listened. I'm sorry about eavesdropping, but where you are concerned, I want to know everything. I was telling the cows that I didn't want to come to supper because I figured that it would be the last time that I would ever see you. I didn't think that you would come to breakfast with me tomorrow because you wouldn't want any awkwardness." Shaun stopped talking and looked so fierce.

Trish put her small hand on his arm and gently squeezed it. Shaun looked at her hand and slightly smiled again.

"Trish, you heard everything. Do I need to say it all again, my darling girl?" Shaun's eyes pleaded his case.

She glanced at the large bandage on his hand. She stooped and gently kissed it. When she looked up, her eyes were full of tears. Gazing deeply into Shaun's eyes, she softly said, "Well, I *would* like to hear you say, 'I love you, Trish' to my face. And maybe, sometime, you can tell me about Sheila, but no, you don't have to say everything else again."

Shaun kissed her hard for those words and then let her go. He held her hands, his fingers automatically tracing circles. He breathed in deeply and said, "Trish Newberg, I love you so much. Even when I was hurt and angry with you for running away without giving me a chance to explain, I never stopped loving you. I should have told you that when you first got back to Dalton. Remember? We were in your tornado shelter, and you were so frightened and vulnerable. That was before Carlos came and everything got so crazy. I foolishly thought that I would have lots of chances to tell you that I never stopped hoping that you would come back to me. I love you, and I always will love you, my darling Trish."

He kissed her again but stopped when he remembered the rest of her request. "I promise that I will tell you about Sheila, but not right now. This is our moment for reconciliation. Sheila caused us both such heartache. But enough about me. I want to know what you feel about all of this, Trish." His blue eyes were dark with hope and trepidation.

Trish reached up and put her hands on either side of his face. She gently pulled his head down until she could cover his lips in a very short and sweet kiss.

Then she looked deeply into his eyes and said, "Dear Shaun, I have never stopped loving you, even when I was mad at you. I spent three years in Brazil berating myself for running away and letting Jenny end our engagement. I was just looking for a chance to come back to Dalton when Jenny called me and told me about Mom's stroke. I couldn't pack my bags fast enough. When I saw you and Mary buying candy in the store, I realized that you might still be so angry with me that you wouldn't want to talk about the situation with Sheila anymore. Then, after the tornado, I had hoped that we would talk, but we didn't. So much time passed, but there were always so many people around that it became too difficult to broach the topic. Then, at Cheri's wedding I saw Mary, who told me that she was in love. I thought that it was with you. I didn't want to mess up anything between the two of you. I cared about both of you too much. Everyone in town was speculating whether you two would get married. I realized that it was too late for us. You told me then that you did not trust me anymore and that we could only ever be neighbors. I was so hurt, but I was determined to stay out of your way. As I said, I believed that you would marry Mary. I looked at my wedding dress every day and hoped that a miracle would happen and that you would somehow come to love me again. I couldn't bear to see you living happily with Mary, so I decided to move away from Dalton. Starting my yarn shop in the strip mall gave me the perfect excuse. I told Carlos how I felt, and he told me that the new house that he was building could become my home. I didn't want to run into you in town with your new wife on your arm . . ." Tears were falling in earnest down Trish's face. These were difficult memories to talk about.

Shaun held her tightly and tenderly brushed her tears away. Then he gently kissed her wet cheeks. "I heard from the whole town that you were likely to marry Carlos. He's a great catch. He's handsome, wealthy, and generous. It would have been a great life for you. He could have given you everything you ever wanted. I'm a poor farmer. I don't have much to offer you . . ."

Trish stopped his words by putting a finger to his lips. She leaned forward and replaced her finger with her lips. She kissed him softly and said, "Shaun you have always had enough for me. I was looking forward to being a farmer's wife. Your love and farm are still enough. You must know by now that I am not swayed by money or material things. I'm a hard worker. I can and will work for the things I want. Carlos has been a great friend. He's known for two years that I still loved you. He has more money than he can spend on himself, and he generously wants to help his family and friends. He was married young, but he lost his beautiful young wife and unborn child in a terrible plane crash in Brazil. He's been lonely and in need of a friend. He and I have never been attracted to each other. Almost as soon as he landed in Dalton, he fell in love with Jenny. He picked my brains about how to get her to notice him. That's probably why we spent so much time together. Both Jenny and Carlos are ecstatically happy now—Josh, too. There has never been anyone except you for me, my dear Shaun. I love you."

They stayed sitting on their bale of hay for two hours, talking, hugging, and kissing. They didn't notice the time passing, but Andrew and Ella did. After eating their supper, Ella put the leftovers back on the stove. It would be lucky if the food didn't turn to ashes after all the re-heating it had gone through.

*Oh, well,* Ella thought, *I can always serve them a nice deli sandwich if they are still hungry.* She was hoping with all her heart that Shaun and Trish were finally talking and pounding out their differences. Maybe, even now, they were making up and kissing.

Ella told Andrew that she was going out to the shed to see what was holding up Shaun and Trish. Andrew looked at her with a slow smile. His hopes were the same as Ella's.

Ella quietly opened the shed door. The lights were on, and the three cows were quiet, chewing on their cud. She couldn't see or hear Shaun or Trish. *Could they be talking in the car?* she wondered. Just as she was about to leave, she heard Shaun's soft chuckle and him saying something quietly.

Curious, Ella walked further into the shed. She could just make out, in the dark corner, Shaun with his hands in Trish's curly hair, and he was holding her head still while his lips were locked on hers. Trish's arms were around his neck, and she was straining to get closer to him. They were oblivious to anything else but themselves.

Ella looked on with a huge smile for a minute before quietly leaving the shed. As she walked into the kitchen smiling so happily, Andrew rolled over to her and took her hand. He was smiling, too. She told him what his son was doing at that moment. They both chuckled as memories filled their hearts.

Ella had known that the shed was Shaun and Trish's favorite place to kiss when they were engaged. They never said anything, but Trish's wild curls and red lips said enough. Shaun had always had a fine flush on his face, too. He had told her once that Trish and he were not going to sleep together until they were married. That is why Ella was so sure that Sheila was making up stories when she told everyone that she and Shaun were having a physical relationship. Shaun loved only Trish, and he respected her, too.

Ella was so happy that she sent Trish out to the shed. Maybe she had unconsciously known that Shaun and Trish would have their talk. Time was running out, and Trish would be gone by tomorrow.

Finally, after talking and hugging and kissing for almost three hours, Shaun looked at his watch and realized the time. He chuckled and said that his parents were likely dying of curiosity by now. He knelt in front of Trish, took her hands, and kissed them. He wished that he had her ring with him, but it was in his dresser drawer. Still, he wanted to propose in private, with just his cows as witnesses.

"Trish, my darling girl, will you marry me? And this time, no long engagement. I need you by my side right now. I've been praying for a second chance for happiness."

Trish, with her big, wonderful smile, squeezed his hands tightly and said, "I've prayed for that, too. Yes, Shaun, I will marry you. I already have the dress, so I guess we can get married quickly. After all, we've had a really long engagement already."

They both laughed. Shaun picked up his petite little Trish and swung her around. Then he just held her tightly in his strong arms. He plastered her mouth with a long and hard kiss.

He gently set her on her feet. Trish's leg was aching, but she disregarded the pain. *Who cares about a little pain when I'm so very happy?* she thought to herself.

Trish looked at her sore leg and Shaun's bandaged hand and chuckled. "I guess we're both members of the walking wounded brigade," she said.

Shaun realized that Trish was probably in some pain, so he swung her up into his arms and held her close to his heart. After a quick cuddle, he walked with her to the door of the shed. He opened the door, looked at his cows, and said, "Good night, ladies. Thanks for being with Trish and me tonight. I'll let you know tomorrow about the next chapter in our lives."

Trish laughed softly. Sometimes Shaun was just so sweet. He grinned at her as he turned off the light and closed the door. He carefully walked up to the house with little Trish still in his arms. She was so light and fragile. He would do everything possible to help her gain back those six pounds and fit into her wedding gown. It worried him to see Trish so thin.

Ella was looking out the window, and she saw Shaun carrying Trish up to the door. He had his hands full, so she opened the door. He grinned at his mom and said, "Mom, Trish is fine, very fine. Her leg was hurting a little, so I decided to carry her over the threshold of her future home."

He stopped to give his fiancée a sweet kiss. It thrilled him to say that. Trish and he were re-engaged and about to marry soon. His bright blue eyes were twinkling with happiness. Ella had not seen this happiness in her son's eyes for more than three years. She was grateful to Trish for making Shaun so happy again.

She closed and locked the door for the night. They would probably be hungry. When she went into the kitchen to look at the leftovers, she knew that she couldn't serve such slop to them. She hummed while she made them some great submarine sandwiches. She didn't want little Trish to lose any weight. In the few days that Trish stayed with them, Ella was confident that her good meals had helped Trish regain one or two pounds.

Ella brought the food to the table. Shaun and Trish were sitting on the couch in the living room. Shaun sat down with Trish still in his arms, so now she was perched on his lap. They were kissing again. Trish looked so small on Shaun's lap. Ella never realized how small Trish was compared to her big strong son. She knew that Shaun would always take care of Trish and cherish her and their babies. Speaking of babies, Ella pictured all the baby clothes she would knit for her beautiful grandchildren. Her heart was nearly bursting with grateful happiness.

Ella smiled widely and loudly cleared her throat. Both Shaun and Trish looked up, startled. They both blushed, and Trish scrambled off Shaun's lap. They walked to the table, together. Ella called for Andrew to join them.

They sat at the table and ate Ella's impromptu meal. In between bites and sips of cold milk, they explained a little of their story. Some of it was just for them, but Shaun's parents could fill in the blanks. They had once been young and in love, too.

After eating, Shaun excused themselves for a few minutes. He took Trish into his bedroom and sat her on the edge of his bed. He took her ring out of his dresser and looked at it. How many times had he looked at this ring in the last three years? It seemed like a million times to Shaun.

He knelt in front of Trish and proposed again. When she smiled and said yes, he kissed her briefly and gently put her ring on her finger where it belonged. It was loose and twirled around a little. After kissing her finger, Shaun looked at Trish in a mock stern way.

"Young lady, you are going to have to gain a little weight back. I don't want this ring to fall off. Also, your wedding dress might be too loose. Do you think that Mom can fatten you up a bit more in the next two weeks? I want to marry you before Christmas. Will you do that? It's quick, but everyone will help us. That way we can use the Christmas season for our honeymoon. You can go anywhere in the world that you want, as long as I am part of your luggage. Is it a deal, my little love?"

A wicked little look came over Trish's face. "Anywhere in the world, huh? Boy, that's going to be difficult for me to decide. I guess that I could take you with me." Trish gurgled with laughter.

Shaun loved this fun and quirky side of Trish. They walked out of his room and back into the living room where his parents sat patiently. Trish was still looking at her ring. How she missed wearing it! It was a small diamond that they had picked out together. She always thought that it looked so good on her slender finger.

Trish held it up so that her future parents-in-law could see it. She was so happy that, in addition to her dear Shaun, she was gaining two perfectly wonderful new parents.

They talked for an hour or so about the wedding plans. Both Andrew and Ella were happy with Shaun and Trish's wish to marry within the next few weeks.

Shaun and Trish intended to talk with their pastor tomorrow to see if he was available to marry them in two weeks. They knew that everyone on both sides of the family would gladly help them pull everything together within that time.

Trish's family would be here tomorrow and would very much want to be involved with the planning of such an important event.

Trish went to bed so happy. She promised Shaun that she would be up early to eat breakfast with him. It was kind of their thing. Trish's family would probably arrive to pick her up in the afternoon. They would be so happy and surprised to see Trish and Shaun engaged again.

CHAPTER

# Sixteen

When the happy travelers arrived at the Healy home the next afternoon, they were full of questions. Even before Jenny could open her mouth, she noticed that Shaun and Trish were sitting very close to each other and holding hands under the kitchen table. She was dumbfounded. Trish stifled a giggle at the surprised expression on her sister's face.

Trish related details of her accident and how she ended up at the Healy farm to recuperate. Her family was concerned about her injury, but Trish's big smile soon gave away her secret. She and Shaun finally talked and were reengaged. She was gratified to see the huge smiles on everyone's faces.

Jenny and Lila jumped up to hug Trish while Carlos strode forward to clasp Shaun's hand in friendship. No matter how adamantly Trish said that Shaun was through with her, Carlos believed that Shaun would find the courage to tell her that he loved her. It seemed that his belief in Shaun was validated. Carlos was so happy that Trish would now have the same kind of happiness that he had with his own darling Jenny.

Ella invited them all to stay for supper so they could plan as much of the wedding as possible. Shaun and Trish had spoken to their pastor that morning and found out that he was available to marry them on December 15th.

Trish asked Jenny to be her Maid of Honor. Shaun intended to ask his cousin Bill to be his Best Man. Trish wanted Mary to be her Personal Attendant, Carlos to walk her down the aisle, and Josh to be an usher.

Trish's favorite color was green, which was perfect since it would be nearly Christmas when the wedding was held.

Trish wanted to go shopping with Jenny, Mary, and the two mothers as soon as they all had a free day.

Everyone wanted to lend a hand and help Trish get ready for her opening day. Trish had already hired Carrie, a high school friend of hers, to work part-time at the store since Trish could not work all the hours that the store would be open. Trish planned to ask Carrie to work full-time while she and Shaun were on their honeymoon. She decided that she would have to hire another worker to cover Carrie's part-time hours.

Shaun, with his arms securely around Trish's waist, softly whispered to her that it might be smart if she hired that new part-time person permanently. He reminded Trish that she would be a busy wife and might soon be expecting their first baby. He didn't want her tiring herself out by working so many hours in her shop.

Her joy at his whispered words erupted into a shy grin. It appeared that Shaun still wanted to have some babies, and maybe right away. Well, she was in her thirties now. It might be a good thing to have their babies within the first few years of their marriage.

Trish whispered back to him that she enjoyed hearing him talk about their son and daughter when he was talking with the cows. She liked everything that he said about their future children.

Shaun hugged Trish tightly. He had waited so long to marry Trish. Now, finally, in two weeks his heart would have what it wanted.

* * *

Amid the final preparations for her store opening, Trish set aside time to call her dear friend, Sarah Thompson. To her surprise, Sarah answered after only a few rings.

"Sarah? Hi, it's Trish. I hope that this is a good time."

"Oh, hi, Trish," answered Sarah, a little breathlessly. "Yes, it's a great time! I was just thinking about you earlier this week."

Trish could hear Christopher's giggles as Sarah tended to him.

"Excuse me, Trish. I just caught this little rascal before you called," laughed Sarah. "He's crawling now, and he can really motor! I've just set him in his playpen so that we can have a nice chat."

"I've got some happy news . . ." Trish began.

"You're engaged! I just knew it," Sarah gleefully interjected. Both laughed out loud with joy.

"Yes, Shaun and I are getting married on December 15 at 1:00 p.m. in our church here in Dalton. We really hope that you and Paul can make it to the wedding." Trish's fingers were crossed.

The two friends chatted for several more minutes. Trish told Sarah to expect a formal invitation in the mail. Before hanging up, Sarah assured Trish that Paul and she would try their best to come.

Opening Day at the mall was everything Trish hoped it would be. It seemed as if the whole community came out, mostly out of curiosity. Trish, along with her two employees, were busy finding products and ringing up sales for the happy customers. Trish did more talking than anything else. Everyone in town had heard of her reengagement to Shaun Healy. They were eager to talk with both Trish and Shaun. It was not really the time or place, but she couldn't stop her neighbors and friends from asking their questions.

Ella Healy and Shaun were on hand to help in any way necessary. Shaun went on errands for Trish, which included getting everyone lunch from the Food Court, getting Trish more change when she ran out, and gallantly carrying large purchases to customers' cars. Trish could not have survived the day without his willing help.

When Trish tried to thank him for his awesome help, Shaun just grinned and said that he would accept her hugs and kisses as payment. They met a few times in her back room just to get away from the crowds and do some of that hugging and kissing.

Trish's two employees looked knowingly when Shaun and she came out of the back room a bit flushed and with disheveled hair.

Trish's customers liked her merchandise, and many of them ordered colors of yarn that were not available in the store. Registration for Trish's classes was now full. She had twenty-one people who wanted to take her knitting classes. Since she was going to be a very busy gal through Christmas, the afternoon classes would begin the second week in January.

Just back from their honeymoon, James and Mary briefly stopped at Trish's shop and helped them during an especially busy time. Mary's face radiated with joy. James looked like a different man, too. Gone was his usual stern look, replaced by a look of contentment.

As they finally closed the door of Trish's shop at 5:30 p.m. that day, they all sighed with relief. It had truly been a long but rewarding day. Carlos, Jenny, and Josh had walked around the stores in the mall and made sure that everything was going well. Carlos was extremely happy that his tenants were satisfied with the way things had gone that day.

Carlos and Jenny took Trish's staff and volunteers out for a celebratory supper. The nearest place to go for a nice steak dinner was Mason City, so they all piled into their vehicles and followed Carlos' Mercedes there. He had Jenny call ahead to reserve a place setting for the eleven people who would be having dinner.

Carlos was already thinking about putting up a great new steakhouse near Dalton. He thought that there would be enough interest from the community to warrant it. He would wait to talk with the Newberg family until Shaun and Trish came home from their honeymoon.

* * *

The last week before Shaun and Trish's wedding was so crazy. Besides the yarn store, they had to buy everything for the wedding. Shaun and Trish planned to have the reception in The Old Barn, where Bill and Cheri were married. They both wanted to have it there, even though it held some recent bitter memories for them.

Someone had to put up and decorate the two huge Christmas trees that would grace The Old Barn's front area. New hay bales would need to be brought in and arranged just so.

Since Trish wanted to spend part of each day at her store, much of the wedding arrangements and chores were left for her family to do. Shaun helped when he could, but Carlos, Jenny, and Josh volunteered to do most of the work. They were just so thrilled about Shaun and Trish's wedding that they would happily do whatever they could to make Trish's life easier. Jenny didn't want Trish to get so anxious that she stopped eating again.

Trish's big weight loss through her depression and lethargy had truly concerned the whole family. Jenny had been so excited about her own wedding that she didn't see the warning signs. Lila had also been caught up in Jenny and Carlos' wedding, and she hadn't noticed the telltale signs of depression either.

Trish and Shaun had chosen their wedding decorations to be a velvety green and rich red—Christmas colors. Carlos offered to pay for the wedding, but the Healys and Lila would not allow that. He could pay for one thing for his dear friend's wedding but not everything. Regardless, Carlos and Jenny insisted that they help with any last-minute shopping.

While they were shopping, Carlos had a great idea about giving the guests a small memento of the Newberg-Healy wedding. The townspeople had waited to celebrate a wedding for months. They had been cheated out of James and Mary's, as well as Carlos and Jenny's weddings.

Walking past a craft store, Carlos saw a beautiful bunch of glittering perfectly white crocheted snowflakes, stiffened with iridescent glitter, and he knew that they would be perfect as a gift for the guests. Josh and he could make some labels stating "Shaun and Trish 12/15/2014" to affix to the backside of the snowflakes. The delicate snowflakes would be wonderful ornaments to hang on those two huge Christmas trees. Each guest could take one home as they left the wedding. Any that were left over could hang importantly on Shaun and Trish's own Christmas trees in the future. Jenny told Carlos that he was a genius.

CHAPTER

# Seventeen

The wedding day dawned cold and clear. It snowed yesterday, so everything looked crystalline white. The roads and driveways had been plowed, so it was easy to get around in town.

The church was packed to overflowing with friends and neighbors. They had waited for this wedding for a very long time. Most of them were so grateful that Shaun and Trish had finally reconciled and were getting married. Everyone thought they made such a wonderful couple. Most of them wanted to get a good look at the other two new brides, as well. Both Jenny and Mary were at the wedding, and the townspeople wanted to talk to them about their weddings, too.

Jenny's bridesmaid dress was lovely—a long sleeved velvet green dress with beautiful sequins and pearls on the front bodice. The full skirt and fitted bodice showed off her small waist. Her long blonde hair was up in an elegant chignon.

Trish looked lovely in her pure white silk dress. Since she wasn't a woman who liked anything overly fussy or ornate, the silky flowing dress' only adornment was seed pearls on the fitted bodice. Trish wore a minimum of makeup and left her curly hair loose, except for pearly combs to keep hair out of her face. Shaun, who loved Trish's wild hair, had specifically asked Trish not to put her hair up. He liked to see it flowing freely around her face.

Lila and Ella wore beautiful green dresses that complemented Jenny's dress. Shaun, Carlos, and Josh wore black tuxedos with green velvet cummerbunds and black ties. Jenny carried a Christmassy bouquet of red and white roses and carnations and dark green ivy. Trish's beautiful and fragrant trailing bouquet was made with gorgeous red roses, white Narcissus papyraceus and poinsettias, and dark green ivy. It looked lovely next to her silk gown.

That morning, Lila and Jenny fed Trish her favorite breakfast in bed. She loved the blueberry waffles, bacon, cut up fruit, and coffee that they lovingly prepared for her. Everyone had been trying to fatten Trish up a bit before the wedding. She had gained back the six pounds that her doctor requested of her. She was still a bit underweight, but she had lost that gaunt look. Her leg was nearly healed, just in time to dance at her wedding. Dr. Peyton and Caroline were so happy that Shaun and Trish reunited and were getting married. Trish invited them to the wedding, and they were thrilled that they could attend.

Instead of getting a limo to come out from Mason City, Carlos drove the wedding party in his new black Mercedes. He had loved driving the rented Mercedes so much that he finally bought his own. He would use it whenever he was in Iowa. It could live in the three-car garage at his new house. When Jenny, Josh, and he visited from Brazil, whoever picked them up at the airport could drive it to meet them. When they returned to Brazil, someone would drive them in that car and return it to his garage.

The church looked very festive, and beautiful Christmas flowers adorned almost every surface. The old church smelled so fresh and clean.

Lila, Jenny, Mary, Ella, and Trish sat comfortably in the Bride's Room waiting for the right time to go into the vestibule and await the beginning of the Wedding March. Ten minutes before the wedding started, Josh knocked on the door to escort Lila and Ella to their seats. Andrew had already been escorted to the spot next to the front pew where his wheelchair could sit.

Both ladies kissed Trish and told her that they loved her. Trish smiled at them. Her future mother-in-law was almost as dear to her as Lila was.

Carlos enfolded his dear friend in a careful genuine hug and told Trish that she looked lovely. He kissed her cheek and told her to be happy. He was very happy himself and couldn't stop the huge smile that lit up his face. He was honored that Trish had asked him to escort her down the aisle.

Jenny and Bill walked up the lacy white aisle and waited for the song to signal the processional. All eyes were on the sweet bride. Trish looked so happy and pretty. They all watched Shaun waiting so patiently at the altar for his Trish. He looked confident and handsome. Trish was aware of all her friends and neighbors during her first few steps, but then she focused on Shaun. He looked strong, kind, and loving. His strawberry blond hair was tamed into a thick smooth cap on his head. It was usually messy and wavy—often sticking up all over (which is how Trish liked it the best). His face was calm, but his blue eyes were twinkling with happiness. His tux looked so good on his tall, lean, muscular physique. Farming was hard work and kept him in tiptop condition.

Shaun looked at Trish and thought how beautiful and serene she looked. Her face was a bit pale, but her eyes were excited and happy.

The service was simple, yet beautiful, and the large congregation sang with gusto. After the pastor told the groom he could kiss his bride, Shaun expelled a sigh of relief. They were married! He had finally married his sweet Trish, after waiting for her for so many years.

Shaun's kiss was sweet and tender, and they both enjoyed it so much before reluctantly breaking apart and facing their guests.

As Trish scanned the congregation, her gaze fell upon Sarah and Paul Thompson. Sarah looked beautiful in a feathery white Christmas hat. Paul was as handsome as ever, and they still had the look of newlyweds. Sarah waved and blew Trish a kiss.

Carlos drove the wedding party to The Old Barn for the reception. It was dressed up for Christmas, looking beautiful and elegant. Trish smiled widely. Her willing helpers decorated it exactly the way that she wanted it to look for her special day.

Snacks provided on the tables were there to tide people over until the wedding supper at 5:00 p.m. Many of the guests were farmers, who would go home for a few hours to do their chores, returning later for supper and the dance.

The afternoon was a blur for Trish and Shaun. So many people wanted to hear their reunion story. A simplified version was shared since they did not think the whole town needed to be privy to the entire story.

Carlos and Jenny stopped by with none other than the Thompsons in tow. Trish was thrilled to see Sarah.

"Oh, Sarah, I'm so glad to see that you could make it!"

Before a beaming Sarah could respond, Carlos said,

"My dear Trish and Sarah, if you turn around, you will see some people who have come a very long way to remind you just how much you mean to them." Carlos gestured, and when everyone turned, their eyes beheld a group standing near the entry.

Not believing her eyes at first, Trish began, "Angie . . . and Dave . . . oh, my . . ." Then, Sarah, her eyes suddenly wet with tears, continued, "Mary . . . Ted! Oh, my goodness, Carlos . . . how?"

Happy to see that both ladies were moved, Carlos called out to the weary travelers, "Please, come over, and reacquaint yourself with your friends."

Familiar faces surrounded their former workmates and their husbands, and a joyful cacophony ensued while everyone tried to talk at once. Eventually, calm prevailed as embraces and updates were shared.

Since announcing their marriage, Shaun had seen Senhor Santos in a different light. He could now clearly see why Trish was his friend, and how so many benefited from this man's goodness.

While Carlos and Paul chatted briefly about business, specifically, Carlos' interest in partnering with Paul on some projects, Trish and Sarah found a few minutes to converse.

"Trish, I never imagined a reunion like this—at your wedding, no less," began Sarah.

"Me neither," replied Trish. She sat because bridal shoes seemed to never be designed with comfort in mind. Besides, her injured leg was screaming for attention. "Do you and Paul have to leave right away? It will be two days before Shaun and I leave for our honeymoon and, apparently, Carlos has arranged a few days' lodging for our surprise guests. It would be great if you could stay as well."

"I can happily report that we can. Paul just told me. He got us a room at the Dalton Motel." Then, Sarah discreetly added, "We're both so blessed to have our men. I have to say, I'm so happy for Carlos, too. You and I can agree that he finally got a second chance for happiness. He and Jenny look perfect together."

Noticing the small line of well-wishers queuing behind Trish, Sarah gestured to Trish, who nodded and said, "Duty calls." They hugged, and Sarah arranged a time to call Trish the next afternoon.

Shaun proudly held Trish's hand as they walked around talking to their guests. He made sure that Trish sat down periodically so her leg did not get too tired. He wanted to dance with his wife later!

The supper was great—pot roast with all the fixings, veggies, fruit, bars, and finally the amazing cake. One of Trish's neighbors at the mall made a delicious three-tiered cake dressed in sparkling Christmas decorations.

Shaun led Trish in a beautiful waltz for their first dance. Later, he requested their song, and all eyes were on them as they performed their spirited two-step dance. They were out of breath and laughing when their song ended. They had quietly sung the song to each other while they were dancing. Those words meant so much to them. Forever and ever, forever and ever, amen . . .

Carlos had given Shaun and Trish permission to use his new house for a few days before they left on their honeymoon. After a two day stay in his house, they were flying to a luxurious vacation in the Caribbean for ten days. Now, instead of having the two days to themselves, they would plan to spend some of that time with their

Brazilian friends and Sarah and Paul. Neither Trish nor Shaun minded. They would have the rest of their lives together.

Carlos and Jenny dropped them off at his new home just before midnight. They stood outside on the driveway. The night air was clean and crisp. Jenny hugged her impulsive independent little sister one more time. She knew that Shaun would now take over, looking after Trish.

"Be happy, little sister. You are now married to a wonderful man who will keep you in check. He can handle all the things that you might come up with. I love you so much. You're going to love being married to the man you love more than anything," Jenny said quietly.

Jenny looked lovingly at Carlos as she said that. He smiled gently back at her. Carlos gave Trish a big hug and shook Shaun's hand before he and Jenny left them alone.

Trish looked at Shaun, who looked tenderly back at her. He picked her up in his strong arms and carried her over the threshold. Trish laughed softly as she looked up into his dear face. They had made it! Her miracle had come true.

Shaun quickly kissed Trish's upraised face as he carried her into their temporary home. They would make wonderful memories at this place. It would be their haven whenever they wanted to get away from the farm. Carlos, Jenny, and Josh would only need it one weekend a month while they were visiting from Brazil.

After Shaun gently set Trish on her feet, they walked together into the kitchen to open the champagne that Jenny had left for them in the fridge. They toasted each other, all snuggled up on the couch and talked about their wedding day.

Before they got too sleepy, Shaun put down their champagne glasses, picked up his bride, and carried her into the bedroom. Trish smiled at Shaun, and he saw all the love for him on her sweet face. His face looked exactly the same for her.